Chon

Chon

The Story of a WWII Japanese Spy
Who Became a South Texas Vaquero

RICARDO D. PALACIOS

MCM Books, February 2018

Copyright ©2018 by Ricardo D. Palacios

Published in the United States by MCM Books, Corpus Christi, Texas.

ISBN: 978-0-9967473-2-5

Library of Congress Control Number: 2018931114

Colophon

Designed and edited by Alfredo E. Cardenas.

Illustration of Chon on front cover by Mary Treviño.

Typefaces used were Cloister Open Face BT for book title and Adobe Caslon Pro for the chapter titles and body text.

DEDICATION

I dedicate this book to my four children, Ricardo Jr., Gabe, Tony, and Ginna, who grew up hearing many excerpts of Chon; to my daughter-in-law Heather, who kept pushing for final publication of the book; and to my girlfriend Sarah Lynn Appling, who helped me make my way through Word software, and helped with proofreading the galleys.

BOOK ONE
Tokyo Plantation

Chapter One

Akechi Massaki scurried around the small dark office stuffing his briefcase with business papers, as the sun set through the blinds on the two west side windows. A short, fat man, Akechi breathed heavily as he moved around, speaking to himself in a sing-song.

"I mustn't forget the garlic papers, I mustn't forget the garlic papers," he hummed and sang, in a low huff.

"And get the onion information for Israel, and get the information for Israel." He continued like a fly trapped in a dark bottle, humming, buzzing, and groaning as he moved. Then he stopped and stared at the wall in front of his desk. There was no sound, except the huff of his heavy breathing.

"The murder!" He shouted out suddenly. Then he said, in an almost inaudible voice, "Soon. I've got to tell Chon how his father was murdered. I'll tell him how his father was killed. Soon; I'll tell him soon."

He paused for a few seconds, then fell back into the sing song, and kept working, and humming, and buzzing.

Akechi was getting ready for his fifth trip to México, and he wanted to see the boy Chon one more time before he left. He had planned a long ride through the plantation and planned to take the boy with him.

Akechi walked out of the plantation mansion, which served as headquarters for his extensive business holdings. He breathed in the fresh cool air. He walked slowly through the shaded gardens. The yard was cool, lush, and green. He walked until he came to a clearing beyond the gardens where he saw sunlit fields as far as the eyes could see. The bright emerald green turf surrounded by the dark green tree lines was topped with a blue gray haze.

He took a breath of fresh air, then turned to walk toward the blacksmith shop, next to the horse stables, and the truck garage. Only the voices of a dozen or so workers in the area competed with the sound of the crunching twigs, grass, and leaves, as he walked.

"Where is the boy?" He asked Yoshi.

"He's over by the shade," Yoshi said while pointing to the boy. "He's been there for about an hour waiting for you."

Akechi looked over at Chon sitting in the distance. "I'll tell him soon, I'll tell him soon," he thought.

"Come, get into the truck," Akechi said, motioning to the boy to come. He slammed the truck door, turned the key, and pressed the starter button. The motor cranked, then roared, as the cylinders pumped. It was a 1927 Ford Model T Runabout and Akechi remembered the day he bought it in San Diego, California. "You can get any color you want as long as it's black," he remembered the salesman telling him. "What a peasant. What a senseless riddle. Only the Americans would say something so stupid and laugh about it. Peasant!"

The thirteen-year-old sat quietly next to him, trying to figure out why Akechi had an annoyed look.

As the ride began Akechi thought briefly of his family's long samurai history, and the events that led to his ownership of Tokyo Plantation and the worldwide produce and spice conglomerate he owned.

"How is your karate?" He asked the boy.

"It is fine Akechi san, it is fine. Nagi san is a great teacher. He said someday I'll be just as good as my father Tengzeu," Chon answered with a tinge of pride.

"Oh yes, I hope so," Akechi replied with a strained sigh.

Nagi san and Tengzeu had been sent to Tokyo to work in a

Massaki warehouse, and had learned KarateDo from Gichin, then brought the art back to the plantation.

"Your father used it well," he said with a pause. "You know, of course, that he was my bodyguard."

"Yes, Akechi san, Nagi san has told me all about my father," the boy answered politely.

As they continued down the road, Akechi looked over at the boy again. Chon was a good looking young man, and Akechi had made sure that he got the best the plantation had to offer. It was the least he could do. Chon was very intelligent, and teaching him was a pleasure for the plantation mentors.

Chon's mother Massa was grateful for the special attention Akechi gave her son, though she knew someday she would lose Chon to the world Akechi was building for him. The attentions and favors had multiplied a few months after Tengzeu's death when Akechi's own wife died in childbirth, as did their son.

"He'll be educated, he'll be a modern day samurai, a polished stone, and an intelligent and good businessman perhaps, but definitely finished and polished," Akechi thought as he drove on. Akechi looked older than his thirty-two years. His hair was already graying. His thick arms hung out, away from his short and rotund body carried by thick legs.

After he lost his friend Tengzeu in 1920 and his wife Kiku in 1921, he immersed himself in the business and succeeded beyond his expectations.

He supported dozens of families, scattered in small camps or villages about every five hundred yards around the perimeter of the plantation. Each camp consisted of several families living together in small wooden houses, painted white and impeccably clean. Each of the camps bore the name of a person, animal, thing, or event significant in the history of the plantation.

Akechi enjoyed the tours of the plantation. It was as if every small house was his own, and each employee his family. The employees sensed this and reciprocated with loyalty and love. Akechi was not like other lords they heard about from friends.

He looked around the Camp of the Cow proudly. The camp was spotless, meticulously manicured. Chon walked around talking with the people at the camp.

Akechi looked at Chon and admired the young man's size and strength. Broad shoulders, muscular arms and trunk, and long strong legs. He also admired the young boy's manner of interaction with the workers and their families.

"Someday a polished stone," he repeated under his breath.

They resumed their tour in the truck, admiring the growth of the crops. At the Camp of the Duck, Akechi and Chon spoke to the camp's leader Hiro, who explained to Chon the art and science of raising the crops. Akechi watched as the two discussed the intricacies of caring for the crops.

"Little by little," he mused. "His lessons are going well. He can read and write perfectly, he is the best in karate, he is an expert horseman, and he understands the operation of the plantation, sometimes better than I."

"Little, by little. But he needs to know about the philosophies of the world, about art, poetry, and geography. He cannot be a good samurai without these," Akechi sighed heavily.

"I'll have to find a way. What a shame to leave this diamond uncut, and without a setting," he mumbled as he waddled back to the truck.

As they neared the mansion, Akechi was pleased they had visited all the camps. The shadows were long, and the big house could barely be seen among the heavy dark shade of the trees and the smoke that hung over the small houses that surrounded it.

Akechi stopped the truck, turned the engine off, and sat quietly for a minute. He finally mustered the energy to explain to Chon how his father died. It was on a trip, he and Tengzeu had taken, Akechi told the boy.

"We were attacked by three men. Your father gallantly fended off all three men, while I made my escape. Unfortunately, a fourth attacker came out from the shadows and stabbed your father in the back."

After a tense, tearful moment, Chon and Akechi hugged each other. After they recovered in a long silence, Akechi started the engine again, and proceeded home.

The evening air chilled them. The day had been long, but approaching home, they were warmed by seeing Yoshi and other servants waiting to attend to them.

"Chon," Akechi said with affection, "I will walk you to your mother. I want to bid her farewell. I am going to México, and will not see you for several months." He put his arm around the boy and walked toward the servants' quarters, surrounded by pretty bonsai trees and rock and water gardens. The servants stared at the contact between the two. They knew, of course, that throughout the last ten years Akechi had accepted and adopted western ways more and more. Akechi had explained to them that it was better for business if he acted like his western contacts and competitors.

Akechi felt their stares, and thought about how much he had adopted western mannerisms. He realized the boy was adopting these customs as well. He refused to believe that it was bad for Chon to learn these ways. "It will make him a better samurai," he thought.

"Chon, I try to teach you everything," Akechi said, as he embarked in a long, planned litany. Akechi breathed heavily, as if short of breath.

"I want you to be a good son, and someday a good father," Akechi said in a fatherly tone. Someday I want you to be something special.

"You have a gift," Akechi said, pausing to measure his words. "You make friends and get along with everyone, especially the workers. You learn fast. You can make decisions. I will share with you, what I know."

"Not all good things are Japanese. You cannot be like the ostrich. You must look. Keep eyes open."

"Tomorrow I leave," Akechi said with a sigh. "You be good. Go to classes. Visit the camps for me."

"Go now, see your mother. I will bring a gift to make you a better samurai," he said with a grin.

Chon stood up and bowed toward Akechi. "Good night Akechi san. You are kind. I will miss you, and think of you every day of your trip," Chon said as he bowed again.

Akechi felt a lump in his throat, turned and walked away. He did not look forward to the long, boring ocean voyage, but it was inevitable and it would give him time to think, to sort things out.

It was the spring of 1933, and Akechi was troubled by what he saw around his country. Because of his prominence, Akechi had met Emperor Hirohito at the Imperial Palace two or three times and felt uncomfortable with the emperor's leadership.

"The ignorant goat should be preserving the peace instead of listening to all his war mongering generals," he said to himself.

Chapter Two

As the ship prepared to dock, Akechi stayed in his room and wrote letters. His messages were quick and laconic, although he took a little extra time to write to Chon. He also wrote out a schedule. He planned to visit with his partner Israel Saenz for several weeks, then spend time with Sebastian Gutiérrez Ayala in Acapulco for a couple of weeks. He expected to meet with Sebastian to discuss several shipments of garlic.

Akechi wanted to talk to the ship's captain about the rest of the trip, but did not want to disturb him while he was docking. He waited at the ship's bow. The dock faced the setting sun, and the approaching ship cast a huge shadow on the dock itself. He had difficulty spotting his contact, but after a few moments his eyes focused and he saw his man Israel Saenz on the port side waving at him.

The people that Akechi dealt with throughout the world owned or rented their own warehouses, offices, and other plants, but each knew that if it were not for the Akechi organization they would not exist.

So, whenever they had the opportunity to host or help Akechi, they did their utmost to make him feel at home. Israel and his people were no exception. In actuality, they wanted Akechi to feel like he was coming to check on his own business.

Finally, the ship rubbed up against the wooden beams that creaked from the sudden pressure. Ropes were thrown down and fastened to the huge tie downs. Akechi then made his way up to the bridge.

"Captain we must speak. Please, to the back room," Akechi motioned to the ship's captain. "No matter where we are, I want you ready to leave in an hour's notice," he said, breathing heavily from his walk up the bridge.

"Is there some serious problem lord?" The captain asked.

"No captain. No serious problem, but I am involved in serious business here, and I am a foreigner," Akechi said in a rapid cadence. "The economies of the world are not stable and war could break out at any time. A combination of factors could cause problems at any minute or hour of the day. If this happens, I want to move as fast as possible. To return to Japan without delay. You understand?"

"Of course master," the captain replied. He did not know exactly what the short fat man meant, but it was not up to him to doubt or second guess him.

With the admonition over, Akechi thanked the captain for the hospitality and his attentions. He bowed deeply, and the captain reciprocated.

Akechi made his way to the gangplank, and again searched in the shade for Israel. He began his descent slowly and felt his legs starting to give way. He realized he had been at sea too long.

Israel was a chubby man of medium height with powerful shoulders, legs, and hands. He had a receding hairline, deep set and piercing green eyes, and a hawk nose. He was a perfect example of a mestizo, part Spaniard and part Indian, with features of both refusing to be dominated by the other. This was a part of the Latin American cultures that Akechi found fascinating. The Spaniards had come and conquered the natives, and yet decided to accept them and intermarry with the conquered. The Spaniard had looked closely, he had understood, and he had embraced.

Israel smiled broadly as Akechi approached the end of the plank. His mouthful of teeth and round ruddy cheeks showing a genuine invitation. So much emotion, so unabashed. As Akechi finally stepped on land, Israel embraced him with both arms, brought him close up to his own body, and hugged him strongly in an abrazo. Akechi was surprised, at first, and tried to fight the bear hug, but caught himself, returned the hug, and slapped Israel strongly on the back. It had been awhile since his last visit to México, but the Mexican ways would come back quickly, he thought. He glanced up toward the ship to see if he was being watched by his countrymen. Only a couple of deck hands looked down curiously.

The following weeks were spent reviewing contracts, procedures, manuals, and systems, as well as meeting company clients, key personnel, and outsiders important to the smooth operation of company business. It made no matter to anyone that Akechi took complete command of every aspect of how they conducted their business. Akechi had learned Spanish years before and was fluent enough to be understood.

During the days that followed, the men met early at the warehouse office and Akechi began with the training procedures, with Israel looking closely over his shoulder. The sessions went on for hours without rest.

Everyone sat around tables and stared at Akechi in awe. He noticed their trans-fixation. "Are they looking at my slanted eyes, or the color of my skin," he asked himself. "Of course, they are mesmerized by my business acumen and the new systems that I am teaching them," he surmised.

He had an understanding with Israel and Sebastian, and others like them throughout the world. They were to do business with him, and he could almost guarantee them success. He gave them the necessary capital, but they had to follow his instructions.

Israel had been with him from the beginning, and although he did not understand the Japanese language or culture, he eased Akechi into his own. Israel and his staff hosted Akechi everyday at the evening meal. Akechi took it all in, relishing every moment. Israel and the warehouse men talked about situations at the office, the women joined in the laughter, and the children played in the background.

Between business meetings and social gatherings, Akechi's thoughts often wandered off to Emperor Hirohito and the clowns that surrounded him, filling him with thoughts of war. "Would the warmongers likewise join in the fight?" He asked rhetorically. He did not think so. "So who cares?"

Several weeks later, Akechi announced his departure for the Gutiérrez Ayala warehouse. The staff was relieved.

For many reasons, but especially because of the tremendous intellectual debates that Sebastian generated, Akechi considered México the most special of all the foreign operations. He had not traveled it extensively, knowing only its southern tip and its western coast, where his Mexican associates grew the vegetables and spices he marketed throughout the world. Nevertheless, throughout the years he had grown to love the country and its people.

Akechi had read of the early oriental tribes who came over the Bering Strait thousands of years ago and had migrated for hundreds of years, thousands of miles to México, Central, and South America, and of the many Mexicans with slanted eyes who resembled his people and other orientals.

He also never tired of hearing the history of Sebastian, even though he had heard them many times. Sebastian Gutiérrez Ayala was a wise but wild man. Everyone knew that he was a wild man. He was forty-five years old. His long, dirty blonde hair framed a long thin face. He had piercing green eyes, a long thin nose, a pencil mustache, and a reddish gold complexion. At about six feet tall, he was taller than most men in the area. He had a muscular upper torso, but below his chest he was a slim person. Sebastian stood out in a crowd, at least in a crowd of Mexicans and Japanese.

Akechi loved to see Sebastian, because he was the only person Akechi believed was more intelligent than himself, and was the only one who had taken the trouble to learn Akechi's language.

Akechi enjoyed the mental gymnastics. The days were so enjoyable, with the toying and arguing. While Israel brought out a more relaxed and serious Akechi, Sebastian made Akechi joke and play around, experiencing an almost total personality change.

Akechi sat in his hotel room staring out the window and remembering his old friend from Acapulco, Daniel Márquez, tell Sebastian's story, while they sat around a campfire in a field, the golden fire reflecting off their faces.

"Sebastian's mother came from Madrid. She was brought to México, at the turn of the century, by her young husband, Miguel Gutiérrez. Miguel was a creole, born in México of Spanish parents. He worked with his father in the produce fields of southern and western México," Daniel began his tale, speaking in a high tone, pausing between statements as the fire crackled its presence. The old man twirled his gray mustache as he told and retold stories of Sebastian's life.

"The marriage between the maverick Mexican and the uppity Spaniard was like a volcano, and it barely survived to allow for the birth of the first child, a son, named Sebastian after his paternal great grandfather.

"Early on in their marriage, the parents realized they could not get along, did not care to raise the boy, and sent him to boarding school with the Jesuit priests. Although abandoned by his parents at the convent for years, the boy was intelligent, and his stay with the Jesuits permitted his mind to flourish, the flower to bloom. He emerged as the brightest student in all his classes, and actually the brightest in any group of which he was a part."

Akechi had gone to Sebastian's warehouse several times and did not find him. "Where could the dirty bastard be?" Akechi asked himself. It was embarrassing.

"Everything I have done for this sorry piece of slime, and he doesn't even come to greet me," he growled under his breath. Daniel's story interrupted Akechi's thoughts as he returned to the story of Sebastian's life.

"It was no wonder then, when at age thirteen the boy announced that he had experienced a call to the vocation as a Jesuit priest. To no one's surprise Sebastian grasped theology and philosophy as easily as he grasped the math, geography, and literature of his earlier teachings. Some of the veteran priests even shied away from arguing with the young man. They were no match, and hastily resorted to faith arguments. The years created a genius, but a young novitiate totally lacking in humility," Daniel would say as he paused to let his story set in. "Many times this character flaw was called to his attention, to no avail."

Akechi had imagined that sooner or later Sebastian would yield to temptation. That was happening now, that he could not find him. Sebastian was avoiding him. Akechi would never admit it to anyone, but it really hurt him.

"How ungrateful of the scum sucking pig."

He went back to Daniel's story. "Eventually he was sent home. Sebastian was hurt and confused at first. His mother did not know what to do with him, and preferred not to be around him. His father Miguel suddenly realized that he had a beautiful son and took him in with open arms."

Daniel spoke with his hands, and the yellow light of the open campfire followed the motion.

"Sebastian, at seventeen, was a very handsome figure. Miguel found himself suddenly proud and endeared to the son he had forgotten. Why should he give this fine specimen up to a religious order? Miguel swept the young man off his feet with the fatherly love that the young man had never experienced and could not now understand, but was delighted to receive.

"It did not take long for Sebastian to learn the agronomy, marketing, and economics that had taken his father years to learn. By age twenty Sebastian controlled his father's operation, and made most of the daily operational decisions.

"It was inevitable that the striking young lad would be exposed to the many temptations of the street; having been deprived for so many years, he gave in to those temptations easily. Only his superior intelligence permitted him to run a large enterprise and be able to carouse until the wee hours of the morning. A normal person could not have done it. Any business would have folded under similar management. But not Sebastian's. He was young and strong, of course, and that helped him immensely. But it took superior intelligence to keep his business going while he chased women and drank all night."

Daniel smiled and laughed as he told the story.

"The young lad was soon known as El Güero. To the people of Acapulco he was something special, someone they could gossip about. A young, rich, almost priest, womanizer, good looking, intelligent, entrepreneur. The market district always had stories to keep them excited.

"Sebastian never returned to the Jesuits. He chose the dark life instead, probably out of spite for being rejected. He continued with his carousing, but business thrived under his astute leadership. Sebastian never married. If he had married one of the lovely young women from the many commercial families, perhaps it would have settled the trouble quickly."

Daniel's big eyes rolled, as he concluded the tale, using his arms and hands as if conducting a symphony.

Years earlier Sebastian had started out like a ball of fire, but his bullishness eventually got him into trouble. Finding himself in financial straits he grudgingly teamed up with Akechi Massaki.

When the two men met for the first time, the topics rolled unto the table, and for the first time in months both of them were genuinely submersed in real, long intellectual conversation. Akechi did not stand a chance with the young man's glib charisma.

Soon, the short visit expanded into the wee hours of the morning. The cognac numbed their senses, but sparked their tongues, and the chatter went on until daylight. Each was fascinated with the other, and with the possibility that each could use the other in their own business affairs.

It was no secret that Sebastian needed more capital, and Akechi knew that he could add a new contact to his operation. There was nothing to force Sebastian to play with Akechi, but the temptation of getting into a world class operation was too much to resist. Sebastian knew that once you agreed to go along with Akechi, there was no quitting or withdrawing. If you quit or tried to quit you were out of the entire game.

Akechi got out of the taxi, paid the driver, waddled into the warehouse, thinking of the ingrate bastard that had failed to show. He had expected to find everything in complete shambles, warehouses empty, staff gone, and things in disrepair. However, after a couple of hours he found that some minor things were amiss but everything else, was in fair order. He asked about Sebastian, and no one knew where he was, where he had gone, nor why he did not show up. Akechi sat down with Manuel, the office manager, and after an extended discussion Akechi began to get the full story.

There really was not much to tell. Sebastian had been his usual brilliant self in maneuvering people, money, and markets, and was extremely successful. He did not follow the "company policies and regulations," carefully and found himself in dark corners and crossroads. It was not wanting to face the embarrassment that he did not show.

Akechi insisted on a field expedition the next morning, and was not disappointed with the condition of the fields. In certain small areas he could see that his advice was not followed. The failings were not major, in fact, they were minor. He was puzzled. Why had Sebastian not met him at the dock.

He interviewed Manuel extensively. Why? Where? Who? When? What? He could not detect anything so materially wrong, such as would cause Sebastian to abandon the company.

Sebastian had understood perfectly what Akechi wanted and required. He understood so well that he immediately undertook to please Akechi, while fulfilling his desires at the same time.

His gambling addiction grew slowly at first, but now, he could not stay away. It was card games and dice mostly, although horses and other dares enticed him just as easily.

Sebastian had planned to follow the rules set down by Akechi and then "borrow" enough money to place his bets, double the stake, return Akechi's money and continue gambling with his winnings. As with most gamblers, the plan did not work, and, not only did he not recoup his own winnings, he lost all of Akechi's money. The cash came from the business of course, and consisted of Akechi profits and operating capital. Sebastian timed his devious plan to coincide with Akechi's absence from Japan, thus eliminating the possibility of early detection through weekly reports mailed to Akechi.

It almost worked, but the last night just as he prepared to cash in and walk away a victor, he hit a losing streak and lost everything. His last loss came at about six-thirty in the morning just as the sun cracked above the horizon. He was exhausted after an entire night of drinking without sleep, but the worst was the horrible empty feeling of betrayal that he felt stabbing the deep recesses of his stomach.

Sebastian had known that Akechi was due within the week. What could he do? He would ask for credit and try to win back all the losses. He tried, but could not borrow even one hundred pesos.

Sebastian paced through the villa for days. He needed to make things right. He had betrayed one of the best friends and finest people and partners that he had ever known. He rationalized that the crops were still in the fields, and that they could be salvaged. Similarly, the warehouses were full of dry products, shipped from the coast. It was not as if he had stolen the money. He did not intend that. His rationalizations continued in an attempt to assuage his guilt. He would explain the entire matter and Akechi would understand. Gambling was honorable and manly. Akechi would understand. The Japanese love gambling, he thought.

When Akechi finally landed, Sebastian could not bring himself to face him, notwithstanding earlier feelings of honor and manhood. Several bottles of cognac did not improve his will. On the twelfth day after landing, and after a very long day, Akechi advised Manuel that he was going to the small restaurant around the corner from the office. He always sought the open air patios. He enjoyed the beautiful odor of the meat cooking on brazas, and preferred the soft outdoor lighting and the ever present trio singing old favorites that he had grown to love.

He chose a small table off to one corner close to the outdoor fire pit. The patio was rectangular in shape and was enclosed by an eight-foot high brick fence, with a gate on two sides, a small hostel on one side, and an open outdoor kitchen built up against the fourth side. The two open sides were lined with banana trees.

The night breeze was cool, and the cold beer went down easy. Akechi told Manuel that he preferred to be alone on this night. He was enjoying the privacy, the music, and the cooking.

After a short while, Akechi noticed a man standing among the banana trees at the far end of the patio. He recognized him. It was Sebastian. He knew then that his privacy was over, and that Sebastian had finally decided to talk with him. He had mixed emotions. He wanted the evening alone, but he also wanted to talk to Sebastian and find out what had happened to him. After all, through the years of their association, Sebastian had become a very good friend, and he was always loyal and true. His only solace was that the matter would be behind him by morning.

Sebastian approached slowly. They could not avoid smiling at each other. Despite the nature of the problem, there was no ill will or anger. Akechi could tell immediately that Sebastian had been drinking. Sebastian offered his hand, and Akechi shook it, motioning simultaneously for Sebastian to sit. Sebastian began his confession. Akechi did not speak one word. Akechi knew that Sebastian would not create a story to cover up for the misdeed. So it was, Sebastian quickly explained the truth. He had squandered the money gambling. Sebastian begged for help.

"You can have everything that I own. The properties that I own far exceed the money that I have taken. I am so ashamed of taking the money," Sebastian said, bowing his head to avoid looking at the friend he had betrayed. Then he looked at Akechi and in clear Japanese continued his confession.

"The truth, my friend, is that I am completely finished. I have not been able to adjust from my hopes of becoming a priest to a life as an ordinary man. I cannot go on in business, unless as a lowly employee. I cannot lead. I have lost the edge in making trades and closing deals."

Sebastian sobbed quietly as he continued talking. Throughout Akechi did not say one word. Sebastian spoke of their friendship through the years. The good times, some bad, and the early formative years. Sebastian slowly mitigated what he had done. He explained all the good that was accomplished and all that remained unspoiled and to be accomplished.

"I come to you asking and begging for forgiveness. I also come to you helpless, as a brother pleading for help. Please help me," he went on crying softly with tears flowing down his cheeks. "I cannot go on, I need your help. In your huge organization surely there is somewhere where you can place me so as to enable me to repay the money that I have stolen, and somewhere where I can help you, somewhere I can be happy without the responsibility. It is the responsibility that I do not want, I cannot cope with it. Please help me, please, please."

Akechi did not believe what he was hearing. Finally he spoke.

"Not only do you come and openly confess a stupid theft, and ask my forgiveness, but you have the balls to ask that I take you in like my little brother," Akechi growled in a deep voice through his teeth. "If you were in Japan I would have you boiled in hot oil and skinned."

Akechi glared across the table at the crying, broken man. It seemed like five minutes passed and neither man spoke or moved, both oblivious to the singing and movement around them. Slowly the adrenalin subsided, and Akechi simply stared at what had once been a proud, intelligent, and energetic man. He slowly remembered the long discussions they shared on so many topics; religion, philosophy, war, peace, business. Very memorable occasions. Akechi continued to stare at Sebastian pitifully.

Sebastian finally stopped sobbing, and realized that the confession was over, started to push his chair back to leave. Akechi looked at him and spoke quickly.

"We leave for Japan in three days, you will go with me. There are two conditions. You leave all your properties here in my custody and control, and you must obey every order I give. If you agree, see me at the office early in the morning on Wednesday. Bring your belongings. It will be a long stay. Now please leave."

Akechi had just found the philosopher, poet, and intellectual that would make Chon, the gifted young boy, into a total and complete samurai, who would polish the rough stone. He was pleased, Chon would be delighted, and Sebastian would have to enjoy being a teacher.

The stone would be polished.

Chapter Three

C hon was bored during Akechi's absence. The only things that kept him going were the karate training with Nagi san and the anticipation of receiving a nice gift when Akechi returned. Akechi had never failed to bring an exciting gift.

His mother, tried to distract the boy by encouraging him to go visit with Yoshi and learn something about the "automobile trucks," but he was not interested. She reminded him that Nagi san would have a special training session that day.

This excited the boy and he immediately prepared for the afternoon session.

Having changed into his gi suit, Chon again returned to lounge around and bother his mother who was trying to finish some laundry. Every suggestion by the mother was turned down.

After what seemed an eternity, the field hands who lived in the Tiger Camp began arriving home. This signaled Chon to go to Nagi san's training barn. It was a large barn, which also served perfectly as a small gymnasium where Nagi san taught judo, karate, and the finer points of being the perfect samurai.

Nagi san was tired from a long day in the field, but he took his job as instructor seriously. Most of his charges had been with him about six years. There were special matters that were left for special moments, celebrated in special solemn sessions. On that day they would observe such a special matter and moment.

Nagi san was a short, muscular man. His hair was cut short, and he spoke in a high pitched voice. He told the young men only that it would be a special, righteous session, worthy of their gi suits.

When Nagi san walked into the barn, he found the young men sitting quietly and anxious. There was no laughing. Nagi san had inculcated in each of them the idea that the business of a samurai was absolutely serious and not a childish matter.

He ordered the boys to cover the windows of the barn with black sheets, thus almost totally darkening the room. There were four small lanterns lit in each of the four corners of the large room. Then he asked three of the boys to construct the altar as he had taught them. The altar consisted of several straw mats, a wooden platform, arranged in rectangular fashion, and faced the group of young men. There were two large bronze bowls on either side of the open space, incense burned in each. Nagi san ordered the boys to a back part of the room to warm up with several karate exercises. After about twenty minutes, the boys had worked up a slight sweat and Nagi san called them over to the altar.

Nagi san sat and crossed his legs in front of him. The boys did the same. Nagi san then began a long litany of prayer and chanting, and the boys followed as they had on many occasions. Finally, the praying stopped and Nagi san began a lecture in a very quiet, precise, and clear speech.

"We are all of the same clan. We are all from the same family. We are all of the tiger. We are sons of Hachiman-shin, the god of war and protector of the Japanese people," he said, speaking in a high tone. He stopped briefly, as if to let the statements sink in, then he began again.

"We are samurai, we are sons of Minamoto Yoritomo. We are sons of Minamoto Yoritomo. We are sons of Minamoto Yoritomo. We are sons of Hachiman-shin and sons of Kami-no-Kaze the god of wind. We are samurai," he said, speaking slowly.

"As samurai we must be faithful to each other, we must be strong, and do without, if we have to. We must be loyal to our friends and patrons, to each other, and to ourselves, and everything that we stand for, but above all we must be brave. We must be brave. We must be brave. We must be brave."

The room was hot and stuffy. Sweat formed on foreheads. The praying and chanting continued. Nagi san bowed deeply as did all the boys. When the praying stopped, the quiet was deafening. Nagi san stood, and the boys followed.

"Above all a samurai must be brave. A samurai does not fear anything. A samurai confronts his enemy calmly and without fear. A samurai fights ferociously and without fear. Fear, and the fear of hurt or death paralyzes a good samurai, therefore we must learn to dominate fear.

Above all, a samurai must be brave. A samurai must be brave in battle, a samurai must also be brave in service to his community. A samurai must be brave in victory. A samurai must be brave, and this means that a samurai must be brave in defeat and in death, until his last breath. Today we learn to be brave in defeat and to die bravely."

He reached to his right side under the straw mat, pulled out a small long bundle. He placed the bundle in front of him, and gracefully unwrapped it, slowly removing the red silk finally exposing what was within. The young men saw a short aikuchi dagger. It shined, with a pearl handle covered with the traditional cross lacing. The boys stared in awe.

The chanting and prayer began again, and continued for about five minutes before Nagi san continued with his lecture.

"Since samurai Tametomo we have been taught to die bravely, even in defeat. A samurai is never taken prisoner. A samurai does not survive defeat to be taunted, teased, and tortured by his victors. A samurai hates defeat. A samurai would rather die than accept defeat. A samurai would rather die than submit to ridicule or torture. There is nothing more honorable for a samurai than to die in battle, whether in victory or in defeat."

"This," Nagi san continued, "is your way of dying honorably in defeat. This is the aikuchi dagger. It is used to commit harakiri." The silent room seemed even quieter, as the boys realized the solemnity of the session.

"Since many centuries past our forefathers have chosen to die honorably in defeat through suicide. It is an honorable thing to commit suicide when you need to, it is a very dishonorable thing not to commit suicide when you should."

Chon sat in total and complete awe as the thought of dying from his own hand sank in. He tasted the unfamiliar taste of bile on his tongue, as he felt the upper part of his stomach tighten.

Nagi san removed his shirt and demonstrated the technique, slowly reaching down for the dagger, separating it from its scabbard, wrapping the blade in rice paper, then turning the point toward the body, and holding the handle with both hands and jerking inward.

He repeated slowly and he described each movement to the young boys. He then urged them to remove their shirts and imitate each motion.

"The secret is that the blade continues to the huge artery that all animals have next to the spinal column," Nagi san explained. "There is a big difference between simply opening the stomach cavity and stabbing quickly and cutting the artery in back. Death comes quickly, intelligently, honorably, in this fashion."

The boys could visualize the entire gruesome scene. Chon could not remember any lesson or session so vivid and impressing. Nagi san knew, of course, that the boys were shocked, and he wanted them to be shocked. He wanted them to be impressed. Harakiri is special after all, he thought, and should not simply go the way of a side kick. To bring them back down, Nagi san began chanting again and then shifted into a soft yell session. He yelled softly and the boys echoed his yell.

"We are samurai."

"We are samurai," the young men answered.

"We are loyal."

"We are loyal," they chanted

"We are honorable."

"We are honorable," they responded.

And on he led them through bravery, death, suicide, bravery, death, suicide, and on and on.

Nagi san dismissed the boys with the admonition that they not discuss any of the day's events ever with anyone. This was the way of the samurai, they were told, and these secrets were not discussed with anyone.

Chapter Four

S mooth seas permitted Akechi's safe return to Japan. Akechi, however, refused to speak with Sebastian throughout the trip. "Let him suffer," Akechi thought. "I do not want him to think that all is well, because it is not." Sebastian was starved for conversation. His anxiety over the lack of human interaction made him feel like he was going crazy. Akechi had instructed the captain and crew to be tight with the liquor where Sebastian was concerned.

The ship's docking occurred without incident, except for the stares of curiosity towards Sebastian from those on the dock.

When they arrived at his mansion, Akechi quickly gave orders about the tall, white fellow and his lodging. He would occupy the small gray bungalow at the far end of the south yard.

"He is a special guest, he is a king from a far land," Akechi told everyone at the plantation. "He is to be treated with silk gloves. A special guest. I will explain more later."

The suitcase and trunks were taken away in various directions.

As Akechi started into the house, he glanced off to his right and in the distance saw Chon staring at him, excitedly awaiting recognition and attention. Akechi smiled, but did not have time to talk and visit with him.

Akechi hurried inside and called to Shimazu, one of the office managers, to follow him into his office. He asked for, and got, a quick summary of recent developments. Akechi was satisfied, and said that he wanted a long, detailed report later. Akechi then explained Sebastian's presence and ordered that under no circumstances would Sebastian be allowed to get involved in the business unless Akechi ordered it in writing and he was present.

Akechi spent three days with his staff. The first day was with the international communications group, finding out what was going on with his worldwide operations. He also asked about the military situation in Japan. He spent the second with his accounting staff checking the purses. He was pleased that his plans were working so well. The third day he spent on the plantation inspecting the fields and crops.

He had looked forward to the third day because he would be able to examine the land, which he loved to do. He had grown to love the feel of sand grains slipping through his fingers, or of mud between his fingertips.

Also, he would get to see Chon.

He went over to the stables as he always did on field inspection days, and greeted Yoshi, who by now had taken the black pickup out of its parking space. It was pointed south and ready for Akechi to get behind the steering wheel to begin his rounds.

The motor was running. Chon approached and bowed at Akechi. It seemed that the young man had grown five inches. He controlled his urge to hug the boy, western style. The others might be shocked. Before long Sebastian would have all of them exchanging abrazos, Akechi thought with a half smile of approval. The day went as usual, but Akechi was so preoccupied in conversation with Chon that he did not inspect very much.

A week after their return, Akechi summoned Sebastian to his office.

"Sebastian, you have caused me great problems. You have dishonored yourself, and now you seek to change your life and your ways. I do not know if all this is possible," Akechi said with obvious disappointment. "I do know, however, that you have asked for help, that I have agreed to help you with conditions, and you have accepted. Now, let me say that I have not brought you here to boil you in oil and skin you."

Sebastian chortled, finding the comment somewhat humorous, but being relieved nevertheless, that he would apparently not be cooked into chicharrones.

"As far as your properties and your business are concerned, you do not need to be concerned," Akechi assured Sebastian. "Things will continue as they were, but I will control them for the next few years while you will stay here on a special mission. After a time, if you desire, I will take you back to México, and then you can resume management of the properties and business. I only caution you the following. Once you take over the business again, if you fail again, then I will have no mercy.

"Now, here you will have private quarters. You may socialize and eat with me or my staff whenever you desire, but your day will be spent teaching and educating a young boy," Akechi paused as Sebastian furrowed his brow curious about his new assignment.

"This boy is named Chon. He was born here on the plantation. When the boy was only a baby, his father Tengzeu was assassinated while accompanying me on a trip to China. The man gave his life so that I could live. I decided that it would be a small thing to repay him for my life by helping his son be a special person. Therefore, I have trained the boy to be a samurai. A modern day samurai. The boy has responded well. He is fourteen now, and is the smartest and strongest young man that I know. He grasps everything quickly and will not disappoint you. He continues his training, but he lacks some things," Akechi said, pausing to see if Sebastian had any questions.

"He must be taught the business of languages, of geography, of philosophy, of logic, of world history, and of theology. He is a piece of coal that must be transformed, that last small bit, into a diamond. You Sebastian, will guarantee me that this will occur. The boy will be in your complete charge. Only Nagi, his samurai instructor, will be able to demand the boy's time as you will. The boy's mother is named Massa, and she will be told of your job. She will not interfere. You may teach him anything that you please, as long as it does not interfere with Nagi san's teachings. Do you have any questions?" Akechi asked Sebastian in a demanding tone.

"Suppose I do not want to teach your young charge? What then?" Sebastian fired back.

"Sebastian, two weeks ago, you came crawling to me for help. I could have killed you then. Instead I took you in and agreed to rehabilitate you. Now, I am offering you the simple task of bringing a young boy into manhood. Do not disappoint me," Akechi replied firmly.

Sebastian realized that he had overstepped his limit and withdrew. "Massaki, do not worry, I will teach the young man, and you will be pleased. You will be proud," he told him, referring to Akechi by his first name since they had been longtime friends, not just business partners.

Akechi called out for Chon. The boy entered slowly and Akechi formally introduced and advised Chon of his new mentor.

"You know as I, that a samurai is not complete, unless he can discuss matters of the world intelligently, I mean like literature, music, history, geography, religion, philosophy, and the foreign tongues of the other parts of the world," Akechi said quietly and slowly, breathing heavy as he did.

"In addition to all these things, Mr. Gutiérrez Ayala will also teach you the principles of business. This is a part of the training that you must have," Akechi explained to Chon.

With all the attention focused on him, Chon smiled broadly.

"Do you have any questions?" Akechi asked in western fashion. Chon stared, then shook his head slightly to indicate he did not.

At that point Sebastian walked straight to the boy and looked down at his face, then began walking a slow circle around the boy, examining every part of his body. To his amazement, Sebastian noticed that his movements were being mirrored by the young man, as he too carefully examined every part of the tall, skinny, white man.

Akechi asked everyone else to leave. He wanted some privacy with Chon. Akechi walked slowly to his desk and sat. He motioned to Chon to come closer to the desk.

"As on all of my trips, I have brought you a gift. This time I have brought you something special indeed. Sebastian is a very special person. You will soon see. He is one of my very best friends. He is very intelligent and can speak on just about any subject. The reason he is so important to you is that he can show and teach you so much, to help you become the most important and special of all samurai. As you know, a samurai is not just a soldier. You must also be a very well versed gentleman, a poet, a philosopher, a teacher, an artist, and so on. A very refined warrior. His instruction is my gift to you," Akechi continued the explanation and Chon listened attentively and understood, but Akechi noticed the anticipation in the boy's face.

"But, as with all my other trips I usually bring you a little gift, a bauble or other similar thing. This trip is no exception." Akechi opened the bottom drawer on the left side of the desk, and pulled out a small package. It was long and narrow and wrapped in brown paper. Akechi began to unwrap it and inside was a wrapping made of rice paper, finally a third wrapping, one of red silk.

Chon's heart beat sped up in anxiety. He had received many fine gifts from Akechi, and he was sure that this one would be no exception. Akechi's gifts were special of course, they were not paper and cloth toys, but each of these gifts were durable and meant to last a lifetime. Akechi continued to unwrap, and finally came up with a beautiful brand new aikuchi dagger. Its pearl handles were covered with the traditional crisscross lace and its scabbard was made of beautiful pecan wood. The grain of the light colored wood looked almost like a wooded scene.

"I must confess, I got this for you here in Japan before I left for my trip, knowing that Nagi san would teach you the importance of the aikuchi in a samurai's life," Akechi said.

Akechi pulled the knife out and the new silver blade shined. Slowly, sweat beads formed on Chon's forehead, he could feel his stomach turning. He again tasted the bile at the back of his mouth. He forced a slight smile. Akechi offered the gift across the desk. Chon moved forward and accepted the beautiful knife. He bowed and showered Akechi with thanks and compliments.

"You may go now," Akechi said. Chon exited in a hurry, and rushed home and stuck the new gift under his mat.

Akechi called for Sebastian who hurried over to the palace. He would be teaching the young boy named Chon. Only the details were lacking. He imagined that Akechi's call was about the boy. He was right.

"Just south of your bungalow is an open shed, which we call a tea house. It will serve perfectly as a teaching area. You can fix it up any way that you need. Yoshi, the blacksmith, has been told to help you. He'll get you a table, board, pens, paper, whatever. In inclement weather, you will use the extra office just next to this room," Akechi motioned to his right. "Do you have any questions?"

"Is there any limitation to anything that I can teach or do?" Sebastian asked.

"There is no limitation. Teach him as if he were your own son. Prepare him for the world. Make him better than I, make him better than yourself. Be proud of him. Please do a good job."

As if to seal a pact, Akechi brought out a bottle of cognac, and poured two drinks. They were off on a new discussion, this one on teaching methods of the different parts of the world. They went on into the wee hours of the morning. They separately thought at different moments that Sebastian's stay was going to be enjoyable.

* * *

"My name is Sebastian Gutiérrez Ayala," Sebastian told Chon, speaking in the Japanese he had acquired over years of dealings, both business and social, with Akechi. He went on to explain the origin of his name, the origin of his family in Spain, and their immigration to México.

As the classes progressed, he read from his own library, translating to Japanese as he went along. *Treasure Island* and *Don Quixote* were the first books he translated. The boy was especially spellbound by *Treasure Island.*

Months went by and Sebastian had not required Chon to participate in the exchange. It was Sebastian doing all the talking. No questions were asked of Chon requiring a response.

Gradually they had slipped into about an hour of language during each session, starting with the alphabet in Spanish.

Sebastian conferred with Akechi about the boy's progress. They both shared amazement at the boy's intelligence. Sebastian requested, and got permission, to follow the boy's movements during the day. In this way he got a chance to see how the samurai shaped up. He shook his head in wonderment at the boy's physical abilities.

The young men would gather at the old gray barn and go through their routines as Nagi san, the sensei, shouted out instructions. Sebastian, in all his worldly exposure had never seen the fighting like the one done at Tokyo Plantation. They called it karatedo. Sebastian was awed by the hand to hand maneuvers, the flipping over of bodies, the rabbit punch, and how the young men broke boards and bricks with their bare hands. Later he examined Chon's hands and found both to have thick calluses on the bottom back side of the palms.

Sebastian thoroughly enjoyed this samurai business, and on many occasions, he invited Akechi to come see, so they both could enjoy the exhibitions of the afternoon, whether in horsemanship, marksmanship, sword fighting, spear fighting, kendo, karate, or some other skill. The two watched excitedly as they had done on many occasions watching bullfights, boxing matches, and baseball games in México.

Meanwhile the teaching continued, as his young charge continued to improve in languages and in reading of the Spanish and English books that Sebastian had brought with him. The boy had a voracious appetite for learning.

"Your name, Chon, is a nickname for anyone in the Latin Americas whose name is Encarnación. Anyone who is named Encarnación is called Chon," Sebastian explained to the boy. "I have several friends whom we call Chon."

He went on to explain the meaning of the name Encarnación, which meant incarnation or the personification of the divine, such as the incarnation of Jesus. The boy was awed as he heard of the child God that Sebastian called Jesus.

Sometimes, when Sebastian was teaching, he would affectionately call the boy Encarnación and the boy learned to respond to his teacher's pet name for him.

"You know Chon, there are many people in México and the other Latin Americans that look a lot like you. There is a story, that many hundreds of years ago, many tribes from this part of the world could not live at peace, because of a shortage of food, and because of warring, and other reasons, and therefore they decided to move and go elsewhere.

"At a ceremony, they prayed to their gods to help them in this journey. Their prayers were answered by a vision, one that explained their voyage to them and told them how and where to go. They were told in the vision that they should not stop their sojourn until they saw an eagle with a snake in its beak, as it rested on a cactus."

Sebastian pulled out a map of the world and laid it on the table, and continued his story. "The story goes on. These orientals were told to proceed north. They traveled north through Manchuria for decades," Sebastian pointed to the map and sketched with his index finger. "Then on through this part of what is now Russia, and then over the Bering Sea. The story says that the Bering Sea was frozen over and made crossing possible for these tribes. The groups totaled several thousand people.

"They continued for several more years through what is now known as Alaska, Canada, the United States, and then into México, where it is said they finally saw the eagle resting on a cactus plant, with a snake in its beak. This supposedly happened at a site close to present-day México City. There the tribes settled, prospered beautifully in the marvelous climate and fertile soil, and multiplied. From there they spread throughout all of Latin America. So it is not at all uncommon for us to see many people in the Americas that look like they belong on Tokyo Plantation. There are many people on the other side of the world that look very similar to you, my dear Chon," Sebastian said, winding up his story.

"As time goes on, Chon, I will teach you more and more about more and more things. Eventually there will be a time when I will have to teach you things that only you and I will know. When we finally come to these subjects you must keep everything I tell you absolutely secret. I will be like a big brother telling you the special secrets of life, and I do not want you telling anyone, and I mean anyone, about these things. Not even Akechi. Do you understand?" Sebastian finished looking inquisitively at Chon.

"I understand perfectly sir, and I will not divulge any of these matters. Through the months I have grown to appreciate you and like you immensely and I trust you as a big brother or an uncle really. I will keep a secret of course," Chon responded, but wondering if he could actually exclude Akechi from any secret. The others were no problem, but he owed loyalty to Akechi and did not know if Sebastian's request would betray Akechi.

The months passed, and suddenly it came to be a year of them being together. They talked and argued and covered every imaginable subject. They discussed Plato, Nietzsche, Freud, Aquinas, Jesus, Buddha, Cervantes, Octavio Paz, Benito Juarez, Abraham Lincoln, Thomas Paine, and many other giants from history.

Sebastian wondered what Chon would do in life? Surely he would end up running the Akechi produce empire. What a waste, he thought. Far too much intellect for simply running a large business. A mind like that should be put to better use. That would not be his worry. That plan had been made by Akechi many years ago, and there was little that Sebastian could do to change it.

"Today is a special day," Sebastian announced to the young man. "Today, little brother, I will teach you a secret special thing about this beautiful world that you live in. But we cannot stay here in the tea house in the open. We must go into my house where no one can hear us and see us. Remember I want these special matters to be and remain absolutely secret. No one knows what goes on. We do these things in absolute secrecy, understood?"

"Understood perfectly," Chon answered. He was very curious as to what the secret matters were. Sebastian put his arm around the young man and they walked from the tea house over to his bungalow. They walked in and Sebastian shut the door behind them. Massa glanced out of the palace as she went through the large house performing her duties. Throughout the day, she looked out toward the tea house and proudly admired her son, and thanked God for the wonderful education that master Akechi decided to bestow on him. On that particular day she noticed that Sebastian and Chon were going into Sebastian's house. She could not say why, but she did not like it. Although not being present, she had been told that master Akechi directed that instruction would take place at the tea house, and during inclement weather in the second office, the office next to master Akechi's own office. Why were they going into the little house?

After about an hour they emerged from the small house, and Massa breathed a sigh of relief. She squinted her eyes as she looked at Chon from the distance to see if she could detect any harm. They were both smiling so she assumed all was in order. Nevertheless, she would question Chon tonight.

As the weeks and months went by, the secret sessions continued. Massa looking curiously from the palace. She resented the
sessions, but was helpless to do anything about them. Eventually
the entire palace staff knew about the apparent clandestine
sessions, and began calling the sessions "the black hour."

"There they go, another black hour."

"Chon is going through another black hour."

"Massa, the black hour has begun."

These were the comments.

Chapter Five

Akechi realized that he had been away from Japan too long. He had stayed out of local politics, and had lost the pulse of current movements. Too long, during these uncertain times, Akechi thought. It was 1935, and the noises of war were getting louder and stronger. Japan had invaded Manchuria four years earlier and withdrew from the League of Nations the following year. Emperor Hirohito was being bombarded from all sides by different interest groups. Akechi realized the importance of raising his voice to let the emperor or his generals know his views, but unfortunately time did not permit a continued lobbying effort.

New groups enjoyed attacking wealth, and the older established political powers. The political powers and parties were conservative and preferred to leave things the way they were. The new groups wanted rebellion, and cared very little about the establishment and their antiquated policies and conservative rules.

By the end of 1935, the war movement had built up to a fever pitch. Militarism was on the rise. The sons of god began to take all of the land that they needed. There was no turning back, there was no failure. In fact there was not even the thought of possible failure.

Akechi learned, disappointingly, that Capt. Tomiji Oi had been appointed chairman of a new council created by the emperor to direct the military expansion. Akechi knew of course that this was bad, and that bad things would follow. He was powerless to do anything about it, though. He knew that things were bound to escalate, but he did not know when and in what direction. By 1937 the escalation of war appeared inevitable.

* * *

Akechi still took trips around the plantation. Now, however, Chon drove the pickup truck . The boy grew magnificently. He was now seventeen years of age, and tall and very muscular. His long face was slightly blemished with adolescent pimples, but the young man was handsome.

Chon's training with Nagi, Yoshi, and Hiro was almost complete. Akechi made arrangements for Chon to attend the University of Tokyo. He had not yet decided what curriculum the young man should study, but he thought it appropriate that his education should be finished at the university. Chon himself had not yet decided what career he should follow, although naturally he leaned toward agriculture and agronomy. In the last two years with Sebastian he had gotten a taste of every possible subject.

Throughout the remainder of the inspection of the plantation, Akechi discussed the world situation with Chon. He brought him up to date on developments in Europe where a number of civil wars and coup d'états created a very unstable situation. At home, the presence of the militaristic Cherry Blossom Society a few of miles down the road from Tokyo Plantation presented a real threat. Chon had many questions, of course, and Akechi did his best to help the young man appreciate the nature of the world situation.

Chon took every opportunity to discuss new findings with Sebastian, and every news break brought a new history lesson, or a deeper philosophical discussion.

As the young man matured the lessons became more enjoyable and more challenging. In time it was not a boy Sebastian was teaching, but a man. Chon's thirst for knowledge was insatiable. His intelligence made the matter a pleasure.

Chon's prowess in karate ripened and he was known for a flying mule kick and a grunt that followed. He had perfected every sport and skill, and was the best in each.

Chon was the favorite of the plantation. Everyone looked forward to his going to the university. It would be good for a farmer's son to go beyond the farming that most of them were born into and would die in. It was a novel thought that a fatherless boy, one of their own, be singled out by the master of the plantation for special treatment. None of them had heard of such a thing. They were not sure it was proper, but they liked the idea.

* * *

One hot and sunny afternoon all the men were in the fields working. Yoshi and his two helpers were in the stables. Chon and Sebastian talked in the tea house. Akechi and his staff were in the palace going over financial statements.

A gray colored four door sedan sped up to the front entrance of the mansion. Two large trucks sped to the north and south sides of the palace area. The quickness of the arrival startled everyone. Japanese Army troops jumped out of the two trucks and completely surrounded the house.

The door of the sedan opened and a young sharply dressed army captain stepped out. He was accompanied by three aides, younger men with brief cases and typewriter cases. The quartet walked to the entrance of the palace and sought entry.

By this time Yoshi approached the troops closest to the stables, asking about their business. Notwithstanding his strength and his training as a samurai, Yoshi was immediately subdued by the four rifle butts that smashed into his chest.

Seeing this, Sebastian quickly led Chon into the small house. Time would soon tell what the nature of the visit was. The captain made his way into the front foyer of the house and requested to speak to the master of the house. Briefly, Akechi appeared. It was evident that he was angry.

"What is the nature of this intrusion?" He growled.

"Simply the business of state my dear Massaki, whether you and the others realize it or not. The war to restore the great Japanese empire Dai Nippon Teikoku must go on. It must conquer. It's just part of the world," the captain said slowly, clearly, and deliberately. There are thousands of things that we must get in order to achieve our goal in this world. These things cannot be attained without a plan, without an inventory, without finding out who, and what, is around us for our use in the destiny of the conquest.

"For example we must know what is going on here at Tokyo Plantation. What you grow? When you grow it? How you grow it. Are you doing a good job? How many people work here? Are there enough workers? Do you need more? Do you have too many? Do you charge too much for your goods? Can you accommodate more people? Can you spare free provisions for the army? You see, there are many questions that must be answered, and that is why we are here. By the way, I am Capt. Tomiji Oi," he said while bowing.

Akechi could not restrain himself. He shouted at the captain. All that he had held back erupted into a constant flow of hot chastisement.

"You do not belong here, I am a loyal subject. I have always done what is right for the empire. I have always charged fairly. I have hired the right people to do a good job. I have managed to produce more than my requirements. I have clothed, fed, and educated my people. I do not need little imbeciles like you coming around, snooping to see what the Cherry Blossom Society can steal. I will not stand for it, I will not tolerate it. You must get your ass off of my plantation, and I mean quickly."

At this Capt. Tomiji stepped back slightly and a young trooper stepped forward with his rifle angled in front of him and approached Akechi. It was meant only as a gesture of force. Akechi did not appreciate the warning and continued to shout and point at Capt. Tomiji. The young guard slammed his rifle butt into Akechi's mouth.

Akechi reeled back into the back wall of the foyer, blood gushing out of his mouth, his lips severed open from the blow. A small piece of tooth fell to the floor. The steward and two of the household helpers came to his aid immediately. His mind surged back to China the night that Tengzeu gave his life for him. He realized now, as he did then, he was no samurai. He was embarrassed and slumped to the floor, sobbing quietly. He had lost complete face, was dominated and humiliated in front of his staff.

The staff carried Akechi off to his living quarters and Capt. Tomiji moved into the office area and took over. The three soldiers, set up in the same and in adjacent offices. Within the half hour the house had been commandeered. Everyone at the palace was advised of the government action and everyone powerlessly acquiesced. The troops were ordered to go about the plantation and announce to the field hands what had occurred. The field hands did not rebel or take other action. They said nothing. They would have time later to discuss this with Akechi, and take adverse action if necessary.

After a long while Capt. Tomiji sent for Akechi. Akechi's clothes were changed and the cuts on his lips were no longer bleeding. His eyes were full of tears. He was very upset. He slowly shuffled into the office where Capt. Tomiji had established headquarters.

Capt. Tomiji explained to Akechi the new order in Japan.

"I do not know why you have to behave so strangely. You must realize that things are no longer as they were twenty years ago. Now, the new revolution is on. Even the emperor is joining the revolution. Why should you fight it? The whole nation is moving forward, why do you fight the motion? Do you realize now that your resistance is useless and in vain? Who do you think you are helping? I sincerely do not question your loyalty, but I do seriously question your motives. You must now realize that things are under a new regime, one in which you have absolutely no say, and one with which you must comply or you will be expended. Let me tell you, you are completely expendable. Do you understand?"

Akechi nodded yes.

"Then, I am glad that you understand. Now to the business at hand. I must have your cooperation. I want complete lists from you of all of your products. I want to know exactly how you run this plantation, and what this plantation produces, and how it produces. I want to know how many people you have here, and who they are and what they do and what they can do.

"The war effort is escalating, and we must be able to identify our resources. In short, friend Akechi, I want to know every-thing, I want your cooperation, and I want to know it quickly. Do you understand?"

Akechi nodded again.

"Fine, I think that we are finally understanding each other. In the morning we will get down to details. In the meantime, I want you to go and make arrangements to house the forty troopers that I brought with me. I want them housed and fed well. Please do not upset me again, I would much prefer for this operation to go smoothly than to have to beat people and shed blood simply to have the Emperor's will carried out. Will we have your total and complete cooperation tomorrow?"

Akechi continued nodding affirmation.

"Then please leave and carry out the orders that are neces-sary to bed down the troops. I will have dinner with you and your staff."

The ordeal seemed to be over, at least temporarily. But in reality Akechi knew that it was just beginning. He assembled all the men around the house, Nagi san and Yoshi led the group. He explained what he understood about the occupation. He did not know if retaliation was the right thing to do. He would tell them later.

Akechi then went inside the mansion and assembled the plantation business staff. The accountants and economists looked bewildered. Again, he explained what he knew about the occupation. He advised them that their services would be in great demand within the next few days, perhaps weeks, as a total and complete asset and resource inventory would have to be prepared for the government.

"I do know that our nation is at war, and preparing for even greater war. I understand of course that we will have to do our share to help with the war effort. What I still do not understand is why we must be treated this way. We have never refused our government, our nation, nor our Emperor. I cannot understand why we have to be treated like this. One thing for sure, we are all Japanese, and we must be loyal, so for the time being, let us carry out these orders. Later I will see if I can rid us of this howling wolf who has taken over our lives so suddenly."

With that he dismissed them. The entire staff and the field hands and their families were assembled as ordered.

Akechi walked up from behind the nearby house. His lips were still red and swollen. All the men jumped to their feet and bowed deeply. Nagi san led the bow. Akechi walked up to the immediate area and also bowed.

"Please sit down, please sit down. You are wondering no doubt why I did not come earlier. Believe me I would have if I could have. It was impossible. I am sure you are wondering why our own army shows up and acts so wrongfully against us. We are, after all, Japanese and we are loyal and have always been loyal to our country," Akechi said while walking among them, waddling slowly, and breathing heavily.

"Well it is not easy to explain. But I must say one thing. There is no disloyalty to the Empire. I may be guilty of several infractions, but I am not guilty of treason and disloyalty to the empire.

"In truth, I have been against the escalation of war, because I do not believe that it is good for us, and I do not believe that it is good for Japan. When I tried to express this opinion to the emperor, I was refused an audience."

Akechi noticed that several soldiers were listening to his speech to the small group of men. The soldiers approached the group from several directions. "I am not afraid," he thought, as he noticed the approaching soldiers and continued his talk.

"When I tried to tell the emperor that I did not think that war against the rest of the world was a good idea, I was denied the opportunity to speak to the emperor, something that never ever happened to me, nor to any member of the Akechi family. Of course, I voiced an objection to my inability to speak with the leader of our nation, to no avail.

"Notwithstanding everything that has happened, and why it has happened, we must now focus on the real occurrence. Now let us say that it is over. Japan is at war. We are Japanese, and we are loyal Japanese, and we want Japan to succeed in the war. Therefore we must now show our loyalty to Great Nippon and do what is necessary to assure the success of the war. We did not get involved in the war effort because I would not allow it. Now we must or suffer great consequences. It is our duty to support our country.

"In a way, I have kept you in the dark. I was trying to protect you, trying to isolate you from the horrible occurrences of the world. I cannot do this any longer and because I cannot, then things will start to change from now on."

Akechi looked to his right and left trying to look everyone of his people in the eye.

"In the morning I will meet with Capt. Tomiji and I am sure that after our meeting I will receive several orders which must be carried out. As soon as I have this information I will pass it on to you. Now I must go. Thank you for everything that you have done to help me."

The crowd had gradually grown very large. Everyone maintained absolute quiet, even the soldiers who witnessed the private abdication. Akechi had tears in his eyes as he shuffled away. Most everyone else did also.

Akechi invited Sebastian to dinner with Capt. Tomiji. Akechi figured that he needed all the help he could get in trying to analyze the occurrences of the last few days and to try to figure out a defense or a solution to the problem.

"Who is this American? Not only do you drag your feet in getting involved in the battles that your country must fight, and not only have you stuck with the old grandmothers who wish to leave everything in its old stale state, but now I find that you have an American spy living on your estate. What is all this stupidity? I demand to know," Capt. Tomiji shouted at Akechi.

"When I first got here I came to straighten out a few business matters. I never imagined that I would find a spy operation. Now I must know," he screamed, "what is going on here, and who it this spy? I demand answers now."

Akechi had regained his composure after the shock of the sudden visit. After all he was not a traitor, he was very nationalistic.

"Capt. Tomiji, you are completely wrong," he said to the enraged captain. "This man is no American, he is Mexican. He is one of my business associates. His name is Sebastian Gutiérrez Ayala, and he helps my business to prosper with superior knowledge of the produce business. What, or who, helps my business prosper helps Japan prosper. I am completely serious about all this. I deserved to get my mouth knocked in because of my nationalist insolence, but I can tell you sincerely, this man is not a spy, he is not an American, and he is a great help to me and to my work, and therefore indirectly a great help to Japan. Talk to him, ask him whatever you desire, I guarantee that you will agree with me."

Capt. Tomiji looked suspiciously at Sebastian, who smiled back widely. He was sincere and Capt. Tomiji could see this.

The genuineness and sincerity of Akechi's comments cooled Capt. Tomiji. He made a few interrogatories of Sebastian, and was convinced that what Akechi had said was true.

Japan already had a network of spies in México, Central, and South America, Capt. Tomiji thought, therefore not every Mexican or Latin American can be bad. Some were helping already.

As the hours waned, Akechi and Capt. Tomiji joked with each other and spoke to each other like old friends. The mutual distrust was still there, the events of the last few hours would not be patched up for some time yet, but the thaw was on, and given the right circumstances, Akechi and Capt. Tomiji could get along well.

The captain left satisfied that no espionage was being carried out at Tokyo Plantation.

Chapter Six

Akechi arose early, and to his surprise Capt. Tomiji was up and was busy in the office.

"My dear Akechi, I am pleased to announce that all the inventory lists are just about complete. It could be that we will be leaving this afternoon. I am very pleased. If it were not for your cooperation, there is no way that we could have finished this soon."

"You see I can be cooperative. I have always been a loyal son. I think you misjudged my philosophy and I think you overreacted," Akechi responded pointing to his lips.

"Well, for that I must apologize my dear Akechi, but your earlier behavior led me to believe that you were a bad merchant. If I made a mistake please forgive me," Capt. Tomiji replied earnestly.

Akechi inspected the inventory lists. The room was quiet with both men working without making a sound. The silence continued for some time, until the roar of trucks outside of the palace area broke the silence. Akechi glanced out of the window and noticed that ten troop carrier trucks drove through the area and onto the back yard. Akechi turned to Capt. Tomiji searching immediately for an explanation.

"Do you know what is going on? Or is this another horrible thing about to happen?" Akechi asked.

"Of course, I know what is happening. I would not be very good at my job if I did not know what ten troop carriers were doing here. You should not be frightened. It is all a matter of work, and there is no reason to be upset. It is simply that we need to get volunteers from among the plantation people. You see we need more people in the navy. That part of our war effort has gone wanting, because of our emphasis on the infantry and the advancements through the islands that have required so much infantry.

"But if we are going to dominate this part of the world, and perhaps all the world, then we need to expand our operations, and we cannot expand our operations without a good and efficient navy. Those trucks will return to Tokyo and points beyond with two hundred plantation volunteers who will join the Japanese military tomorrow. You should be proud to be able to make such a contribution to our nation," Capt. Tomiji smiled as he finished talking.

Akechi was in absolute shock. He tried to hide his feelings.

"First, you hit me in the mouth with a rifle butt, then you take over my plantation and squeeze out its effort and information into a cardboard box , and now you tell me that you are taking all my farmworkers to help you on some boats that you expect to conquer the world with. I am breathless," Akechi said, stopping for a few seconds, huffing loudly.

"How am I supposed to run a plantation and provide food for the war effort if you are going to remove two hundred workers?" Akechi continued.

"Don't jump to conclusions," Capt. Tomiji shouted back. "I have conducted studies of all the farm operations in the nation, and I find that while yours is the most productive and most efficient, it is also the most heavily populated.

"You don't need so many people. If I really wanted to bring you to common level with the average farm operation, I should take five hundred of your young men. So by this standard two hundred is not very much. I am treating you fairly."

Capt. Tomiji paused, then continued in a low tone.

"Despite our crude entrance ten days ago, I have gotten to know you and respect you, and to like you. By taking only two hundred men I am doing you a favor," the captain said in a defense of his actions.

Akechi knew that Capt. Tomiji was right, he had too many people, and had a duty to support the war effort. There was not much he could say to rebut Capt. Tomiji's point, so rather than say something ignorant or abrasive, he kept quiet, and moved to leave the room.

"I can see your sadness, and your disappointment my friend. I would feel the same if I were in your shoes, but really I have no choice," Capt. Tomiji told Akechi.

"In order to continue to help you, I have the complete list of all young men on the plantation between the ages of seventeen and twenty-three. I want you to go through here and pick the two hundred that you think would best serve the empire," Capt. Tomiji said, handing Akechi the several pages of typewritten lists.

Akechi recognized this as a veiled favor. He was letting Akechi pick the least desirable workers.

"When do you want the list?" Akechi asked.

"I would prefer it as soon as possible, because we must assemble all the men and instruct them on what is to occur. So, quickly please," Capt. Tomiji answered.

Akechi went outside and sent for Nagi san. He knew it would take twenty minutes for Nagi san to arrive. He leafed through the pages, silently calling out the names of the young men that he had seen born, raised, educated and put to work on the plantation. Some of these young men were already married and had children of their own. He continued to look through the list until Nagi san arrived.

He explained the situation to Nagi san, and shortly they began going through the list, choosing, changing, adding, changing, choosing, until they narrowed the list down to four hundred young men. They continued their chore until noon time, when they finally gleaned out two hundred names. Their work done, Akechi ordered Nagi san to spread the word throughout the plantation, that two hundred of them would become sailors in His Majesty's Imperial Navy.

"If they hear now, they will have time to get used to the idea. In this way when their names are called they can be proud of going to serve the nation," Akechi said, returning to the main office and handing the lists to Capt. Tomiji, with the special list on top of the others.

Capt. Tomiji was reviewing the choices with care, when Akechi broke his concentration.

"When do you want them assembled for instruction?" Akechi asked Capt. Tomiji.

"This afternoon at eighteen-hundred hours. I need to give them about one hour of specific instructions about departure. It must be quick. I have no time to waste," Capt. Tomiji barked out the orders slowly and softly.

Akechi and Nagi san knew that the reaction would be favorable. The men were trained properly, and for a moment just such as this. They were good soldiers. They would make the plantation proud.

By seventeen-fifty hours the sergeants and lieutenants had the volunteers lined up in ten columns of twenty each, from shortest to tallest. They were ordered to sit on the ground.

The young men were excited for the chance to prove themselves. Even if it meant death, it meant excitement. To go off to strange and distant lands and fight and prove their bravery. There was not one that did not feel honored to be chosen. The first fifteen minutes they were exposed to nationalistic propaganda, which they did not need.

They were assigned line numbers and instructed on which line numbers would report to which truck. They were told to leave their clothes, and to come fed, as they probably would not be fed for a day or so. They could bring food if they wanted.

Akechi watched the entire proceedings, with Capt. Tomiji watching from behind the scene. A joyous ambiance permeated the plantation. Everyone was excited and proud. Even Akechi felt a sense of pride that Tokyo Plantation could contribute so well to the war effort. He stood, took in a deep breath, smiled, and turned to go back into the house, when Capt. Tomiji confronted him suddenly.

"I know you are not expecting this, so I will be swift. You are going to be upset, but you must trust me. It is the best thing for him. I want the young man Tasaka Chon to join the volunteers in the morning."

"No, you can't, you can't," Akechi screamed. "He is to enter the university this next term. He has a special destiny, you can't do this to me," Akechi's scream turned into a wail.

"I know what you are thinking. That you and only you can mold him finally into the fine man that he will be. That is not true. The empire can and will finish molding this young man. Now please do not make this harder than it really is," Capt. Tomiji finished and turned on a heel and left the room for the evening meal.

Akechi hurried out of the room biting his lower lip. He interrupted a chess game between Sebastian and Chon. He had to tell Chon, so he could go tell Massa and get ready. He hurried Chon off to Massa.

"Sebastian, what do we do? How can we stop this? Oh how horrible," he moaned, in emotional distress. "The only good, really good thing to come out of this plantation in the last twenty years, and this bastard has to come find him. I have great plans for Chon, but Capt. Tomiji says that I may never have a chance to carry them out." Akechi paced the room nervously, breathing heavily. Sebastian watched silently.

Akechi knew, of course, that there was very little that he could do to stop this turn of fate. He was hoping however, that Sebastian might know a sly trick to stop what appeared inevitable.

"Offer him money, a mordida, a bribe, you know how easy and well it works in México. When we want special things done by the government, positive or negative, the mordida always works. Do you remember?" Sebastian rekindled the memory.

"No, no, a bribe will not work with this dog. He's too high up. Damn why didn't we think of hiding him when these chicken shitheads showed up. Instead we showed him off, and naturally our best came to close scrutiny of Capt. Tomiji. And, now he's gone, and there is very damn little we can do," Akechi concluded as he plopped down on a mat in the corner of the room.

"If a good handful of cold cash will not turn the trick, then the only other alternative is for Chon to desert. Leave for other parts. Your organization is so large, that you could hide him easily, you could make him vanish, poof, like nothing. I know that in my country during the revolution, and the first war, my countrymen, when they were drafted to serve in the military, all went to visit some relatives in El Norte, north close to the border, and then poof, they vanished forever, to start a new life in the United States. Why can't you ship him off to Korea, or China, or even México?" Sebastian reasoned.

"It is too late," Akechi shook his head, "if he were not so well known, what you say could be done easily. But it is too late, now they know he is here. If I were to hide him, they would know it was me who was responsible, and they would make life for me and everyone on the plantation miserable. No, it is too late. If we take such a course, it will have to be later, once Chon is already in the service. It is a good thought but it will have to wait," he grumbled.

"If money and desertion do not work, then my ideas are gone. Unless you want to make the boy out a queer, or pretend serious illness?" Sebastian chuckled.

"No, no, we'll just have to wait until a few months from now to see if we can help then, from a distance, so we won't be so easily detected," Akechi said, rising to leave, struggling to get to his feet.

* * *

Chon was ecstatic. All his life he was taught to be a good fighter, a good soldier, and a samurai. Now he was getting his chance. True, he would be in the navy and not the infantry, but there was glory to be won in the navy too.

He remembered reading in the history scrolls and hearing from his teachers of the battles that were won by the ancient samurais thanks only to the ships and their maneuvering that enabled samurais to get a better advantage over their foes.

Massa also had mixed emotions. Her only love in the entire world was now going off to war. The war mentality had become so ingrained in everyone at the plantation that she could not be unhappy that her young pup was to go off to make his mark as a samurai. She fixed a special meal for him that evening and they enjoyed time with each other, talking until the late hours of the night.

At daybreak, the families were present to bid their two hundred warriors farewell. The feeling of pride prevailed at the plantation. When the families realized that Chon was going too, they felt even greater satisfaction that the master's pet was not being singled out over their boys. The small talk among the families rose to a mild roar.

Capt. Tomiji appeared and motioned to the lieutenants and sergeants to start the march. With a few sharp yells everyone fell into formation. Ten columns were formed. All even, except for the one with Chon, who stood out as the odd man. The columns were instructed to move to the assigned trucks and they obeyed. In less than three minutes the volunteers climbed up into the trucks, which began moving out of the plantation, followed by four door sedans. There were only two unhappy persons there, Akechi and Sebastian.

The plantation samurai sang and cheered as they traveled down the highway in the open trucks. They sounded like a group of students on their way to a picnic. Practical jokes on each other were the order of the day. Each truck carried a few armed soldiers. The plantation samurai did not know it but the soldiers were on the lookout for deserters. There was no need to fear anyone from Tokyo Plantation deserting. The boys were proud to be going to fight for the empire.

These men were able. They were specially trained in fighting, in self subsistence, weaponry, horsemanship, survival, and agriculture. They could definitely fend for themselves. As they drove down the highway, they never stopped singing and yelling, such was their joy. After two hours they saw the outskirts of Tokyo. Most of them had never been to Tokyo, and did not know what to expect. Gradually the group quieted down as everyone fell into a trance, staring at the sights in the metropolis.

Chon turned and asked one of the soldiers, "Where are we being taken?"

"I do not know. I am not told these things. Let me suggest that you not be so nosy. Do not ask questions," the soldier shot back curtly.

Chon shook his head at the coldness. He wondered where he would rest his body that night.

Traveling through the streets of Tokyo they could not help but stare wide mouthed at the scenery and the people. They never had seen such sights. The streets and neighborhood housing was new to them. The vehicular traffic was unbelievable. Retail shops on the street were something they never knew, and that they could not quite grasp. The soldiers laughed at the innocence of the new volunteers. After the newness wore off, the boys again spoke, laughed, and yelled as they drove through the streets of Tokyo.

Tokyo was a huge city. They had never imagined that it was so big. They always heard that it was a large place, but having never seen it, it was hard to imagine how large it really was. Soon every block looked like the last one they passed, and the drive became monotonous, although not to the point of being boring. They continued to stare, but now more at ease, less excited. The trucks rolled on. Finally, the trucks drove into a military encampment. The young men cheered. They were home now, they thought. The trucks drove through the fort and stopped at the large tin sheds, which were repair garages for motor vehicles.

A lieutenant came up quickly and barked out orders.

"You shall go relieve yourself promptly and prepare to remount. This is not our destination. We are here for refueling, and shall leave in a half hour. Go," he said as he motioned toward the ditches at the back of the sheds.

Chon and the others ran off laughing, giggling, and mimicking the lieutenant as they went to empty their bladders. The chatter was loud, and everyone joked with each other. As they finished their business they wandered back to the area where the trucks were parked. The sergeants then asked them all to sit in an open area under a couple of shade trees.

Most of the food was already gone. This was not a problem, because working in the fields they were accustomed to fasting for long periods, and eating after the long day's work was over.

* * *

By the fourth week of basic training, it was easy to see that Chon was going to lead his classes. All of them. His classmates liked him, and were proud of him. They had heard of Chon's humble beginnings, about his father, and of Tokyo Plantation, and the way that it operated under its quasi feudal system. This made them all the more proud of him. Chon was everyone's friend and everyone was his friend. They knew too, by now, of the particular brand of hand-to-hand combat that prevailed at the Tokyo Plantation, a new art called KarateDo. A few had already experienced the flying mule kicks.

After the third month, they were given a furlough. Chon hurried home to Tokyo Plantation. Everyone was pleased to see him. Akechi, Massa, and Sebastian beamed with pride. Chon asked about the other volunteers and was sad to hear that a few of them had already been killed in island warfare.

"It's funny," he thought, "I have been so busy training to go kill and fight a war that I have forgotten that the war is already on."

Massa cooked Chon's favorite meals, and Akechi and Sebastian did not leave him alone, asking every imaginable question.

Chon had grown some since his departure. He also gained about twenty pounds. He filled out completely and cut a handsome figure. He drove around the plantation with Akechi and Sebastian, insisting on visiting the camps. The memories were beautiful, and every moment was a genuine pleasure, each like a sip of dry wine. Most enjoyable.

Like all vacations, Chon's came to a quick end. Too quick, everyone thought. Akechi and Sebastian made arrangements to take him to Tokyo. The trio had a good time on the trip. Chon explained that he would not be able to tell them where he was going, because he was not allowed to divulge this information. Akechi and Sebastian looked at each other disappointingly. Their own child, in a manner of speaking, would not divulge his destination. They were curious, of course, but they appreciated his mission, they appreciated his manhood. They had seen a boy leave the plantation, and a man return.

Chon had received orders to report for duty at Officers Training Academy in Tokyo. Prior to reporting for duty at the academy, Akechi insisted on a fancy meal. Sebastian was none too eager. Akechi took them to the fanciest club he could find in Tokyo, the Blue Oyster fish house. Akechi was prepared to drink and eat and talk for the entire evening, and so was Sebastian. They ordered saké and oysters and continued their conversation. They had a lot of catching up to do.

The topic of death eventually entered the conversation. Chon told them sad tales of several deaths that had occurred in camp. The mood saddened at the table. Akechi listened attentively and said nothing for the hour or so that Chon related the asinine aspects of the training camp.

"Chon, I am asking you to immerse yourself in your new assignment and try to forget the awful memory of your father's death, and of your friends from the plantation, and your training comrades that have died," Akechi counseled the young man, for he no longer was the young boy he an Sebastian had been training. "Do not blame yourself. You cannot go through life expecting to protect and take care of all your friends. I know that you do not understand nor agree with everything that I am saying, but please pay attention to what I say, and someday at least some of it will all make sense to you. Please listen."

Sebastian could not miss such a golden opportunity. For two hours of food and saké he regaled them with philosophy, death, sacrifice, friendship, and other topics. Akechi and Chon were amused and shook their heads, it was like old times again. Sebastian's lecture was good therapy.

Chon did not want the talk of death to ruin the warmth that he felt being with his two mentors. The men drank to each other's health. After dinner, Akechi treated them to some entertainment by Geisha girls. Of course, Chon had never had the privilege of enjoying Geisha girls, so this experience was a nice end to his brief furlough.

After several hours of revelry, it was time to leave, and they drove Chon to the academy, where he managed to get without showing any effects of the saké and managed to wave goodbye.

Akechi and Sebastian's trip back to Tokyo Plantation was quiet and somber.

Chon walked upstairs to his room and looked out the window. The sun was almost gone and he could still distinguish the court-yard below. The companionship had brightened the day, and he had not noticed until now the dreary weather. He suddenly felt lonely and homesick. A light drizzle began to fall. He stared out the window. His thoughts wandered off to Tokyo Plantation, and all his friends there. He turned off the light. He laid on his mat. He thought of his military career.

"So far so good," he smiled in the dark.

BOOK TWO
The Making of a Spy

Chapter Seven

Chon had enjoyed a marvelously distracting time with the two old tomcats, Akechi san and Sebastian. His two days on the town helped to get him on his way back to living normally.

Chon ran up the stairs to his room. It was ten o'clock in the morning, and there was a bright sun out, and it was cool. He clicked down the hall and into his room. To his surprise, he found Capt. Shigeru Torisu sitting at his desk. The young sailor had excelled in entry training. Much of it was repetitious of the Tiger Camp training Nagi san had meted out. Despite the beatings, vomiting, and physical and mental abuse Chon thrived in the new environment.

Capt. Shigeru, a sort of wandering inspector with ample Imperial power took a liking to the young seaman. He ambled about inspecting and observing. Even colonels and generals made way when they saw him. Chon's superior abilities came to the attention to Capt. Shigeru, who immediately put Chon on a fast track to advancement. After entry training, Capt. Shigeru moved Chon to officers training where he again excelled. His knowledge of the Spanish language and of México and Latin America did not go unnoticed.

"Ah," Chon uttered, "captain you surprise me, I did not expect you. In fact, I almost forgot all about you. It is very good to see you, sir."

Chon saluted Capt. Shigeru and the captain waved him off.

"My dear young man, I have seen you do so many great things I cannot wait for graduation day. I intend to pluck you out and get you working immediately. You are to tell no one, of our shortcut procedure," Capt. Shigeru said with a wink.

"Well," Chon replied, "to be honest, I guess I am ready. I am ready. I will carry out your orders."

Capt. Shigeru noticed the maturity showing through. The Chon of the entry camp would not have been at this point, but this young officer certainly was. He was dead serious, all business.

"This is great," Capt. Shigeru thought. "The boy is now a man and he is ready."

"I have some good news. Soon you will be using your training. Here are your orders," Capt. Shigeru said, handing Chon a document. "All your classmates have gone to their new classes. There is nothing more for you to do here. I will pick you up at 1500 hours. Get your gear and be ready."

"You will be very pleased with the new challenge," the captain said, staring at Chon. "It is one of the most exciting branches of our military, and will offer you excitement and challenge. I can guarantee you that you will not be disappointed. I have gone through this training, and I loved it. There was not a dull moment in the entire training period. I know you will be pleased. I will see you this afternoon."

As he left, Capt. Shigeru turned and looked back into the room.

"Do not fail me young man, or I will kill you," he said, staring into Chon's eyes with pursed lips and narrowed eyes.

Chon gathered his belongings.

"What am I getting into? Should I run and go back to Tokyo Plantation. If I only knew where I was going. If I ran, Capt. Shigeru would wash me out of the service and into prison, exile, or maybe even death," Chon thought.

He continued with his chore. Would he be working with the devil himself? Sometimes he felt that he would. The night with Akechi san and Sebastian had been good therapy, but now he was dwelling on life's uncertainty.

"Maybe it would have been better if I had refused Capt. Shigeru," he thought. "If I had done that, I would now be out at sea swabbing decks or dead, but I would not be under such a heavy burden to do Capt. Shigeru's dirty work. Whatever that might be."

"What could possibly lay ahead for me?" He wondered as he finished packing. "I know my next step will be more training, but after that, what can I expect?"

Contrary to habit, he ate alone, reminiscing about his stay. It seemed to Chon that he had been training since he was drafted.

The captain picked him up as promised.

"We are dealing with a very sensitive matter, I do not even want to discuss this here. We must go to another building on the base. Let us go," Capt. Shigeru said, as he marched off with Chon at his side. They walked hurriedly through the base until they came to a small building near the ocean with a small sign nailed on its corner. The sign read "I. S." nothing more.

Capt. Shigeru walked in first, and the seamen and other officers snapped to attention. He waved them at ease and walked through to the next room where an overhead light shone directly on a desk.

"All these months you have been training for this moment. I could not tell you because of the secrecy required. I know that you are very happy with the navy. Well, you will be removed from naval service," Capt. Shigeru said as he paced around Chon.

"The next service you will perform for the empire will be the final calling in your military service. You are now a member of I. S., the Intelligence Service. This is what you were destined for, what you will do," Capt. Shigeru said as he stood straight with his chin out. "Our Prime Minister has great plans for our Japanese Empire, but they cannot be carried out without the I.S. and men like yourself."

"Beginning tomorrow, you will report for duty here. You will undergo three months intensive training. You have already been assigned to a project. You will not learn about it for about three months, by then you will know much, and the final month will be spent preparing you for your first test.

"Oh, by the way, you have been promoted to lieutenant, here are your new stripes and bars. Congratulations. You see here at I.S. we don't need to follow the rules exactly. We make them," he chuckled.

"This promotion carries a change of quarters. You will move next door to the senior officer's quarters. Well done lieutenant, and welcome aboard. For your information, aside from my military rank, I am also known as Commander, because I am the chief commander of I. S.," Capt. Shigeru said, smiling through squinting eyes.

Chon walked back to get his gear. He was confused.

"Every time that I think I have reached a plateau, one that I like, this captain, uh, Commander Shigeru devil shows up and rocks my boat. I so like the navy. What if I do not like I. S.? What if it has nothing to do with my previous training? Intelligence service; spying, sneaking, back stabbing like snakes, harakiri?" He was confused.

With his transfer done, he laid down on his mat and turned his thoughts to Tokyo Plantation and Akechi san, Sebastian, and Massa. He smiled. "If they could only see me now. I. S.! Sebastian will be happy. Akechi san will not like it. Mother will not understand it. The samurai, and the others will be proud."

He smiled again. He felt proud. He did not know what he was getting into, but he was proud.

* * *

It was August 1940 and Chon was nineteen-years-old. Were he an older man, he would have tired of so many schools and so much training. But he was strong, had stamina, and had a thirst for knowledge. The man in charge of the I. S. school was Maj.

Kano Kosugi. Maj. Kano was forty-years-old, and had been in the spy game for about twenty years. He had started in I. S. at the age of twenty and worked his way up through the ranks. Maj. Kano was of medium height, thin, and balding. He wore small rimless bifocal spectacles. He loved his profession. He moved about energetically and spoke in bursts, like machine gun fire.

Chon moved into the officers quarters and was ready for school to start. There were only thirty students; the best Japan had to offer.

Chon walked into the classroom and, as usual, sat down in the front row. Soon the room was full of students, murmuring and whispering anxiously. All were excited at the prospect of their new profession. At first, Chon was indifferent, and disturbed at having to go through one more school and continue with his training instead of putting it to work, in the front like the other men from his plantation. Gradually he got used to the idea, and now was anxious to get started so he could finish.

He learned from Commander Shigeru, his latest mentor and guardian and constant companion, that this would be it; there would be no more training. Chon would make it as a master spy, or if he failed in the I. S. school he would be assigned to serve as a useless seaman on some desolate island. This frightened Chon, but at least it represented a change from the captain's promise to kill him if he failed. He would work hard, and try to excel.

Maj. Kano rushed into the room, his arms full of books and materials. He was excited, he smiled broadly, full of energy and enthusiasm.

"Good morning," he bowed at the young men standing in front of him at attention. They bowed, and he waved them at ease.

"Today you begin the most exciting career ever available to any man. You will soon see what I mean," Maj. Kano said in slow deliberate tones.

"Only a very few men are chosen to enjoy a career in the Intelligence Service as agents. Here you have a soldier," he indicated by holding up one fist. "Here you have the other," he said holding up the other fist. "When they both meet," he said, slapping his fists together, "there is a war and one of the soldiers is gone." He held one fist behind his back. "It is suddenly over, or at least it seems that way."

A dull story Chon thought. A very dull story indeed.

"But when you have an I. S. agent, on one hand," Maj. Kano said, lifting his left fist again. "And then you have an enemy agent, or soldier, or army on the other side," he lifted his other hand. "Then, the agent slowly and gradually takes a position against the other agent or army," the major, slowly waved the fist, hand open now, to the other fist. "And unbeknown to the other agent or army, the I.S. agent infiltrates the other's defenses, then walks away," he removed the fist from the other. "Then, three weeks later, the other agent or army is dead, and nobody knows why. That is excitement, and that is a fun way to fight a war," he concluded as he jumped up and down laughing, in glee.

The students laughed, not so much at the story but at the major's antics.

"You see now what I mean. I. S. is where the action is. There are no attacks from I. S. There are no barricades to build. We have no artillery. What happens here is that we work with our mind and," the major paused looking at his students, and then said slowly and in a high voice, "with the technology that our super whiz scientists develop to cause havoc and death."

"We do not need to meet fist with fist, actually we prefer to meet fist with kiss, but in a few days the fist will rot," he jumped again laughing and giggling at himself. The class laughed with him.

"The reason you are here is to learn how to give these dangerous kisses. How to use your mind to defeat an army. How to cause havoc. Yes, you, each of you," he said as he waved his pointed finger through the room, "can cause enough havoc that compares to the military action of three hundred men. I will teach you how. In the next few weeks you are going to learn many things dealing with the general topics of secret weapons, diversions, psychological warfare, germ warfare, disguises, languages, cultural customs and differences, fact gathering, explosives, and many other topics that make up the real ingredients of war. This crazy thing called war."

The major paused as his voice trailed off.

"When you leave here you will not want to fight a naval battle again, you will never want to fight with submarine torpedoes again, unless of course it fits into the more elevated plan of an I. S. scheme or diversion. You will see how easy it is to defeat the enemy by simply letting the enemy lead you to his own weakness," Maj. Kano said, with his voice reaching a high fever pitch, and he was jumping up and down again with excitement.

Maj. Kano's excitement became contagious and the young officers were excited and anxious to learn about this new strange magic.

"Now today we begin with a brief lesson on languages of the foreign countries that we deal with, either as friends or as enemies," the major's voice was now low and serious, it had lost its high pitch. "I have brought with me ten instructors. You will split up into small groups and undergo special observation of a foreign language."

"For you Lt. Tasaka, I have a special assignment," Maj. Kano said, as he pointed at Chon. "I want you to join one of the instructors in the next room. You may go now, the rest of you stay right in this room, and we will disperse into smaller groups."

Chon walked into the next room. It was small and bright with many windows, and many tables in it. Sitting in a corner, close to one of the windows, was a tiny figure writing at one of the small tables.

"Excuse me, I am Lt. Tasaka, I was told to report here," Chon said in a soft voice, trying not to startle the old man.

"Ah yes, Lt. Tasaka. I have been waiting for you," the old man said as he lifted his head and motioned for Chon to move forward toward him. Chon complied. "I am told that I am most fortunate to have you as my pupil for the next three months; that you have shown everyone in your previous schools that you are indeed a superior type of person."

"My name is Miyoshi Hisahide. I used to live in South America, and lived in the United States for some time. I am seventy-years-old now, and my purpose in life seems to be to help you, and others like you, sharpen your skills in the Spanish and English language. I am told that you have a good basic grasp of these languages, is that true?"

"Well yes, that is true. You see, my benefactor brought a man home from a business trip, and he stayed. The man was from México and spoke Spanish and had a working knowledge of English. He stayed so long, actually he never left and is still there at Tokyo Plantation, my home, where I grew up. I must say, however," Chon continued, "that I have not practiced or used these foreign languages since I was drafted two years ago. So I will need the practice, but I welcome it."

For the next few weeks, Chon enjoyed the classes with Miyoshi san. At the same time he learned about cannons and derringers, and piano wire, strangulation, cane knives, smoke screens, diversionary tactics, and other necessary spy matters.

For about a week, Chon and the others underwent lessons in dress and mannerisms. Most of them had never worn anything other than their peasant pajamas on the farms, or their rough city garb, and since being in the service their fatigues and uniforms. Now they were taught to wear western style suits and hats. They donned double-pleated slacks and double-breasted coats with wide ties, and beaver fedoras. They laughed at each other until Maj. Kano interrupted and lectured them on how stupid it was to laugh at something just because it was foreign. They were taught to knot their ties, and were required to do so without a mirror. Through the next several weeks they were taught the mannerisms of the different foreign countries. How to spit, how to walk, how not to bow. In a sense they were being deJapanesed.

There were valuable lessons in geography, hills, valleys, deserts, cities, weather, seasons. Chon was relegated to Miyoshi san for special teaching on México and Central and South America.

It appeared to Chon that he was to be assigned to México or perhaps a Central or South American country. It did not seem fair, he thought, that he be taught to spy on México simply because he had been befriended by a merchant, who had become a very good friend. For the friend's efforts in teaching Chon a little more about his own country, Chon was about to become a spy in that country. That was not entirely right, he thought.

The classes went on for several weeks. Chon learned things that he never thought existed. He learned to pull a long wire from his western suit lapel and use it to strangle someone, if necessary. His ring had a secret compartment that contained cyanide poison. If necessary he should dispose of himself, instead of being captured by the enemy, tortured, and forced to confess his mission.

He was taught the oriental art of torture. Maj. Kano was very proud of his mastery in the matter of torture. He had read all there was to read on the subject, and had spent much time in Korea trying to learn more about it. He was taught that, after torture and starvation, the body and mind eventually weaken to the point of total and complete malleability. He yearned for the day when he had several prisoners of war to use as experiments to prove or disprove the theories.

The students had many field exercises, which could not be taught in the classrooms. They spent days using dynamite and other dangerous explosives. Maj. Kano was only too happy to show the students how to blow up property with explosives to cause a diversion. The "whizzes" as Maj. Kano referred to the scientists assigned to help the Intelligence Service, designed small and portable bazookas and mortars. Maj. Kano showed his charges how to use these effectively. Smoke bombs were also part of their regular arsenal.

Each day was exciting for the young men. Most were from farms and the remainder came from city neighborhoods. None were from wealthy families. To most, the automobile was a very special contraption. The devices and inventions that Maj. Kano showed them absolutely bewildered them, and excited them, at the same time. Everything he taught brought new smiles in amazement at science, trickery, and stealth. The young men shook their heads.

A special emphasis was placed on communications, radio communications and any other type of communication. Chon memorized twelve code books. It was imperative that he learn code if he was to communicate. The code work was hard at first, but then Maj. Kano explained that it was mostly based on mathematics. Knowing this, Chon made easy work of the problem.

They were introduced to hand held radios, which they were told were top secret and had not even been used in the field. They learned to use them expertly. They also learned to repair the equipment. They communicated around the world, as well as with all Japanese bases. The young men were amazed. They shook their heads. They could communicate with submarines hundreds of miles away, and with army bases in China.

Chon marveled at the ideas. It was sad that war was the motivating reason for educating so many people to so many marvelous things and ideas. It was horrible that death was viewed as necessary to take a nation out of the feudal system and into the modern world.

At times, he wondered why life was so cheap and inexpensive in Japan. Harakiri was prevalent. Soldiers were thought of as cannon fodder and not much more. Sebastian had different thoughts on life and the value of life. They never really discussed it in detail, but he grasped from his teachings and thoughts, that in the western cultures, life had an immeasurable value, one that was not easily discounted. One poor man was thought to be just as valuable as a wealthy leader, or so it seemed from the general concepts that Sebastian passed on to him. He had noticed that Miyoshi san shared this thought. Chon could not understand why two areas of the globe had such diverse views on something so basic as life and death.

Chon felt fortunate to know three people who shared so much in common and whom he could love and understand so easily. He wished that he could have some free time with Miyoshi san and Sebastian together. He knew that they would have a wonderful time together.

The young man did not know it but he had been honed to be one of the best in the Japanese Intelligence Service. To some, Chon seemed an accident. A bright young man was not supposed to come from a farm. A farm boy was not supposed to be a samurai. Almost no one in Japan, and especially a farm boy, was expected to know Spanish, about México, and also a little English. It was a strange chemistry.

After officers school, the I. S. school provided the last special training, the final sharpening of the blade. Strangely, those around him knew better than Chon just how talented and sharp he was.

With the training at I. S. school completed, the men were expected to go and show their skills, while Maj. Kano was still in charge of them. During the next six months they were sent out into the Japanese countryside or into neighboring China or Korea. Mostly, they were spying on Japanese, checking on their compliance with governmental rules or regulations. These tasks were not important to the government. But it was good training for the men. In each of the situations, they were supposed to go in undetected, and leave undetected after having obtained the required information. If detected they were ordered to bluff their way out of a bad situation.

If needed, they were under orders to use physical force, as extreme as necessary, and to utilize explosives and armament if required. In each phase of every operation they were expected to be prepared to use everything they had learned. They were especially encouraged to use their radios and to communicate in code.

Chon's experiences were rather normal. The only unusual occurrence happened in Seoul when Chon was discovered as an undesirable snooping around. He was unable to talk his way out of it so he had to resort to physical force. The karate-do he had learned served him well as he sent three Japanese infantry regulars to the ground wishing that they had not been so aggressive in their questioning.

Chapter Eight

Chon and Maj. Kano walked into the Intelligence Service building. They were shown to the larger office with the overhead light. Commander Shigeru was seated at the desk in the back office. He rose and all saluted each other, came to rest, and sat down. The Commander began to speak in a serious, low, raspy voice.

"Lt. Tasaka, at this point I must confide in you and let you know some matters that are considered very sensitive and vital to the welfare of our country and important to the continuing march in our effort to establish our rightful position as a world power.

"You see, it is imperative that we continue to grow. However, there are certain natural resources that we do not possess in our mother country, so we must go out and appropriate them. So far there have been many successes and the Japanese Empire continues to grow. There are those, however, who would like to stop our growth. These powers would like to continue their world domination in shipping and in trade, and they want to stifle the great Japanese Empire. This cannot and will not happen. We must continue forward. Nothing will stop us now," the commander said as he got up from the desk and walked to the window, his back to the two men.

"The ones that primarily obstruct our plans are the Americans and the British. We will not permit anyone to stop us, and we must deal with these pigs accordingly. If they want to stop us and obstruct our progress, then we must respond in kind and do what is necessary, regardless of the amount of force required, to accomplish our mission, and regardless of the consequences, even if it means committing Japan into a wider war," Commander Shigeru said as he walked back to his desk where he sat down.

"Now I will give you the particulars of the plan. Or at least in general terms the particulars of the plan. You see the details are either not yet formulated or are too secret to divulge to anyone at this point in time," Commander Shigeru said and began the disclosure of secret plans to Chon and Maj. Kano.

"The plan is code named Mount Niitaka. All that you need to know right now is that we plan an offensive against the Americans. The plan is to be a two-pronged attack. We will pick our spot and try to render them completely defenseless by a surprise attack. Second we will invade the United States itself. We have formulated plans for both of these operations, but I cannot divulge details. Those will come later," Commander Shigeru said, emphasizing his reticence with his eyebrows and mouth.

"I guess it could be said that we are still exploring the alternatives in each of these attacks. That is where you and I. S. come in. There are other I. S. operatives that are serving on other facets of these projects. You, Lt. Tasaka, will help with the secondary phase of the project, that is, the attack on, and invasion of, the United States.

"Many times when attacking, it is best to seek out the soft and unprotected underbelly of the enemy. That is what we think that México will be in relation to the United States. Intelligence reports tell us that the two countries have been unenthusiastic allies for almost one hundred years. Despite a history of skirmishes, conflicts, and conquests, they get along out of mutual need. They trade with each other openly, and the border they share is almost a subculture made up of the two cultures, American and Mexican.

"Amazingly travel between the two is almost unrestricted. There are some restrictions, but they almost completely open their borders to each other. Since México has almost no military to speak of, and therefore no defense, the United States does not see a great need to protect or defend its border with México," Commander Shigeru explained as he walked over to a map on the wall.

"In addition, the border between the two countries is so large that many Mexicans openly make their way into the United States and stay without permission. They easily assimilate with the large population in the United States that is Mexican by culture but American by citizenship. This is something that can be capitalized on because an unauthorized person could easily make his way into the interior of the United States. We are told that these unauthorized entrants are called 'wetbacks' or in Spanish 'mojados,' because they have to swim across the river that separates the two countries, and are wet when they arrive into the United States. Anyway that is just some general information. You will get a very detailed briefing later," Commander Shigeru said.

"Your assignment," he told Chon, "is to become an operative in México. You will infiltrate into the country and find out everything that you can. We want all the information that you can get.

"You will be transported by submarine to the southwest coast of México. The submarine will remain off the coast to assist you. You are expected to make your way to the capital México City, and then to slowly wind your way up through the country until you reach the American border. When you reach the border, you are to travel up and down the border at least once and retrieve all the information that you can. We want all the information that you can obtain."

Chon fidgeted in his chair, and Maj. Kano smiled excitedly.

"Now please listen carefully. You will be armed, and you are expected to use all the force necessary to insure that this project succeeds. You will take a radio and we expect transmissions to the submarine nightly. The information will be transferred by the submarine to the mainland immediately," Commander Shigeru told Chon.

"Your mission is serious, delicate, and secret. If there is any possibility of detection, you are to destroy all evidence, including the radio, and then you are to destroy yourself. Do you understand?"

Chon and Maj. Kano looked intently at Commander Shigeru. They were completely quiet and took note of the seriousness of the mission. Neither spoke nor made a sound or movement.

"We do not want the Americans to suspect anything at all about a possible entry through México, therefore, I repeat, if there is the slightest possibility of detection you should destroy all evidence of your mission, including the radio, and then yourself. Do you understand?"

Chon simply nodded assent.

"Additionally, I have one more strict order that must be followed. If for some reason something should strain or interrupt the communication with the submarine, you must take extreme measures. Listen carefully therefore. If you cannot communicate with the submarine for ten consecutive nights that means something has gone wrong with the plan, and the project should be aborted. Again, all evidence should be destroyed, including the radio, your weapons, and even yourself. There must not be any detection. There must not be any force used, there must not be any attention called to the project. Do you understand? Now I want an audible response from you, and I want you to repeat the orders I have given you."

"I understand perfectly," Chon replied, and proceeded to repeat the plan, the orders, and direction that Commander Shigeru gave.

"Good then, I am glad that you understand. Now I want you and Maj. Kano to go, first, for a cultural briefing from Miyoshi Hisahide, and then, an equipment briefing and issue, and finally report to the submarine twenty four hours from now. Go now," Commander Shigeru said, motioning them away.

Miyoshi san gave Chon a final briefing on México, from its geography, its people, their customs, their dress, to their food, their habits, and peculiarities. Chon had heard most of the lecture many times before from Akechi san and Sebastian. He was ready.

"Now Lt. Tasaka we must choose a name for you, and we will prepare Mexican identification for you. Do you have a name, I would like to pass on it for authenticity and genuineness," Miyoshi san asked.

"Yes I have a perfect name, and I am certain that it will pass for genuine and authentic. The name is Encarnación Gutiérrez Ayala." He picked the name that Sebastian told him was the source of the nickname Chon and Sebastian's own family names.

"Oh yes, a very good choice. Encarnación, a very good and sometimes common name having to do with the Incarnation of the Christ child. Yes, yes, a good choice, and Gutiérrez, very well-known indeed, and Ayala solid Mexican name. Yes, a very good choice," Miyoshi san said, pleased with Chon's choice.

"Well then, I think you should go and get your forged papers, and other equipment. My dear Lt. Tasaka, or should I say Señor Gutiérrez, I wish you the best of luck," Miyoshi san bowed at Chon and turned and left the room.

Chon provided the name so that documentation could be prepared. He was issued clothing, a duffel bag, a pistol, suicide tablets, a suicide ring, emergency food rations, maps, the vital radio, and a new code book especially prepared for the mission. He was given other equipment. Chon walked over to a corner of the room and inspected each of the items. He wanted to be sure that each was in good working order. He reviewed and inspected and began to memorize the code book.

Mount Niitaka was the codename for the primary project; the secondary project was known as "The Valley". Commander Shigeru was "The Hawk", Chon was "The Lone Wolf", and the submarine was the "Silverfish". Japan was "Mother", México was

"The Company", and the United States was "The Rainbow".
The codes went on. He would have to destroy the book first if
he experienced any of the problems that Commander Shigeru
cautioned about. He removed the radio from its canvas bag and
set it to the correct positions. He screwed on its antennae, and
plugged in the microphone. He hit the switch and moved and
adjusted several of the dials. He monitored military radios in
the area. He broke in and tested for transmission. He was heard
by many. The radio worked. He then tested the pistol.

As he examined the material, a young sergeant arrived with
Chon's Mexican identification papers. He examined them carefully. They appeared to be the genuine article. The papers were
even a little pocket worn, and looked authentic. From today
forward he would be Encarnación Gutiérrez Ayala, with his
Mexican nickname being Chon.

Accompanying the identification papers was a profile of the
young Mexican that Chon was to portray. Miyoshi san compiled
it and there was a note attached to it urging Chon to memorize
it quickly and be prepared to modify it if necessary. Gutiérrez was
twenty-years-old, he was an agronomist by profession. He had
not received a formal education but acquired his skill through
training in the produce fields of San Blas in the state of Nayarit,
a state on the west coast, in the southern part of the nation. If
stopped and questioned, he was to say that he was on a buying
trip, buying seed and supplies. The profile contained the minutest
information, which Chon committed to memory. Birthplace,
parents' names, brothers' and sisters' names, schools attended,
childhood illnesses, and other information that Chon felt sure
he would never need, but memorized nonetheless.

The clothes Chon was issued were typically western in style. He
was given several white shirts, several pair of double pleated slacks,
khaki pants, simple black lace shoes, a couple of ties, and two hats,
one a farmer or modified cowboy hat and the other a common
gray fedora. A short gray jacket completed his new wardrobe.

Chon and Maj. Kano walked to the submarine. At the dock to greet them was Commander Shigeru. He smiled widely as they approached. Chon was the star pupil of the Intelligence Service and he knew much was expected of him. The trio saluted each other then bowed toward one another.

"Good morning, my dear Lt. Tasaka, are you prepared for your mission?" The Commander asked.

"Yes sir, I am quite ready," Chon replied.

"Come then let's board, I have some final instructions that I must pass on," the commander motioned for all of them to board. The three went down the forward hatch. Once inside they walked to the rear and entered a tiny office. There was a desk, a chair, and a small bed. No more.

"Lieutenant I have some details I must explain. You will be dropped off at the ancient port of Acapulco. Here is a short written brief on the Port of Acapulco. Your first assignment once you land is to purchase a farm pickup. The truck will give you good cover, and you will need a vehicle to travel the country. Here is a pack of Mexican and American money in small bills. Do not let the American money frighten you. It is used just as Mexican money in México, as a matter of fact, sometimes it is preferred, depending on who you are dealing with."

The room was so tiny, they spoke within inches from each other in the dark cabin.

"Next, here is a written brief on money, its exchange rates, and the general and suggested prices of items. Try to get a vehicle that is not too old, as mechanical difficulties could cause you major problems. With a new vehicle your problems would be minimum. It will be hard to find a new vehicle but try to get the newest possible. The brief on money contains a page or three on vehicles, brand names, specifications, and the like.

"Next, here is a brief on the journey that you will take. Here, let us look at this map. You will land here," he pointed to Acapulco on the map with a pencil. "Then you will travel northeast to the capital México City, which is also called the D.F., the Distrito Federal. Then what you should do is travel to the western part of the country as soon as possible, then zig into the interior part of the nation, then up to the border and start looking for weaknesses, and providing the usual intelligence information while you are there. Having accomplished that, you will then travel to the west coast, where you will arrange to rendezvous with the Silverfish and journey back to the homeland. We expect the journey through the country to take about sixty days, and it cannot take longer. You must accomplish your mission within sixty days. The submarine is taking on extra provisions, and has made arrangements to refuel at sea before returning," Commander Shigeru emphasized, as they heard the engines going, and the crew preparing to cast off.

"This same brief contains information on all of the cities that you will travel through, and all the operations and factories that are likely to be found in the area. We want you to investigate these facts, and confirm these, and others. This includes American border cities. You will not be able to cross the border to investigate these cities. Even if you were able, we do not want you to risk the possibility of detection. Even without crossing into the American cities, you should be able to gather much data from the sister cities across the border in México, as intelligence tells us that thousands of Mexicans, cross the border daily to work in American factories, restaurants, ranches, and other endeavors. All you have to do is find the right person and you can get much information.

"Now to reiterate, you will establish communication times with the Silverfish, and communicate daily. Importantly, if you are detected, you should destroy all material you have with you, and then destroy yourself. I repeat, you should destroy all material you have with you, and then you should destroy yourself. If you are unable to accomplish this, the Empire will disavow any knowledge of you, you will be a man without a country. You will not be a Japanese; as far as Japan is concerned, you do not belong to her. In short you do not exist, until you return.

"Also, to repeat for emphasis, if the Silverfish is detected, you must abort the mission, and you will destroy all your materials and then yourself. If the Silverfish does not communicate with you for ten straight days, you will presume that she has been detected.

"Lt. Tasaka, it has been a pleasure working with you. I expect to see you walking through the door of my office in a couple of months, and perhaps sooner. Good luck to you. Do not forget your goal of finding the soft underbelly of the enemy. Onward," the commander concluded. The three men rose and bowed.

"It looks like I have much reading material for the long trip," Chon responded with a grin. Commander Shigeru exited, walked through the sub, and up the hatch. Maj. Kano rubbed his hands together, smiled, and nodded. "Sayonara, Lt. Tasaka," he said as he prepared to climb the metal ladder.

The submarine captain got the ship under way immediately. Chon asked for and received permission to stand on the tower with the other officers, as the ship left port Kure in Hiroshima. It was a bright sunny day, and he enjoyed the fresh ocean air pushing on his face as the ship made its way out to sea.

After a couple of hours they went below. The captain ordered the ship to travel at full speed. They had a very long way to go. The officers knew that they were taking Chon on a special mission, but they did not know the nature of his mission.

For the next few days, Chon immersed himself in the written briefs and material that Commander Shigeru gave him. He smiled as he read on. "I am going to be more of a Mexican than Sebastian himself." He memorized geography, learned about factories, cotton fields, cotton gins, copper mines, zinc mines, antimony mines, and railroads. He would need to update and confirm much of his material when he was on the scene. He was particularly curious about the border culture and how it seemed that the nations coexisted as one in a trade zone atmosphere. He kept this goal in mind; "find the weak part of the underbelly."

After three days, the captain appeared at Chon's room while he reviewed notes and briefs.

"Well Lt. Tasaka in forty eight-hours, give or take, you will land. I have been ordered to advise you of this milestone. I am told that now you must make your last minute preparations. Let me assure you that foremost in my mind is doing the best that I can for the Empire, and believe me, I hope to see you in a few weeks so that we can travel home," they bowed to each other and the captain exited.

Chon tore up the paper material. The destruction took three hours. He sent for a seaman to take the torn material and dispose of it. Having purged the area and the ship of signs of his mission, he pulled out his gear and began the last check. He removed everything from the duffel bag, and again inspected each item, one at a time. The clothing, the survival kit. He loaded the weapon. He started the radio, and checked it with the bridge. He caught the bridge radio man by complete surprise, and toyed with him briefly, then explained that he was in his quarters checking his radio. He was ready. He decided to sleep, and get rest because he did not know when he would get sleep again.

The ship came to its destination about ten miles north and west of Acapulco. It sank to the bottom and rested. It was three hours to drop off. Chon was advised to get ready. He changed to his black diver's suit, and packed everything away. He had three items to carry, the duffel bag, a suitcase, and the box case which contained the radio. Chon walked down the hallway to the bridge area. He spoke briefly to the men there. Their excitement and enthusiasm made him proud of the mission and of his country, and he felt honored that he was chosen for it.

The captain ordered "surface", and a flurry of activity followed. Chon felt the ship rise slowly. At first it seemed to turn over to one side, off balance, then righted itself, and continued to rise. The captain lifted her and it took five minutes to surface. Chon was given the signal to go forward to the hatch and exit, carrying the suitcases. He handed the bags to the seaman topside, then followed through the small hole. It was dark at 2100 hours. Chon was surprised at the warmth that he felt in the air. It felt strange. It was late October 1941. He had expected cool air. He walked forward on the submarine. The rubber raft was already in the water and there were three frogmen tending it and ready to help him board. There was a short ladder leading to the raft. There was another frogman in the raft waiting for him. He handed one suitcase to the frogman and then the other, then he followed. Being in the raft, the frogman climbed the ladder onto the submarine. The other three frogmen followed the first and boarded the submarine and went below. This was the signal for Chon to shove off, and he did, paddling feverishly toward the beach. He was a mile from the shore. There was total darkness. When Chon was about fifty yards away, the officers on the conning tower went below and a minute later, the submarine submerged. The loud suction noise startled him.

He felt completely alone, and scared. He thought of the monumental mission ahead of him. He caught himself in fear. "Calm down, calm down," he said to himself, "soon you will see that there is nothing to be afraid of."

He landed fifteen minutes later. He jumped out of the raft, and ran onto the beach pulling the raft behind him. He did not pause, but continued his pull toward a thick growth of vegetation about fifty yards away. He tugged the raft about ten yards into the forest and then stopped to catch his breath. The ocean waves and the rustling of the trees in the wind provided Chon some calm. He rose from the rest and took off his rubber suit. As he rose, he noticed the moon was rising. "I am sure that this is Miyoshi san's doing," he thought, "who else would know that on this day, ten minutes after I land, the moon would rise to provide me with the light that I need to prepare for entry. It had to be Miyoshi san," he said to himself with a chuckle. He deflated the rubber raft, and hid it and the rubber suit in the underbrush, finishing with a healthy cover of sand.

He wore black oxford shoes, gray double pleated slacks and a white long sleeve shirt with the sleeves rolled up to the elbows. He chose not to wear a hat that night, thinking it would be suspicious looking on someone carrying three suitcases in the night. He began the ten mile walk into the west side of Acapulco. He walked rapidly. He came to a turn in the beach and then saw the many lights of Acapulco in the distance. Acapulco was a sleepy fishing village, and the reason it was chosen as a beginning point was its close proximity to México City, which was only seventy miles away.

Shortly after midnight Chon walked into town. He was apprehensive, but he was mentally prepared for all possibilities. The town had some street lights, which together with the dim lights from the homes and shacks provided the illumination he needed to keep walking. He finally came to what appeared to be the business part of town and found a place to lodge, the Hotel Miramar. He self-assuredly walked up to the desk.

"I need a room for the night," Chon spoke to the desk clerk.

"Why yes, of course, we do have a room," said the desk clerk. The clerk was tall, skinny, balding, and wore glasses. He seemed like a taller and quieter more reserved Miyoshi san, Chon thought.

"Very well," Chon answered, "I'll take the room. I expect to be here no more than three nights. I have no dog, nor pig, nor goat so you should have no problems with me. But if circumstances should change I will advise you immediately."

The old man asked Chon to sign in and demanded one days rent in advance. Chon signed in, for the first time using his alias, "Encarnación Gutiérrez Ayala". The old clerk explained that he would have room number eight up one flight of stairs, and three doors on the right. Chon went up carrying his three bags. He slipped the key into the keyhole and reached for the light switch, and one bulb lit up the single room. There was a large bed, a chest of drawers, a mirror on the wall above the chest, as well as a wash bowl and pitcher of water on top of the chest. There was one chair in the corner, and that was it. The room had one window that faced the ocean. However, the ocean was ten blocks away. Chon put the clothes suitcase in the closet, and immediately, opened the other and began removing the radio, the collapsible antennae, and the microphone. He started almost in a whisper, "Silverfish, this is the Lone Wolf, do you read me?" There was no response. He waited for about a minute.

"Silverfish, this is the Lone Wolf, do you read me?" A crackle pop and static, later he heard "Lone Wolf this is the Silverfish we read you loud and clear." He was relieved, and almost forgot to respond. He snapped out of it. "Silverfish, I am in, and I am surrounded by good company, I am in place. I cannot speak loudly but I am in place. I will communicate tomorrow. Do you have any questions?"

The sub answered, "We understand Lone Wolf, we are with you, we wish you luck, we will talk as scheduled."

Chon was ecstatic. He had landed, the radio was working perfectly, and he was on his way. So far everything was working as planned. He was happy; he was pleased. He quickly disassembled the radio, and put it in the suitcase, and then in the closet. It was late, he was tired, and he laid down to get some sleep, but instead his mind wandered to the events of the day.

His Spanish went well apparently, as there was no problem with the desk clerk, no raised eyebrow, no grimace. As far as his appearance went, Sebastian, Akechi san, and Miyoshi san were right, even in the dark streets of Acapulco, he had seen several Mexicans who looked like they belonged right in the middle of the streets of Tokyo. He was surprised that they were correct on this point. How could these people halfway around the world, look like Orientals, look like Japanese, look like Chinese. Was it the Aleutian Straight explanation, or were the continents together billions of years ago and then separated, and some people got left on both sides. "Who knows," he thought, "and really at this point in time who cares? I am here, I am happy, my project is working, and so far I am undetected, but most of all I'm tired."

He dosed off to sleep.

Chapter Nine

Chon rose early. He was fully rested. He looked out the window and investigated the entire street below. There was a grocery store, a butcher shop, a dry goods store, and a pharmacy. It seemed benign enough. A typical main street area for thousands of villages around the globe.

He was hungry. He did not see a restaurant in the stores below, so he would have to search one out. He groomed, dressed, and prepared to leave his room, but he hesitated; should he leave his baggage or must he carry it off with him, he thought. He did not feel like hauling the bags around, but he feared that the baggage might be stolen. Without the baggage he would be lost. The decision was easy, the bags must come along. He brought them out of the closet and shut them tight, opened the door, and left the room.

As he descended the stairs, a lady desk clerk noticed him as he started for the door.

"Are you checking out now? Aren't you the gentleman from number eight that came in last night?" She asked.

"Yes, I am the one that came in last night and got room number eight, and I am not checking out," Chon answered.

"Then why are you carrying out your bags?" She asked. "And where are you from? You speak funny, you do not speak like you are from here," the desk clerk pressed him.

Chon gasped for air, while the adrenalin in his veins choked him. His training was meeting its first challenge sooner than he expected. He grasped for an answer. He took a deep breath.

All of his feeling of conquest from earlier in the morning was gone and lost. He took another deep breath. "Stay calm, stay calm," he thought. "What would Commander Shigeru do in the same situation, how would Sebastian and Miyoshi san handle it as Mexicans? He calmed down, prepared his response, and after what seemed like an eternity, but was only a few seconds, he replied.

"First, my bags are my business and not yours. Didn't you have robberies here about a couple of months ago?" He bluffed.

"Secondly, I am from the north, and if I talk differently it is because we are the ones that speak correctly and not like you lazy southerners," remembering what both Miyoshi san and Sebastian had taught him, he fired back, staring across the desk at the surprised woman.

The lady dropped her head and turned around obviously defeated. Chon pulled off the act, and he was pleased. He was also sweating. He had to think real fast, and that made him very uncomfortable, but he drew on his resources, and they did not fail him. He was learning that he could trust his instincts, his training, and his intelligence.

He walked out of the hotel in a hurry, and made for the closest restaurant. After three blocks he found a little neighborhood cafe, and went in to eat. After breakfast he set out to check out the rest of the town, more importantly he needed to buy a small truck. He walked around and watched, listened, and observed. Late that morning he found a pickup truck for sale that was only three years old. An old ranchero was hard up for cash and needed to sell it. At first, the ranchero offered to rent it, but Chon insisted he wanted to buy it, no strings attached. The mission was not consistent with rental payments. The rancher explained that he bought the truck in Texas and bribed the Mexican customs officials to get it into the country, and that this cost a lot of extra money. He tried to jack up the price, but Chon was having none of it. He knew from his training that the world, México included, was just barely beginning to recuperate after a horrible worldwide economic depression, and he also knew that things were not going all that well for México in the present economic situation, so he stood firm. All he would pay was five hundred American dollars. The Mexican did not know it, but he was up against a world class haggler and trader when he traded with any Japanese. He did not have a chance.

Chon drove off in the pickup. He felt good. He thought only about Tokyo Plantation all day as he drove around. He remembered his driving days with Akechi san. That night he raised the Silverfish and reported that the day had gone well. He added that he had not investigated anything and had no data to report, but that he had achieved the goal of buying a truck for transportation, and the next day would move north to México City.

The next morning, a day earlier than anticipated, Chon began his journey north. The trip to México City was short, relatively speaking, and he was surprised to find that México City was huge. He had read about it, Miyoshi san told him about it, and Sebastian described it in detail. The briefs that he received also described it in detail as a very large city, but somehow all of this went unappreciated until now. This city was not nearly as big as Tokyo, but it was huge. Earlier, he had made mental plans to spend a week in México City gathering data, but seeing the size of the large city, he knew that he would do better by scouring the countryside instead of concentrating so much time on México City.

On the third day he began his journey in earnest. He traveled east first to Veracruz and the neighboring towns and villages. Each night he found a small hotel and each night he raised the Silverfish and reported statistics on growing crops, population, power plants, natural resources, military strength.

Then he went to the tip of Yucatan collecting information as he went, and reporting back to the Silverfish. He established a pattern, and it was now routine for him. He continued up the coast to Oaxaca, and then on back to México City.

He was starting to feel exhausted and told the Silverfish that he would not report for three days as he needed to get his truck repaired, which was partially true since he did have to get a flat repaired. Also, because it was hard to get fuel and oil. Mostly though it was because he needed the rest. It was not easy to go out in the countryside of a foreign nation, not being sure about its language, its customs, or anything else about it, and spying on it, and to be and remain casual about the entire operation. It was nerve wracking and very stressful and he needed a break and he took one.

At times he felt sorry for the people he spied on. They were generally very kind and friendly and always wanted to help. They seemed hard working and were very honorable. But a job was a job, and he had his, and he did it to the best of his ability.

The northern part of the country was much different from the other parts that he had traveled. There was much more desert or dry country in the north. He also noticed that the people in the north were more independent, and more vocal. They were not docile and easily led as the people in the south of the country.

In the north the people stood up for what they believed in, and seemed to be more serious about their desire to improve the quality of their lives.

Included with the dry parts and the desert, were some beautiful areas, and some fascinating large cities. The cultures varied even within the country, not unlike Japan. In about ten days he made his way to Saltillo, in the northern state of Coahuila. The temperature there was just beautiful. It was a very cool climate. The next stop, however, was Monterrey where Chon spent a very hot week taking inventory of the factories that permeated the city.

Chon's assimilation into the Mexican culture, though forced, occurred very rapidly. He embraced it and this acceptance made his job easier as it made his detection harder and more remote.

Chon finished researching Mazatlan, the seaport on the west coast of México. His plan was to go northward along the coast, and after reaching the border with the United States, turning abruptly and heading along the boundary in a southeast direction.

"If things work out just right, I might have an opportunity to cross over into one of the American border towns. I'm sure I can get a three-day permit from the U. S. consul," he thought. What he was not sure of was the probability of detection. He knew, of course, that if detected, if the Americans did not kill him, Commander Shigeru certainly would.

It was December 5, 1941. He reported to the Silverfish the night before and informed them that he was taking two days off to rest. He had not rested since México City. He inquired of the Silversmith's location and was told that the ship was in the Gulf of California, the long sliver of ocean between the Mexican mainland's west coast and the long peninsula known as Baja California. They had been there for ten days.

* * *

Unbeknownst to Chon, the next morning Commander Shigeru hurriedly assembled a War Conference in Tokyo, after learning that the Western powers had refused to meet the Empire's demand to control their part of the world. Many of those called to the War Conference knew of the coded messages that had come from Washington. Commander Shigeru called the assembly to order. Most of the generals, colonels, and admirals were present. Only those actively carrying out the war effort were absent.

"Please, please, I require your silence, and your attention. We have much to discuss," the commander said, tapping a pencil on the podium urging the crowd to be quiet. Those present were leaders that could be trusted with the highest secrets. He had to explain very sensitive matters and was glad that he did not have to worry about information leaks.

"We have received the signal from Washington that things have not gone well. Of course, if what you want or desire is aggression, then I can report to you that things have gone very well in Washington. The Americans and the British have refused to meet our demands. We have explained very carefully that we must be allowed to control our own part of the globe, and our desires have been rejected."

Looking out over the assembly, all Commander Shigeru saw was a small sea of short hair and bald heads.

"This means, of course, that we must take matters into our hands and do what needs to be done by and for the Empire. This means that the Mount Niitaka project is on, and we must strike immediately," he said, smashing his fist into the podium.

"Although we expected the Valley project to be ready with the Mount Niitaka project, it is not, and therefore we cannot have the one two initiative as originally planned," Commander Shigeru said, and then paused. The entire cadre bowed to him and to each other, speaking in short phrases and in a low murmur.

The Commander interrupted. "Before we go on, I would like to remind you that these matters are of the utmost secrecy. You must not forget that. You must be very careful. If word of this leaks out, it could mean the failure of the project, and of our entire well-planned strategy. It could mean the success or failure of the war, and that means the success or failure of the emergence of the Empire to its rightful place in the world.

"I must insist that you suppress the excitement of the moment and assure that everyone under your command receive the orders they need, in secrecy, and proceed to carry out our missions. I plead, please go now for the Empire."

The cadre walked out in a hurry, each almost bursting with the news they wanted to share.

* * *

Chon called his own two-day holiday for Saturday and Sunday. He had traveled the entire Mexican countryside in a hard-driving pickup truck and was exhausted. He rested on the beach on Saturday, and likewise enjoyed the sun on Sunday.

Like Akechi san before him, he had gotten to know the Mexican culture first hand and loved it. His preference, likewise, was for the open air restaurants, the guitar music, the sun, and meat cooked over brasas. Unfortunately, cabrito asado was not a dish common to the coastal city of Mazatlan so on this Saturday night he had settled on broiled lamb.

Chon rested on Sunday. He first went to the beach for a swim and some sun. By about one o'clock he returned to his room, changed clothes, and went out to find a restaurant for lunch. After lunch, on a park bench under many shaded trees, he read the daily newspaper for more leads on the information he needed to finish his report. By about four o'clock he began to nod off with sleep. He gathered his newspaper, and walked behind the park bench and laid down on the grass, placing the newspaper on his face and went to sleep.

Mazatlan was a very large city. Chon was apprehensive about walking about with two huge suitcases, one containing the radio. To avoid this problem, he decided to hide his illicit cargo outside the city. He found large hills east of the city, explored the terrain, and found a cave. The entrance was hard to find. The cave was small, but had one large room about ten meters square. Chon searched its interior carefully and found several small niches where he could hide his survival equipment and the radio. He covered the bags with vegetation.

Afterwards, the park was filled with people. Chon was intrigued by the Mexican custom of going to the park on Sunday and of the young people going to the plaza Wednesday and Sunday nights. The people walked around the plaza's cobblestone walks over and over. Everyone enjoyed the day. At about sunset, he gathered his stuff and walked along the park, staring at and studying the people. He had advised the submarine that he would not communicate until Monday night. He entered his room and reviewed his notes over and over again, making mental note on what he reported and what was still to be reported.

After a few moments, he turned off the light and went to bed.

Monday morning December 8, 1941 Chon awoke early and went down for breakfast. Since he had not eaten supper, he was starving and wanted a big breakfast. The hotel restaurant was not open yet so he sauntered down the street looking for an open restaurant. He walked a couple of blocks and ran into a newspaper boy hawking the early morning news.

"Señor, buy my newspaper, there is big news, the Americans and the Japanese are at war. Muchos explosiones and sinking boats yesterday. Big news señor, don't you want a copy," the young boy asked.

Chon could not believe his ears, "What war? Americans? Japanese? Explosiones? What are you talking about?" He interrogated the young boy vigorously.

"Mire señor, I don't know Japoneses and I don't know Americanos, and I don't care about explosiones, and ships, so you want to buy my newspaper or not?" The boy offered an ultimatum as he prepared to run.

"Just give me a copy," Chon said under his breath, as he handed the boy a five centavo piece. He sat on a park bench and began to read. "Mount Niitaka project has happened, and they didn't even tell me. Bastards. Here I am in a remote foreign country, counting sheep, cows, and lead mines, and the one two punch had already begun, and without my help. Dirty bastards. How could they leave me out of such a tremendous offensive? I will complain to Commander Shigeru when I see him next. I am not pleased."

After he had read the newspaper over and over and over, it hit him. "I can't linger around for the rest of the day. I must move. I have to take some action now. Hurry, hurry," he thought "it's time to move, to ask and find out what is happening." He ran to the hotel, and quickly picked up what few belongings he had with him. He rushed to the lobby and checked out. He hurried to his pickup and got in, started the motor, revved up the engines until he felt that it was ready, and drove off to the eastern boundary of the city of Mazatlan. In his hurry, he passed the hills that he chose for his hiding place, and had to double back.

He parked the pickup under some trees about three hundred meters from the road. He felt sure that it could not be seen from the road. He hurried to his secret cave. Chon arrived at the cave entrance, and he slithered in. He was exhausted, he panted for a few minutes until he regained his breath. "I must not panic, I must not panic."

Finally, he could breathe easily. He scurried around and built a tiny fire. He needed light as the cave was dark. He arranged his bags, and opened the suitcase and took out some food and his survival kit. He uncovered the radio and other gear that he brought earlier. In his usual methodical manner he arranged everything in his new room, as if he planned to stay for a month. It was ten o'clock in the morning. "Silverfish, Silverfish, this is the Lone Wolf, do you hear me? Do you read me? Silverfish?" He was anxious and his tone of voice revealed it.

For five minutes there was no response. He tried again. "Silverfish, this is the Lone Wolf can you read?"

He waited. Finally a crackle came over the radio. "Lone Wolf, this is the Silverfish. We read you fine. Lone Wolf have you heard the about the Mountain?" The submarine queried.

"Yes Silverfish, I have heard about the project? Have you communicated with Mother about our project?" Chon asked.

"Lone Wolf, we have instructions. Please listen carefully as we will not transmit twice. There is a shark in the water here, and we must be discrete. Listen. You are to destroy everything except your kit and your transportation. After destruction, you shall drive to the pick up point on the coast where you will destroy your transportation and any other thing in your possession, except your kit and then wait until 2400 hours. By that time, we will have arrived, and we will come in to get you. Do you read? Do you understand?" The message from the sub was over.

"I read and understand, this is the Lone Wolf clear and out," Chon responded.

He gathered all his data, clothing and everything else that would burn, and slowly began to feed the fire. The flames rose and brightened the room. Soon only the radio, the clothing on his body, and the survival kit were left. He positioned two large flat rocks in front of him, and then dragged the radio over toward him, he unscrewed and pulled, and began to disassemble the radio. As he pulled parts from the equipment, he placed them on the rock in front of him, and crushed the parts, rendering the part incapable of identification. Whatever remnants that would burn were tossed into the fire. The rest, he buried in a shallow hole outside the cave. He took several deep breaths and took inventory. The only things left were his clothing and the survival kit, and of course the truck below. He scurried down the high hill.

Chon rushed toward Mazatlan. He could not forget about the attack on Pearl Harbor, he kept going through the newspaper account over and over in his mind. "Planes, bombs, submarines, ships sinking, it must have been one beautiful day," Chon said to himself.

He drove carefully through the downtown area and found the highway that led south of town. He still had to destroy the pickup truck. Before leaving town, he found a gas station and filled up the tank. He drove off.

When he had traveled eight miles, he came to a huge creek or canyon on the side of the road. He stopped in tourist fashion and pretended to view the deep gorge. When he noticed there was no traffic, he opened the door, and placed the gear in neutral and began pushing the pickup toward the edge of the gorge. He finally got it rolling slowly, removed his kit, and let it go.

Chon woke up on the beach about seven o'clock. He was ready to be picked up, but of course he had to wait until midnight. He yearned for the radio. Chon walked up and down the two hundred yards, which he mentally marked as his pick up perimeter. Twelve midnight rolled around and he held his survival kit anxiously. He waited for a rubber boat or something similar to float up on the beach. He listened closely for a call, or for a sound, a human sound.

By two o'clock he was too sleepy to keep waiting. He slept five feet from the water line. He was certain, he told himself, that he would hear someone approach. He slept, and finally awoke at 0530 hours when the sun began to creep up behind him from the east. The submarine had not come. Surely there must be something wrong, but not that wrong, he hoped. He was sure that Silverfish would come.

He thought of Commander Shigeru's words, "If anything goes wrong with the Silverfish, I want you to destroy everything, including yourself. Do you understand? I do not want any evidence found that we were even attempting an action against the United States through México. Do you understand? If anything goes wrong I want everything destroyed, even yourself. Do you understand? If something happens to the Silverfish, I want everything destroyed. Do you understand? If anything major goes wrong, I want everything destroyed. Including you, do you understand? I do not want any evidence left in México that you have been there, if something goes wrong. Do you understand? If for any reason the submarine has to leave the area and leaves you stranded, I want you to destroy everything, and then be honorable and destroy yourself. Harakiri, do you understand?" The words echoed in his ear for the rest of the day.

By six o'clock in the evening he was still at the beach. He was going to wait again until midnight.

The night was a repetition of the one before. He waited, he paced, he laid down, he sat, he paced, he listened, he laid back, and finally at three o'clock in the morning he dozed off on the beach, feeling comfortable that he would be awakened by the crew of the landing craft sent to retrieve him.

The sun rose slowly up again on the east side of the beach. He felt the warmth and awakened, now in acute desperation. The ship had not shown. There was definitely something wrong. He sat back and gathered his thoughts. "What should I do?"

He began the long walk to Mazatlan. Chon walked through the dusty streets. He was on the edge of town. He walked without noticing anything around him. The shanty homes, the people, the dogs, the children all went unnoticed. He prodded on.

Eventually he got to the downtown area. He rested on a park bench at the central plaza called the Alameda. He had been there several times, and was in familiar surroundings. He rested. He relaxed.

An urchin walked up and begged for a penny. The child was selling newspapers, but sales were not good, so he shifted his trade to a straight plea for a coin. Chon raised his vision and saw the little beggar. He thought about how many times he had waved these little bastards off. Sometimes they would go away, sometimes they were tenacious as hell and would not leave. He looked at the boy's face, and it was dirty, and he had a runny nose. The boy looked pitiful. The face was a cinch to garner at least a nickel.

He looked at the boy and examined the rest of him slowly. He looked under his arm, and noticed he was carrying about six newspapers. The boy pleaded for a centavo again. Chon started to wave him off, and the boy turned slightly and revealed the headline of the newspaper. Chon almost lost his breath.

He reached into his pocket and almost threw a cinco at the beggar, as he grabbed a newspaper from the boy's arm. The headlines read:

AMERICAN SHIP SINKS SUB OFF MAZATLAN

He read it over and over. He could not believe that it was possible. Slowly he inched into the article. The kill was confirmed by the U.S. Naval Station in San Diego, California. There was evidence recovered. Several Japanese code books were found, clothing, uniforms, a deflated and torn rubber raft, a lifesaver, and certain items containing the ship's identification as the I201.

Chon sat on the bench going over the newspaper for two hours. The sun shifted over the shade of the trees. He was in the bright sun, but he did not move. He was oblivious to the world around him. He sat.

By four o'clock, Commander Shigeru's orders were haunting him. "If the missions fail, you will be expected to destroy yourself. Is that understood?

"If for any reason the I201 cannot make it back, or if it is destroyed, or if it must leave the area without you, all must be destroyed, including yourself. Is that understood?"

The sun went down, and Chon sat on the bench. His mind raced. He was trying to find a way to evade the matter of harakiri, and finally came to the realization that he could not. He spent three hours psyching himself to take that final step. Finally he rose. He picked up his survival kit and walked out of Mazatlan, traveling east. Eventually he came to the hill, and the cave. The only sign of his earlier presence were the ashes. He went outside and brought in firewood, and lit a small fire.

The large cavern lit up. It was golden orange throughout the large room. By this time Chon had regained his composure, but was still in a semi trance. He knew what he had to do and he was making all preliminary preparations. He opened the survival kit and removed everything.

The fire was about in the middle of the large room. In front of the fire, but toward the entrance, Chon placed a large flat rock. On the flat rock he placed the cyanide suicide ring and his aikuchi knife, the suicide dagger that Akechi san had given him years ago.

The rest of the items in the survival kit, he placed in a corner. He thought that he should go outside and bury them, but he decided that he would get to that chore momentarily. He removed his shirt and slacks, and dressed in a set of light cotton karate pajamas. He sat in front of the fire and fed it ten small sticks. The fire popped. The room lit up brighter.

As he sat there he thought of the barn at the Tiger Camp with Nagi san and the short lesson he gave them in the art of thrusting the aikuchi. He thought about that for a long time. Nagi san's method of doing the deed quickly and severing a major artery was a major departure from just sticking yourself in the gut. The Massaki way was quicker faster and more efficient. He began to chant Buddhist and Shinto hymns. He stared at the fire.

He continued to chant and pray aloud. Then he stopped and he began to pray quietly. He prayed continually for about an hour. The moment finally came. He picked up the cyanide filled ring. He brought it up to his face, and stared at it momentarily. He spoke to the ring.

"You, little round circle of shit, I do not want you and will never see you again," he tossed it into the fire. Then he grabbed the aikuchi knife, and brought it in front of him with both hands, he held both arms outstretched in front of him.

"And you, bastard knife, I do not need you either, but I will not destroy you, I will keep you as a memento of what I am and from whence I came." He put it down on the flat rock. He let out a huge sigh. He sat on his butt, and stretched out his legs and laid in front of the fire to rest. He was exhausted. He had lived five years in one afternoon. The intensity of the meditation drained him. He had been through the worst ordeal of his life.

He had decided to live. Suicide was not his to commit. He would go on as best he could. Right now all he could do was thank God, whether the Japanese Gods or Sebastian's Jesus, it did not matter to him at that moment. What mattered was that he live.

He rested. The next day he would begin to put the pieces of his life back together.

BOOK THREE
Becoming a Mexicano

Chapter Ten

After the fire burned out, it was dark and cool in the cave when Chon woke after a long sleep. His nightmare was over. Although he had tossed and turned throughout the night, he had begun to build a framework for a new life during his sleep. The plan was simple.

He dressed, put on his shoes, and rushed into Mazatlan for provisions. He walked through the general store and purchased the basics and staples he would need. A razor, a toothbrush, soap, clothing, food, a tin pan and cup, a saucepan, and a set of utensils. He did not want to buy too much because he would now spend his new life as a drifter. He also bought a small cotton bag to carry his goods.

He returned to the cave and, with water he had found nearby, he washed and groomed. He also washed his clothing. Then he brought up some wood to rekindle the fire and he prepared and ate a meal of rice and vegetables.

With the camp in order and everything clean, including himself, he sat outside under a shade tree and contemplated the problems he faced. For several hours, he analyzed several alternatives, combining alternatives, adding and changing them and finally came up with the final plan.

Since he had overlooked destroying his identification papers, he would continue with the same identity and alias, Encarnación Gutiérrez Ayala.

"To survive I must bury myself in Mexican society as deep as I can. I must go underground. I have violated and disobeyed

Commander Shigeru's order to destroy myself. If I am ever caught and taken back to Japan I will be executed immediately," he thought. His goal was to go undetected in México for the rest of his life. He could never return to Japan. His ties with Japan, Akechi san, Sebastian, and his mother were over. As far as they were concerned, they would think that he died in action, and they would never see him again.

He would go back to the basics. He was well trained in many things. He could hold down any job, but chances of detection would be more remote in a low profile menial job or position. Therefore, he chose to return to farming and agriculture. He would be Chon Gutiérrez, a farmhand. He was resigned to be a farmhand for the rest of his life. This would be his way of avoiding his pledge to commit harakiri.

He stayed in the cave for another five days, thinking, meditating, praying, preparing, and psyching himself up. Then, he was ready to move, to travel. He packed all his things, including the remnants of the survival kit, his only link to his former life. He emerged from the cave a new man. Dressed in white pants, white shirt, a flat straw hat, wearing thick leather sandals the Mexicans called huaraches. The portrait of a typical farmhand, a peasant, a peon.

For several days, he walked north and then east. He walked mostly at night. When he had traveled a sufficient distance from Mazatlan he began walking during the day in search of a farm where he could work. He looked for a large plantation. Finally, as he came up on a hill, he looked over to the north and saw hectares after hectares of green fields. At the center of the fields he saw a green clump of huge trees, signifying the main house and other buildings. The headquarters of the hacienda was not unlike Tokyo Plantation, the headquarters was surrounded by smaller farms and ranchitos.

He walked up a lane bordered by about twenty large shade trees on either side. As he neared the main house, he decided to divert his route to the outer buildings and look for the caporal. He walked around the main building and yard and came to various barns and sheds. The whole area was shaded by large trees in contrast to the bright sun, which came down on the fields adjacent to the buildings. There were many wagons, tractors, farm implements, and other tools in and around the barns and sheds. Many people were lying and sitting in the shades of the sheds and barns. It was the noon hour, the siesta as it was called in México. It was customary for the trabajadores to rise as early as five in the morning to take advantage of the cool morning air and then take a break during the heat of the early afternoon. They would return to the fields as the heat abated and would work into the evening darkness.

There were two small fires where a few corn tortillas and a couple of pots of beans were being warmed on bare coals. A dog barked at him and challenged his approach, otherwise, hardly anyone even noticed or seemed interested in his arrival. He walked over to the nearest man to him, sitting under the shade of a tree.

"Hola," Chon said.

He got no response. The man looked up and examined him from head to toe. Chon imagined the man asking himself questions, as his eyes surveyed the situation. Chon had committed to become a farmhand and as part of his new identity he was required to hide his eyes. An intelligent, confident, or stern look would surely give him away. It was not easy, but he must hide his eyes and guard his speech.

Again Chon tried, "Hola."

Again there was no response.

"I am looking for work. Do you think I could get a job here?" He asked.

There was no response.

"What do you think? Is there a chance of getting a job around here? " Chon kept probing.

Finally, the man spoke. "Mira hombre, if there is a job or not around here is no concern of mine. You need to wait and talk to el señor Luis. He is the caporal. He will be here later this afternoon. I cannot say. One thing I can tell you is that if you come to work here you better be ready to work hard. This here is no fiesta."

He stopped speaking and returned to his rest.

Chon wondered whether he should make an about face and walk out of the depressing place? "Did I pick the wrong farm or are they all like this?" Chon thought. For an instant he almost walked away but decided he would stay and see what happened.

He sat on his haunches a few feet from the man.

"What are the crops?" Chon asked.

After a long pause, the man answered. "Watermelons and cantaloupes, right now, and some corn and squash, but we grow everything. This is good soil, and the water from the river which is brought up with machines, uh, engines, uh, pumps, is good. We have good crops."

After about five minutes, Chon asked, "How much is the pay?"

The man looked at him, "Two pesos a day," he replied and turned away.

Chon searched through his memory. From the economic data that he had memorized before starting his mission he remembered that five to ten pesos per day was the average wage for simple laborers. Why was the wage so low on this farm?

Chon dared to continue probing, and although slow to respond, the man continued to cooperate.

"What's the name of this place?" Chon asked.

"This is La Hacienda San Rafael," the man said.

"Who is the owner of this plantation?" Chon asked.

"Tomás Resendez Peña, Don Tomás," the man answered.

"What is your name?" Chon asked.

"Antonio Reza Ponciano," he answered. "Tonio for short. Hijole mano, you sure ask a lot of questions."

Tonio laughed as he looked at Chon. Tonio liked him after that day.

"Who is the caporal?" Chon asked.

"His name is Luis Carranza, and he's a real cabrón, a bastard. You will see," Tonio replied.

"What do you mean?"

"You will see, you will see," Tonio warned, "and by the way, what is your name mano?"

"My name is Encarnación Gutiérrez Ayala, Chon for short."

Chon noticed that several of the smaller groups of people were starting to move towards the fields. Tonio got up, brushed off, and stretched.

"What is it you are doing today?" Chon asked.

"We are thinning out the cantaloupe," Tonio answered.

"Can I go with you, I promise I will not get in your way?" Chon asked.

"Sí hombre. Come on and watch and don't get in the way."

They spent the rest of the day thinning out the small green plants. Tonio was pleased that Chon knew what he was doing.

Chon enjoyed it thoroughly, with memories of Tokyo Plantation, filling his head. He had not been out in the field for many years. He smelled the dirt and it smelled great. He felt great. He knew he was going to love his new life. He worked side-by-side with Tonio, and Tonio enjoyed the new companionship.

The other workers noticed that Chon worked well and fast. As the hours went by Tonio and Chon got to know each other better and better. Chon talked about his past, his made up past of course. He told Tonio that he was from below Mazatlan, a place named San Blas, and had been a farmhand all his life. He had to leave his village because of bad blood between him and his brother. He did not elaborate, and he was hoping that he never would have to.

Tonio and Chon were about the same age. Like Tonio, Chon was not married. Tonio had been a farmhand all his life too. As the afternoon passed, Tonio explained more and more about the situation at the plantation, with Luis Carranza in charge. The situation had gotten worse as time went by. Carranza had been one of the workers. He always got along well with everyone. He was older than most of the men on the plantation, and more experienced. He was quiet and did not cause anyone problems. He had been a caporal for about five years, and every year he got progressively worse.

At first there was no big change. Gradually, however, Carranza became more abrasive, insulting, and abusive. First he began wearing cowboy boots, discarding his huarache sandals, then he discarded his white cotton pajamas for blue jeans, and a khaki shirt. Later he took to carrying a small whip, a small leather bracelet attached to it hanging on his wrist.

At some point in time, Carranza began to drink alcohol excessively. At times he carried a pistol. Typically, he would show up at mid-morning, yelling, screaming, and occasionally whipping a younger boy, a woman, or an older person; he would push his horse up on anybody he chose. If anyone tried to defend themselves, they had to fight the horse, the machete, the whip, and possibly even the pistol. A few of the younger workers had tried to stop him, but they were no match for his arsenal of weapons.

If Carranza needed more work done in order to achieve a certain goal or project, he would yell, scream, and threaten until he got it done.

"But why don't people leave, if the situation is so bad?" Chon asked Tonio.

"Because, we have heard that it is just as bad no matter where you go. And besides, we have a job, we cannot afford to quit, and then maybe have to travel fifty miles or so to get turned down or end up with the very same situation," Tonio explained.

"But surely there must be something that can be done to stop all this," Chon insisted.

The sun was setting. The golden shades of light strung out across the green fields. The workers walked in small groups down the lanes, toward the oasis that was the plantation headquarters.

This was Chon's favorite part of the day. It was cool, and the colors were beautiful. The sun hiding behind the western clouds was a rich gold, surrounded by red, orange, gold, and even dark gray clouds. The breeze died down now, and sounds were crisp, voices carried a long way.

Tonio and Chon walked toward the houses, still intrigued with each other's company and conversation. Chon had not enjoyed extended conversation since Intelligence Service School, and he had much catching up to do in becoming sociable again, except that now he must keep his speech, expression, and manner guarded, in keeping with his new identity.

They arrived at the barn and shed area, and everyone sat down or laid down under a shed, or under a tree, or on some lumber, much like they did during the lunch hour. Chon expected them to go to their shelters, shacks or houses, clean up and begin preparing the evening meal. He expected one or more large fires to go up immediately, but only one small fire at the end of the open space smoldered. It was very shady in the area, and one could still look out to the bright green and gold beyond the fields. It was like looking from the inside of a cave to the bright outdoors.

Chon looked to Tonio for a lead. "Tonio aren't you going to build a fire and fix a meal? Where is your house? I do not understand why the people just lay around instead of going to their homes and clean up and prepare for the evening."

"Well Chon, it used to be that way, before Luis took over, but since then it seems that things just deteriorated. Those small houses over there they are filthy and abandoned. People sleep under wagons and under tractors, they eat when they get the idea of doing it instead of when they should. And that includes me. Things are different now, and nobody cares. We used to get a regular ration of food, but now we do not, so we eat when we get something, and sometimes we do not get anything. It would take too long for us to go into the village and buy provisions, even if we had the money.

"We used to have water piped in from irrigation canals for cooking and cleaning, but the pipes rusted out long ago, and now the water is half a kilometer away. We go when we have to, but not otherwise."

"But why don't you send someone into the village to get merchandise for everyone, why don't you fix and clean up the houses, why don't you dig a trench and bring the water closer? I just do not understand?" Chon said with bewilderment in his face.

"Well it is not easy for me to explain," Tonio said, shrugging his shoulders.

"And besides," Tonio added, now feeling a bit embarrassed for all the conditions that Chon's questions were bringing to light, "if the house needs something fixed, we have to ask Luis, and that means a beating or a good cussing out, and nothing gets fixed. If the pipe needs fixing, that means we have to ask Luis, and that means a beating or a good cussing out, and the pipe does not get fixed. And if we do not get enough food, we have to ask Luis, and that means a beating or a good cussing out, and we get no more food.

"We used to have beds for the shacks, but when we moved out, we used them outdoors, and they soon rusted and were no good, so now we don't have beds. The mattresses did not last without beds, being outdoors. We tried to explain to Don Tomás, but we are never able to see him. He never comes out, he handles all the business through Luis.

"We have even tried to communicate with him through some of the household servants, and that has been impossible. Either he does not believe it, or he does not want to do anything about it. He is rarely seen." Tonio paused.

"I don't know, I don't know. You are just going to have to see to understand. It is easy to ask questions," Tonio concluded with a sigh.

Chon could not tell for sure, and he still had much observing to do, but what he had seen thus far, was a whipped people; they were defeated in body and in spirit. As a matter of fact they had no spirit. They had lost their will and spirit to fight, to live. There was no joy, no happiness. They were defeated. In effect, they were worse than slaves, and did not care.

Chon shared some of his food with Tonio, and they talked around a small fire under a juniper tree until late in the night.

Chon decided he would try to hire on with Don Luis the following day. He knew he could probably get a better deal elsewhere, but he liked Tonio and he wanted to be around him and learn more about him and the people at the hacienda. So he would give it a try.

He was tired from his day of walking and stooping.

Chapter Eleven

Throughout the night Chon tossed and turned and glanced around the camp. There was always at least one fire burning, his. Sometimes there would be one other, but no more. As he looked around, he noticed men, women, and children lying on the bare ground, with barely enough cover. He awoke several times during the night to relieve himself. He looked around and wondered if he made the right decision, but each time he returned to his own mat, made of a bed of leaves, grass, and weeds, and covered himself.

He could see the pink of the morning peeking over the eastern sky. He rose, and gathered his gear, and put it away. He fed the fire, and prepared for a morning meal.

Suddenly, a man on a horse rode through the camp, yelling and screaming obscenities.

"You must get up, you must get up now!" He bellowed. "I need you out in the fields now, up, up, up, you lazy bastards and bitches, up and at it."

The horse reached the end of the open area and twirled around and Luis Carranza dismounted. He was about fifty-years-old, tall, and thin. His hair was gray and he had a black beard. He wore blue jeans, a blue shirt, a flat brimmed straw hat, botines, and a short leather vest. He carried the machete and quirt as Tonio had described. He came swaying toward the open area at an open trot.

"Up! Up and at it, dammit, you have to finish doing the large field soon. If you do not finish, the cantaloupes will grow bunched up and it will ruin the crop. I cannot wait for you, go, go, go, you must move, and you must move now."

The shouting continued, echoing throughout the area.

The laborers moved hurriedly to get ready to return to the fields for the thinning. Carranza paused, and walked slowly through the open area, investigating as he went along. He did not scream. Paula, one of the women, took this moment of silence as a moment of truce, and approached Carranza. She held her two hands together as in prayer and pleaded, "Don Luis, I must ask for some flour. I have three little children, and now we have no food, will you please give us some flour?"

Carranza stared at her. He had fire in his eyes. He breathed heavily. His right hand rose quickly and he struck her with the hand whip across the face, and she screamed a shattering shrill.

"You dumb stupid, bitch," he screamed at the top of his lungs in a high baritone, "I have told you all, never to ask me for anything. I have told you to wait until I bring you the food that I think that you need, when I think you need it. You make me so mad that I cannot even think straight."

He got more and more excited, and began flailing with his arms.

All this time Chon sat under a tree quietly, staring at the new intruder carefully, biting his tongue. It was not easy to be quiet, meek, and timid. After a few moments, he sat up on his haunches, then slowly stood as he watched the mad man put on a show. When he flailed his arms up and around, Chon noticed that he had a small pistol stuck in his belt in the left side of his belly. Chon just stared, catching every movement.

The sun was peeking over the horizon now, and Carranza kept walking around the camp, shaking his head in disbelief. "How dare you peones approach me that way," he yelled. He kept shaking his head.

Chon had a decision to make. Should he try his pitch for a job now or wait for a later day. He must suppress Lt. Tasaka, whatever he did, otherwise he would uncover his disguise. What should he do?

Suddenly Carranza raised the pistol in his hand. He kept talking loudly, yelling and screaming. Everyone kept quiet, but largely ignored him. The crisis was going into the second cycle. He continued with gun drawn yelling and screaming. Finally, and gradually, the people began to talk to each other and ignored him again. He was at his absolute limit.

Carranza put the pistol in his belt and turned rapidly, searching the crowd for a face. He turned again and searched. Finally, he approached Lupita, a beautiful seventeen year old girl, who stood nearest him. He ripped off her blouse, and she stood screaming in front of the crowd of people with her breasts exposed, her torn dress top falling to her waist. Her screaming bothered Carranza so much that he struck her and yelled at her to shut up.

Chon tried to remain still, but could not. He was on Carranza in a second. He had to control himself. He grabbed him by the throat and lifted him up and held him there for what seemed like the longest minute. Carranza looked down at Chon in shock. He was shocked that anyone would dare challenge him, and shocked that physically he was hanging from someone's hand overlooking a crowd of very surprised people.

Chon threw him a few yards and lowered his head and shoulders, his thighs tightened as he sprinted toward Carranza with all of his strength. Carranza saw the attack coming, and managed to cock the pistol and get off a shot that went astray. By that time Chon was a meter away and his feet were flying in the air. He came down on Carranza with a thud and a whop!

Carranza flew back about three meters, his pistol went the other way. Chon broke his fall with his two hands and somersaulted up on his feet. He stood in his stance and charged again. He lifted the limp body, placed it on his knee, and screamed as he dealt out three karate chops. He then lifted Carranza and slammed him against his knee. He thought about not going through with the three phase attack as he always had, but he was wound up, and concluded he must complete the job, or else regret it later.

Chon stood up straight and looked down at Carranza, who was writhing in pain, and wind knocked out of him besides. His groaning and moaning did not move Chon nor any of the others. Chon stood above him another half a minute, but Carranza was not going to get up for a long time.

Tonio and the others were wide-mouthed. They had never seen a display of oriental martial arts, and they suddenly witnessed a flurry of it. They had never seen this type of fighting and were amazed. After a few minutes the spell broke, and they cheered and clapped continuously for several minutes. Finally, Chon gave orders for three of the men to pick Carranza up and take him to the horse.

For a long spell there was no movement, no sound. Chon looked straight at Carranza waiting for his next move. There was none coming. Carranza just stared at the ground.

After about five minutes, Carranza finally shook off the cobwebs staggered over to his horse and after three tries, he managed to get on, and moved his horse on over to where Chon stood. He looked at Chon briefly, then stared ahead into open space, he spurred his horse on and galloped away into the darkness.

For a long moment no one spoke, everyone just stared at each other and the fires. Then after the fear passed, everyone began to smile and laugh and finally to jump and slap each other and Chon on the back.

"Hijo de su puta madre, son of a bitch, the stupid bastard is gone," Tonio said with a smile.

The rest picked up Tonio's words and chanted them over and over.

When reality finally returned, everyone asked Chon why he did what he did.

"Chon, were you not afraid? Chon did you not think about the pistol that he was carrying in his hand? How did you know that he would just go away, and not start shooting?"

Chon was bewildered, actually, and would not answer the questions. He returned to his quiet, withdrawn, timid, charade.

"Well," he stuttered, "well, I just do not know what, I mean why I did what I did or why, or why not."

Chon was nervous and did not know exactly what to say. He applied just the right amount of necessary force. Instinct told him how much. Just then Lupita's mother came to talk with him.

"Señor, I just want to thank you. For a moment there I was afraid that he would carry her away or try something worse. I am very lucky that someone as brave as you was here today. If you would not have been here I just don't know," she glared at the rest of the men who stood around Chon, then thanked him again and left.

The small gathering ate, chatted, and enjoyed the conversation, most retelling and exaggerating the confrontation. After a couple of hours, people began to drift away. Chon and Tonio stayed to clean up and remove the caldrons. Finally, they were finished and went to Tonio's house.

Chon laid on a cotton sack and took a deep breath. He had done a very stupid thing. He could not be a leader and pull his punches, he thought to himself. He was so foolish. Carranza could have easily raised the pistol and blown him away. He must never do this type of thing again. There should never be a halfway point. Either he should get into a fight and fight to the death or he should stay out of it entirely. Today, for having gone in at half speed and wanting only to stop a bad situation without guaranteeing that the situation was defused, he could have gotten killed or hurt, or worse, others could have gotten hurt or killed.

Then Chon began walking toward the field that they would work that day. He needed to guide the people on to work. Once the people began to work, Chon pulled Tonio aside for a talk.

"I am not ready, and this is not a good time for me to stand and fight. Also, it would not be good for the people, it will only bring trouble for them Tonio," he said in a low voice. "I am leaving today. I am sorry, please forgive me. It is the best thing, I know to do. I am not running out on you. Please forgive me, I must go."

He grabbed for Tonio's hand and they shook, and then Chon grabbed him and they hugged in the Mexican style, slapping each other's back two or three times. Chon turned and hurried back to camp. Everyone watched in bewilderment as Chon trotted toward the camp.

Chon rushed back to camp, found his bag, and packed his belongings. He had almost finished when Tonio ran up.

"Chon, Encarnación, I must go with you. I am tired of being here. I must go too. Please let me go with you. I know where we can go and what we can do, please, let me go with you," Tonio pleaded. Chon looked at him briefly.

"Well I cannot stop you. Actually I will enjoy the companionship. But Tonio I want you to understand that you have to keep up with me. I am used to traveling alone, and I do not need an anchor," Chon lectured Tonio.

"Encarnación, I promise I will not be a hindrance, I will hurry and I will work hard, I promise, I promise," Tonio pleaded.

"Well then hurry, get your stuff and say your goodbyes. I am in a hurry," Chon ordered.

Chon reached and picked up his bag, threw it over his shoulder, looked around, and picked up a few small items. He had his survival kit. One final look, and, he was on his way. He saw Tonio approaching.

"Are you ready amigo? "Chon asked.

"Sí, sí Encarnación, let us go," Tonio said anxiously.

"Vamonos," Chon said, as they walked toward the front of the main house and out to the road to Durango. They waved goodbye to the others and strode out of the plantation. They walked down the tree lane and did not look back.

After reaching Durango, Chon and Tonio prepared to journey east to Monterrey to look for permanent work. Chon knew that it was a huge city and it would be easier to get lost in a large city than in a small village.

As they were leaving, Chon saw a bus station with a bus parked in front of it.

"Mira Tonio, un autobus, let's go see how much it costs to ride to Monterrey," Chon said. They walked to the ticket office and looked at the fare schedule.

"Well don't ask me because I can't read the tariff. I don't understand it," Tonio said.

"Tonio, I'm sorry but we're going to walk, it costs too much. A peso and twenty five centavos. It's too much money. Let's walk," Chon said to Tonio, who did not hide his disappointment. He knew the long walk would not be easy.

They started out through the dusty streets of Durango. They walked until nightfall, having traveled about two miles out of the city. Chon found a good spot under a tree, and they made a small fire and warmed some food that Chon had bought in Durango. They talked and joked by the fire. They reminisced about the fight, and wondered how Don Tomás would solve his problem.

They were in no hurry. They basked in the excitement of their new adventure, and their new friendship. Although it was winter, it was cool. It had been a full and hard day. They thought they would stay up late, but they were both asleep by eight o'clock.

They rose early, made a fire, and ate.

"Be sure to eat well because we may not get a chance to eat for a long time," Chon warned Tonio. They loaded up, then began their trek. Chon had bought a small canteen at the general store for five pesos. It was expensive, but Chon knew how valuable it would be.

By mid-morning they had walked about fourteen kilometers. On the hacienda, they walked and stopped and carried and hauled and pulled all day long. They were in good physical condition.

They traveled another couple of hours. On occasion, a car or pickup truck or large truck would drive by. They motioned and thumbed for a ride, but none stopped. Tonio was very discouraged. Chon knew better and kept walking. At noon they rested again.

Tonio wanted them to take the bus on into Torreón. He was getting so tired. Chon on the other hand did not mind the walking. He was enjoying getting back into training. He knew it would be good for him to get his stamina back. He also knew that it would be best for Tonio to get some stamina. So despite Tonio's strong hinting, Chon knew that he was not going to get a bus ticket into Torreón.

Chapter Twelve

The sun was almost down over the horizon on the tenth day of their journey when the pair cleared an area of weeds and dry grass and made room for themselves and their baggage. They made a fire, then went on to a nearby river to wash their clothes, and to wash and bathe. After the bath, they changed clothing and sat by the edge of the water and talked.

"Well, let me tell you something Chon," Tonio began. "In our land, there are many people that are mojados. They earn money and then return to México, and some go back every year for more work and each year the cycle repeats itself."

"Are you suggesting that we go on and become mojados?" Chon asked.

"Exactly," Tonio replied. "You know I have three cousins that are mojados, and every year they come home to Durango and they bring lots of good American clothes, and other things, and they bring money. I have spoken to them.

"They tell me about how they walk to the American border, then swim across the Río Bravo. Sometimes they walk very long distances, and then they finally get to a ranch or farm and get the job that they want.

"They also tell me bad things, how they walk without food and drink for days, and how they get sick, before they finally get somewhere and get food, drink, and work. But that could not happen to us Chon, we are always careful to have the canteen full of water, and we always have some food, and we know how to walk good and long," Tonio said with pride.

Chon realized what Tonio wanted, for them to become wet-backs. Tonio went on.

"They also say about a special border police, they all call La Migra, and the Rinches, and these police chase them because they say they are not supposed to be in the United States without papers," Tonio explained.

Chon paid special attention.

"They also mentioned about how some of the gringos with blond hair and blue eyes, you know the güeros, they do not like Mexicans, and sometimes they treat them very bad. Sometimes they do not feed them, at other times they try to beat them, and other times they run them out of restaurants and movie houses, and other places. Yeah, they told me all, and some of it sounds bad I know, but most of it sounds good. We get good work and good pay, you know," Tonio told Chon.

They sat quietly. The fire popped, sparks fizzled. After a few moments Chon spoke up.

"How would we get there?" Chon asked quietly.

"Oh, it would not be hard. From here we go straight to Monterrey. Then from Monterrey we either go north or go east to the Río Grande River. I have heard that many go north but I have also heard that a lot go east, as there is more work because there are more fields in what is called El Valle of the Río Bravo. I know my primos always go east to El Valle, and there are many farms. There are ranchos also, with much cows, and horses, but there are lots of farms, fields, with lots of irrigation, and crops. It sounds to me just like San Rafael, but just the pay is much better, and there you have no peoples that you grew up with like San Rafael, and no wimmens, only new friends," Tonio wrapped up his story of el otro lado.

Again they both laid quietly watching the small campfire. A spray of stars formed their ceiling. After a few moments of silence, Tonio broke in again. "What do you think? Should we keep talking about this or not?"

"Tonio, tomorrow we rest. Let us stay here under this tree and rest. We have this river here, we can wash our clothes. We have soap. We have food. Let us spend the day resting and talking and thinking about things," Chon said.

"Tonio, you might have a good idea about going to the fields in the United States, but it is something that we must think about. So let's take a day to think about it. Está bien?" Chon asked his new friend.

Chon knew from his training that there was risk involved in getting into the United States.

"O sí amigo, quite frankly, I am now ready for a rest. Oh sí, we can wait, and have a day to rest. I would like that. I was wondering when you were going to stop Chon, amigo."

At their camp the next night, Tonio seemed very tired and frustrated. After the evening meal Chon broke the silence as he stared at the campfire.

"You know Tonio, I think that we ought to go on to the United States, and be wetbacks," he said in a firm and low voice.

"Que, que? You really want to go to the Norte? Chon I am so glad, I know we we'll like it and that things will go well. Chon, I think we made the right decision. We'll do all right, you'll see. You just stick together with me and we'll do all right," Tonio rose to his feet and danced around. Wringing his hands over the fire, smiling broadly as he talked. Chon smiled back.

"Yes tomorrow, we go straight for Monterrey and then for the border," Tonio said excitedly. "I am tired of wasting time here looking for work. Let us go and find adventure. Let us go and know foreign lands, and make lots of foreign money. Let us go give it a try, and maybe we get to know some little gringo girls, yeah some pretty ones, huh, Chon, yeah and shapely ones."

With a wide smile, Tonio motioned with his two hands in an hourglass pantomime. The next day they hitched a ride on the back of a cargo truck headed for Monterrey with a load of bananas from the south. They had to lay on top of the huge load and were warned by the truck driver not to damage any of the bananas. So they had to "lay lightly" and be careful. The trip was uncomfortable, but it was cool. Laying on the very top of the load, as the truck sped down the road, provided a constant breeze. Sometimes it rained, but mostly it was sunny and windy. The wind was so strong, they could not even talk to each other without yelling. Mostly they just lay there as time passed.

The driver felt sorry for them, and that was the only reason they got a ride. The driver knew that if his company found out about this gesture they would fire him. It was against company policy to pick up riders or hitchhikers. The driver, who was named Juan, was a deeply religious Catholic and every time he saw a hitchhiker he visualized Jesus Christ himself disguised and testing him to see if he would help the Redeemer himself, and either win or lose heaven. Though he passed many hitchhikers eventually he would capitulate, and compassionately take one or two suffering souls to their destination.

While the driver stopped to eat in Saltillo, two hours away from Monterrey, Chon and Tonio made a small fire and fixed their own meal. The weather was very cool. Chon loved the cooler weather, and was very happy when the driver decided to spend the night. Chon and Tonio enjoyed the cool outdoors. The next day they rose early and again warmed by the fire. The truck took off at six thirty and began the trip to Monterrey. Chon and Tonio grabbed onto the bananas as the truck slowly descended the mountain trail. By the time the truck approached Monterrey the weather had turned hot and sultry. The truck was traveling slower now as it approached the big city, and the breeze subsided. Chon and Tonio laid on top of the truck perspiring heavily, and looked around at the houses, people, animals, and streets as they entered Monterrey. Chon laid pensively, thinking of his trip through the streets of Tokyo in what seemed like a decade ago.

Eventually they rolled into the downtown district, moving slowly through the paved streets, and arrived at the marketplace.

The driver backed the truck to a produce stand, and within minutes, several workers, and Chon and Tonio unloaded the bananas. The driver thanked them.

They were in the middle of Monterrey and walked to a dry river bed. There were no trees and no running water. There were many people in the bed of the river, mostly kids playing soccer or baseball. Chon and Tonio sat on the high bank of the river and watched the people.

They stayed at the Santa Catarina River bed for two hours just watching, then Chon suggested that they walk around. They walked for hours, watching, enjoying the plazas, the magnificent shade trees, the beautiful churches and other buildings, the people, particularly the beautiful women. Chon finally started the walk out of town, north toward Nuevo Laredo. The pair walked through the dusty, noisy streets.

"Tonio, why are we going to this place? Is it ugly and dry like this?" Chon asked.

"No, well, yes, no. Well let me explain. My cousins tell me that it is very hot and dry on the way. Then you cross the huge wide river, the Bravo. Then it gets hot, but there is lots of water and fields, but then in certain areas, there is hot and dry just like here. Just cactus, mesquite, rabbits, and no grass, so no, yes, no, yes. You see what I mean?

"But don't worry they tell me that in the big farms, they have lots of big shade trees, and grass and houses, and barns, just like San Rafael, and it's lots of fun, and in the winter it is just right, cool, but in the summer it is very hot, but the breeze it cools off all right, especially at night. They say it is like the desert. It is hot in the day and cool at night," Tonio finished retelling what his cousins had told him about el otro lado.

Chon shook his head left and right as he heard the long litany, and smiled at Tonio as he went on and on.

"Well, we will see," was his only response.

Chapter Thirteen

Tonio yelled and jumped up and down, knowing that they would not travel through the desert for the next three days. Chon had agreed to take the bus for the remainder of the trip to the Río Bravo. They walked to the bus station and bought tickets to the border. The bus, they were told, left in one hour so they waited at the station, watching people. There was an old lady with a chicken, a young mother with five children, a vaquero, three boys with a pair of goats, and a skinny lady with a huge pig. These would be their companions on the trip to the border.

The windows on the bus were open throughout the entire trip. Only forward motion forced the hot air into the bus and kept the dust out. It could be worse, they thought, and were content with the air flowing through the vehicle. At least it kept them dry.

The novelty of the trip wore out quickly, and they had to adjust to riding with the animals, on a bumpy and dusty road. It was uncomfortable, it was hot, and it was smelly. No one talked. It was boring. Chon sat erect, and looked forward the entire trip, with a half-smile on his lips. As far as he was concerned it was better than walking through the hot desert.

The bus arrived at about five o'clock in the afternoon. The bus station was two blocks from the Río Bravo and the international bridge. All traffic and all attention seemed to point toward the street that led to the river that separated the two countries. They were anxious to see the river.

"What do you think? You wanna go see?" Tonio excitedly asked Chon.

"Yeah, I guess so, let's go see," Chon said, feigning excitement.

They noticed that everyone that was on the bus that did not carry an animal, made a beeline for the bridge. They were going to cross into the United States. Chon could not understand. How can these people simply walk off the bus and go over to the American side. He followed them, curious. They walked under the huge high shade at the Mexican Customs station. They came up to a toll booth, and Chon noticed that the rest of the passengers paid their toll and kept walking.

The bridge was about thirty feet above the surface of the water. The river was about sixty yards wide. Chon and Tonio walked up to the high bank and investigated in silence. It was a muddy river, and traveled at a rapid speed. From his intelligence briefing, Chon knew that it started in the state of Colorado, and emptied into the Gulf of México at Brownsville, Texas. The Spanish colonists had named it the Río Bravo, the rough river, fierce, and vicious. They stood on the edge of the railing and stared at the mighty flow of water for about twenty minutes, mesmerized at the natural monument. They walked alongside the river, south and east.

Chon saw where a large creek emptied into the Río, and hurried over to it for shelter for the night. The trees were tall and shady. They barely managed to unpack and settle down before the sun went down. By that time they had built their fire, and began the evening meal.

For a long while, they sat and warmed by the fire. Each in his own mind was thinking of the adventure that lay ahead. The United States of America. They stayed up late, talked, and reminisced. Tonio spoke about San Rafael, Chon joined him, but remembered Tokyo Plantation, and thought of Akechi san, Sebastian, his mother, Nagi san, and the others. Of course in his conversation with Tonio it was San Blas and not Tokyo

Plantation. He was a long, long way from home, and he would never go home again. A tear welled up in his eye.

The next day they walked down river. They had decided to walk to an unpopulated area to make their crossing. They could still see the twin cities of Laredo and Nuevo Laredo above them. They walked until noon, and came upon three men sitting by the river. They stopped to talk. Chon felt uneasy. The possibility of an ambush coming to mind. The day was hot, but the breeze off the water cooled them. There was a blue gray haze over the water. The roar of the river made hearing difficult.

"Pa dónde van?" One of the strangers asked.

Chon elected to keep quiet, but Tonio blurted out.

"To the United States, al otro lado," he smiled widely.

"Let me tell you something amigo, it is not going to be so easy," the stranger told Tonio. "First you got that awful river out there to tickle your balls as you cross. It has speed, and it has whirlpools, it drags you down to its bottom, and it won't let you up until you fill your lungs with its water, then it spits you out, and then what the hell are you good for when you drown.

"Then if you happen to make it good from breathing the water like a fish, then you still gotta worry about the Migra. They're afraid that us little Mexican farmworkers gonna take over the whole damn country, so they gotta spend money on these guardias to keep us out.

"Then if that ain't bad enough, now we gotta watch for the military policía from the army fort. So let me tell you, hermano, if you gonna cross, you better be ready for hardship and problems."

The man finally stopped his tale of horror, and everyone there stood, listening to the roar of the river.

Chon focused on two phrases, "the Migra" and the "military police." That upset him. He could see ten rifle barrels pointing at his head and firing. No blindfold.

"Let me ask you about the Migra and the policía militar. Are they out looking for people like us or do they just sit back and wait to see if we approach their guarded areas?" Chon asked.

"Naw they don't come and look for us. The Migra, they don't have too many men to just sit wait and see who walks into their hands. Every once in a while they drive up to the ranches and farms and check everybody out. So, if you ever see the green jeeps drive up, you better get going out to the monte, and hide, and stay until you are sure that they are gone. Otherwise, you get a free ride to the capital of México, the great D.F.

"The soldiers, is a little different. They don't give a shit about nothing except getting drunk every night and going across the river to Boys Town, you know to see the putas, so they do not bother you unless you get too close to the fort, the one in Laredo. So, that's easy, just do not cross close to the fort."

"I guess you've been there then," Chon said.

"Sure I been there. All I want to do is work and get a little better wage, so I swim this cabrón river, and I cross, and I go to try to find work, and I go through hot and dry, with no water and no food, and I drag on the ground, like a lizard, until I crawl up to a rancho or a farm, and I beg for work, and I work hard.

"Then one day, here come the Migra, and chases us where we have to starve and go without water again for several days, until we can make our way back. It's hard for us to understand. All we want to do is work hard, and get good vegetables for the soldiers to eat, so they can beat the shit outta them Japs and Nazis, and they won't let us. They keep catching us, and throwing us back to México. I tell you friend, it is hard to understand."

Chon dwelt on the words of war. To beat the Japs. That was him and all his family and friends. He thought for a long while. He took a deep breath and shook his head.

"Well, we thank you friend, for your advice, but we must be going," Chon looked concerned and waved his hand from his forehead.

The experienced mojado stood to see them off. "Yeah, all right, we'll see you and good luck to you. One other thing I forget to tell you. Stay off the roads. The Rinches, the migra, they patrol the roads, cause it is so easy to see someone walk along or cross an open area, so don't be so stupid as to stay on the road, and when you cross, cross at night so they can't see you.

"One more thing, take some food, and if you can, take some water. I see where you got a canteen, that's a damn good idea, yeah, that's good except that sometimes you got nowhere to fill it up," he laughed heartily. "Remember that sometimes there's no water and there's no big river, it's a desert, just a desert, and you gotta crawl around like a snake sometimes."

He finally stopped and sat down as abruptly as when he started talking. By this time Chon and Tonio were yards away, and again thanked him for the help. They walked away slowly, continuing along the water's edge. They were fascinated by the natural wonder. They walked for about three hours. They came to a bend in the river, and to their surprise saw a low water crossing in the form of many large rocks in the bed of the river. Chon smiled widely as he turned back to see Tonio. They could not hear each other because of the roar. They were in luck, if this was truly a low water crossing they would not have to brave the deep and treacherous waters of the Río Bravo.

The cool from the breeze blowing off the water was perfect. It got them in a good mood. Soon they would be crossing over into the "Promised Land".

"One thing for sure," Chon screamed into Tonio's ear, "since it appears to be an easy crossing, it may be that the Border Patrol or the Migra will be right there waiting for us, so we have to check and be sure it is right."

The river was about one hundred yards wide. They stared across the river for about an hour, looking for any abnormality. They hid the baggage in the brush, then walked down the river for about half a mile. They stared again, and memorized every part of the left bank. They walked back to the crossing. They walked up river about half a mile and again stared and analyzed. They walked back to the crossing.

"All right, we will cross now. We must be very careful. Try to keep the bags dry," Chon shouted above the roar of the water.

"The rocks will be slippery so try to keep good footing. You will get wet, so get used to the idea. Let's be careful. When we get across I will climb over the top of the bank. I will see if there is danger. If there is a problem, I will motion you to run up river or down river, or to follow me. Do you understand?" Tonio motioned that he understood.

They walked down the bank, and came to the water's edge. Chon placed his bag on his head, and stepped carefully onto the rocks on the water's edge. He tested the firmness of the bottom. It held. So far, so good. He walked about ten quick paces and looked back at Tonio who had just begun the test. He turned to continue his own wading. The water was up to his knees and he hoped that it would not get any deeper. By the end of five minutes, Chon made it to the middle of the river. Tonio caught up, and was right behind him. They got the hang of walking the rocks, and made better progress. In short time there were at the edge. They were on American soil. Chon turned and handed Tonio his bag and ran up the bank. It was about fifteen feet high. There was a worn trail up the bank so Chon did not have difficulty getting up. He climbed over the top of the last barrier, and stood there. Tonio could see him from the waist up. Chon looked in all directions. Tonio was getting nervous. Suddenly he saw Chon run back down the embankment. Tonio started back across the river, an alternative they had not planned. By the time he put his right foot in the water, Chon was right behind him, grabbed him by the waist and pulled him back and away from the water.

"No, no, come on down river," Chon yelled at him. Tonio turned, looked at Chon, and then looked up at the embankment, and saw why Chon was excited. At the top stood a giant white Brahman bull, with a huge black hump on its back. It was coming to the river for water. Chon and Tonio laughed nervously as they trotted downriver. They went several meters and stopped and turned around. The bull had descended and was drinking water undisturbed, not even disturbed by the intruders.

"What did you see, I mean besides the bull?" Tonio asked.

"I saw lots of monte, but beyond that, and over a fence, large, actually huge, green fields of growing crops. I did not see houses. I did not see people, and no migra, no soldiers, and no jeeps. So I think we have landed safely in the United States."

He looked at Tonio with a huge smile on his face. They were still having to yell because of the roar of the rapids.

"Let's go find another way up," Chon yelled.

They traveled for about ten yards and saw a clearing and both scurried up the bank. They came out on the other side in heavy brush. After the brush, and over a fence, it was just as Chon described. What seemed like miles and miles of fields of growing crops. The clean and straight green furrows seemed liked they went forever. It was strange. There were no people in the fields. They both felt like they were at San Rafael.

They walked for two hours, and came upon what looked like a camp. They walked up on an old man hoeing weeds. Chon spoke first.

"Senor, we are looking for work, can you use good experienced hands? We will be good help for you," he said to the viejito.

The old man looked up, and then continued to hoe. He finally spoke. "Well, I am not the man in charge here, but if I had to make a wager, I would say that you could not get a job here. You see, there are many people from México who cross over at Laredo. There no one can get a job, because there are too many people who want a job." The old man paused and continued to hoe.

"After they get to a farm on this side of Laredo, most of them are too lazy to move north and keep looking for work," he paused again. "When they get here sometimes there is work and sometimes there is none. It depends on whether some of the people have gone home or not. You see it is very hard to understand the young people that come here. They want work, and they work for two months, they get a little jingle in their pocket, and they are ready to go home and see their wives, or sweethearts."

The old man shook his head and paused again.

"It is hard for me to understand. There are only about nine good working months in the year. We start to work the soil in February, we plant in March, we start irrigating and by May we thin out the plants. In June we work and in July and August we baby the matitas, and in September we pick and harvest the crops. In September, October we plant the winter crops, and start irrigating and the cycle starts all over again. The only time we have need for more hands is when the stupids cannot wait and leave early. But right now no one has left yet. You can go talk to Francisco over there, he might want you to stay," the old man pointed them in the direction of Francisco and kept hoeing.

They had found out there were no jobs.

"Well, tell me viejo, if a man really needed work, I mean good, hard, and permanent work, and he walked up on this plantation, and there was not any work at this one, then where do you think he could go and find good employment?" Chon probed.

"If I understand you right, that you want permanent work, with no foolish vacations?" The man mused and kept hoeing. "I think you should go to a special place that no one really hears about unless they are told specifically to go there. This place is not on the river, you see. It is just off the river on the high, high bank, and it is on the other side of the big gray ribbon, the one they call the hawuey. It is off the main road."

The old man finally stopped hoeing, looked up at Chon and Tonio and looked down his nose, inspecting them from head to toe. Chon understood the man perfectly, and found the entire exchange humorous.

"The place is called Rancho Salinas, and it is a huge ranch with cattle and fields like these. They grow all sorts of crops there and raise cattle. They hire many hombres, and it is owned by a Don Juan Salinas. He and his family live there. To get there you go up the river about ten miles, then head east toward the little pueblito known as Encinal, about twenty miles from the river.

"Don Juan has water pumps to get water from earthen tanks, to pump water to the most fertile fields in the region. Don Juan knows how to do it," he emphasized the last words, slowly spoken as the greatest compliment, "Don Juan knows how to do it. He has one huge and nice rancho."

He stopped and Chon waited for more comment. None was forthcoming.

"About ten miles up, to the large wide bend in the river, then twenty miles east to Encinal?" Chon looked at the old man.

The old man did not speak, he just nodded his head firmly.

BOOK FOUR
Going to Texas

Chapter Fourteen

During the next three days, Chon showed off his survival skills as he killed rabbits, armadillos, picked mesquite beans, wild persimmons, and tunas. Tonio did not know it, but if he were not with a top graduate of the Japanese Intelligence Service he might have never finished the adventure.

On the second day they came upon a young man walking toward them. He was barefoot. His feet were swollen with sores, blisters, and thorns. His shirt was torn to shreds. His mouth was so dry that is was cracking and bleeding. He had not shaved for weeks. He was a pitiful sight. As they walked up to him, he begged for help. Chon and Tonio made him sit down, they managed to give him some water. After a while he calmed down, and explained to them that he had started on a journey just like themselves, but that he did not bring food and drink, and had not eaten now in three days. He had no water. He got lost and wandered around in circles for days in the heat.

Chon began cleaning his feet, and removing thorns. They fed him. They noticed that he had a bag and asked what he carried. He had a pair of shoes, but he removed them because he did not want to wear them out.

Chon sat pensively by the fire that night.

"Why are people that just want to work persecuted by the police or Migra, to the point of causing their death because they had to run through the brush like fugitives?" Chon had heard of some men being chased for miles. Others told of working hard, for low pay, and meager or no food, or of working for food with a promise of pay, and the pay always came late, thus guaranteeing that the workers would not leave. They were given fair quarters, but sometimes having to sleep out in the open, which was all right most of the time unless it happened to rain, or suddenly got cold.

More and more as the days passed, Tonio thanked his lucky stars that he was with Chon. With Chon he did not have to worry about surviving. Yes, they both passed long, hard, hot, and tiring days. Their feet hurt, they got blisters, their huaraches almost wore out, but they always had water, and Chon always found food. Each wetback that they met was on the verge of death because he had no water, no food, and no shoes. Tonio had all three, and he was with the master of the monte, and he thanked the Lord daily for it.

Finally, they could see the ranch headquarters from about two miles away. Actually, all they could see was a huge clump of trees. There were no other tall trees around so they assumed that it was the ranch headquarters. They were right. As they got closer they noticed that it was like the main camp of many ranches and farms that they had seen before, except that this one seemed greener, and the trees larger. There was much vegetation around the main house, including green grass, between the main house and the other buildings. In actuality, it looked more like Tokyo Plantation than any other place he had seen since leaving Japan.

Chon thought it strange that the main headquarters camp could be so green when the surrounding area was so barren. As they walked toward the house, they were walking in desert like land, yet just yards away was this beautiful green oasis. A long tree lined drive led up to the main house. There was an irrigation canal on either side of the lane. The trees were tall and gave much shade. Tonio and Chon walked about one fourth of the mile long lane, when they met up with a man watering the trees.

"Buenos días," Chon greeted him.

"Buenos días, peones," he answered.

He was an older man, and had a white beard. He wore blue jeans, cowboy boots, a tan shirt, and a white straw hat. Other than his dress, he reminded Chon of the old man hoeing weeds in the fields downriver from Laredo.

"We have come all the way from Durango looking for this place, do you think two workers could get a job here?" Tonio blurted.

"Oh sí, you can probably get a job here, but I cannot say for sure. You have to go talk to Don Juan, he is the owner, and if you cannot talk to the owner, then you should talk to the caporal, you know, the caporal, his name is Ramón, and he tell you for sure, but if I had to guess, I would say that you probably be able to get on, yeah," he said, as he kept working the small dirt dike controlling the water that came in to each tree.

"Well, thank you friend, what is your name?"

"My name is Atanacio, at your service," the old man responded as if parroting from grade school indoctrination.

"Very well Atanacio, we are off, wish us luck. Perhaps in a few hours we will be fellow workers," Tonio said.

They continued up the lane. As they approached the main house they could see it was the center of everything. It was surrounded by huge shade trees. At the edge of the house were pretty bushes and flowers. There were several sidewalks leading to different areas of the surroundings. The house faced south, as did so many in this area of the world. They were constructed to take full advantage of the usual south easterly breezes. Even on the hottest day, if the breeze was blowing, the houses would be cool, particularly if they were surrounded by shade.

The main house had two levels. It was white and had a red tile roof, very similar to many houses that Chon had seen throughout México. It had a large porch surrounding all four sides of the house. The white walls of the house seemed to be of the whitest of the whites, and made good contrast with the red roof.

Off to the east side of the house were the remainder of the
buildings. There was nothing on the west side except trees to
shade the main house and yard. The other buildings were also
under the same shade canopy. The vegetation was different, but
the concept, that is, the main building, the yard, and the other
buildings all within the huge trees reminded Chon of Tokyo
Plantation. As was the custom, they skirted around the main
house and approached it from the rear. Walking around the east
side of the house, they could see many people milling around.
Some working, others simply walking from area to area, but all
with an apparent purpose.

As they continued their approach they were met by six dogs
that came out and challenged them. No one called the dogs off.
Those that looked up at Chon and Tonio seemed to say, "You
do not belong here, if you can justify your presence, then get by
the dogs on your own." They turned away to continue whatever
it was they were doing.

As Chon and Tonio rounded the corners to the rear of the
house they noticed several men under a shed off to the east
of the house working around a tractor. They were removing
the tires, and working on the engine. Chon and Tonio walked
toward the men.

"Excuse me, we are looking for Don Juan or for Don Ramón,"
Chon began, holding his eyes to the ground, not wanting to
show his eyes and the confidence and intelligence that they
could show.

From under the tractor, slid a tall big man, wearing greasy
bib overalls, and sat up on the creeper.

"I am Juan Salinas, may I help you?"

Chon was startled to see the owner of such a huge ranch
working on a greasy tractor. From the other side of the tractor came another man, this one in khaki pants, and wearing
a camiseta, and a baseball cap. He was a heavy set man with
broad shoulders.

"I am Ramón, may I help you?"

There they both were and both staring straight and looking very serious. Chon was again startled and surprised.

"Well very plainly, and begging your indulgence, we come all the way from Durango, and we understand that you need help, and we need work. We are both strong, and we both know how to work hard. I am sure that you will not be disappointed," Chon said nervously, and talking too fast.

The other men stared at him. There was a quiet for a few seconds.

Finally, Don Juan spoke up. "Ramón, go talk to them in the other barn, if you think they will work out give them a chance. Lord knows we need the help. But let them know I am not putting up with any bullshit. I want workers."

Don Juan Salinas, laid back down on the creeper, and slid under the tractor. Don Ramón, waved to Chon and Tonio to follow him. They walked to another stall in the same barn. Don Ramón conducted a quick interview of each of them. Both answered well, although by now Tonio was very nervous.

"Well, look muchachos," Don Ramón said. Chon thought it strange that the old man would call them boys. "We do need help, but I want you to understand how things work around here.

"First, we all work hard, and it's important that you understand that. For example, we do not want people hiding behind a building or over in some pasture and loafing while everybody else works hard.

"Second, we do not want people working here a few weeks and then wanting to go home. We want you to stay the season at least, and not go home until the crops are in. Actually we wish that you would never go home, but we understand that you are going to go home, or that you have to go home, we just would like you to keep it to a minimum.

"Finally, we do not want immoral people. There are families that work and live here. You mind your own business and leave them alone. Also, we do not tolerate anyone stealing anything.

That is something that Don Juan cannot stand. You steal one penny, and you are gone. You break any of the other rules I just mentioned and you are gone. Do you have any questions?" Don Ramón asked.

"No sir, we have no questions," Chon answered for both of them.

"Very well then, go on down this lane," he said as he motioned east on past all the barns. "At the very end of the row of houses, there on the right, is a small house. It is your house. Keep it clean or you sleep in the barn with the pigs. Do you understand?"

"Yes sir, we understand," Chon answered. Chon felt good. This was the type of farm or company that he wanted to work for. There were rules, and people worked hard, and things moved along. This was not like San Rafael.

"And, sir do not worry, we will not embarrass you. You made a good choice in hiring us and we will make you proud with the patron. Do not worry," Chon said.

"Well I hope so. We will see," Don Ramón responded.

Chon and Tonio walked away to their house.

"Oh, by the way," Don Ramón stopped them, "we realize that you have been walking for days, so the first day there is no work, clean up and rest, and get some food, ask around, you will find everything you need. Today you do not work, tomorrow, you work hard, starting at day break. "Understood?" Don Ramón asked.

"Understood, sir," Chon and Tonio both responded as they walked away.

Don Ramón walked back to the stall where Don Juan was working on the tractor. "They will work out, they seem to be all right Don Juan," he reported to the owner.

"Well I hope so, I just do not want to lose any more employees. We need all the hands we can get. We have crops out everywhere, and in time we will have to pick them, cut hay and make bales, move cattle, cut calves, vaccinate, earmark, and we need hands, and I cannot operate this place without people. Oh how I wish they all stayed. This business of going home all the time, it drives me crazy," Don Juan said from below the tractor.

"Well I think they will work out," Don Ramón explained. "They said they wanted work, and you know what they did not even ask how much the pay was. I think that is a pretty good attitude, don't you think?"

"Well it sounds good all right, but let's just see what happens."

Chon and Tonio walked toward their new house. "You know Tonio, I think I am going to like this place. It is the only place I have ever seen where both the owner and the number one person in charge are working. Did you see that Don Juan, working under the tractor, all greasy, and in there up to his armpits? That is a good sign, I like it."

"Yeah Chon, and have you noticed how clean it is around here? This place is much more cleaner than San Rafael. Everyone is working, that is good," Tonio responded.

The house was tiny. It had a small porch in the front. One front room with two beds, a small room in back that served as a kitchen and eating room. It was spotless. There was one kerosene lamp hanging in the front room and one hanging in the kitchen. There was a wood stove in the kitchen.

By contrast the camp kitchen, that served all of the workers, was large and rectangular shaped. There was a large wide fireplace on the north wall. Off to the side of the fireplace, and in a corner, was the remainder of the cooking area with a huge wood stove and two large sinks for washing dishes, pots, and pans. In front of the cooking area was a counter about half the length of the long room. During meals, the cooks laid out all the food on the long counter. At the beginning of the line were the plates and the silverware.

Most of the workers did not use these utensils. Instead, two pieces of tortilla were used as scoops. These was the custom in the modest ranches and farms where money was scarce and silverware was a luxury. Chon could use chop sticks and western

style utensils, but in order to keep his cover, used the tortilla
double scoop method of eating. Chon imagined that many hours
of happy conversation and communication were spent in the
camp kitchen. It was a big, cozy room, and probably nobody felt
like leaving when the meal was over, Chon thought.

The similarities between Tokyo Plantation, and Rancho Salinas were astonishing. It pleased Chon. These familiarities made
things easier for him.

The friendship between Chon and Tonio grew stronger. Tonio
learned much from Chon, and had become a much better man
for it. Tonio achieved a good degree of leadership skills and
common sense, thanks to Chon. As close as they became, Chon
still could not trust him with his innermost secret. That would
be left for special ears, if at all.

One of those that befriended Chon and Tonio first was the
caporal Don Ramón. He told them that he was born just a few
miles away from the ranch, in a two room shack with dirt floors.
His father had died when he was three-years-old. He grew up
with his mother and brother and two sisters. Life was hard for
him and his family. He left school when he was in the fourth
grade, a move he regretted. But he had to help earn a wage to
support the family.

Don Ramón talked about how hard it was for him in his
early years. They had no money. He joked about how he would
save a dime for a month so he could go to town and go to the
Saturday night dance. At times the admission was a quarter
or fifty cents, so he waited outside the church hall or school
gymnasium or dance slab until a couple of hours passed and
the admission dropped down to a dime, at which time he would
whirl into the hall and dance until his feet ached. He loved to
dance, he said. He had no vices, other than enjoying a cup of
whiskey on occasion.

"Don Juan made me a man," he said. "A man cannot be a man
without his family clothed and fed, and without a good house

for them to live in, and a man cannot be a man without a piece of ground to own, to work, and to grow crops on. I finally am a man, and I can say that Don Juan made me a man."

Don Ramón preached philosophically. Chon and Tonio learned new things from the old man everyday, things about loyalty, manhood, family, and love. They loved him, and he loved his workers, all of them. Whatever he asked for he got. All he had to do was ask, and they would go to work for him. It was not a one way street either, it was through his efforts that the community showers, and privy, and kitchen were started. Much earlier, he had insisted on the small houses for all the workers. He had lived the misery with all the wetbacks; he saw to it that it was remedied.

Don Juan had heard the stories of the pain, and the misery first hand from Don Ramón, and agreed readily at each suggestion of improvement. He thanked God that he had the money to spend on the improvements.

At night, after the campfire, Chon laid in his bed and wandered about Japan, and the war. He thought of Tokyo Plantation, of his mother, and all the others. What would they think of him for doing what he did? Would he be a traitor? He was certain they would label him as such, with the possible exception of his mother and Sebastian. It was hard to erase a lifetime, and invariably he found himself thinking of the old country. What made matters worse was that he was sure they thought that he was dead. There was no way that they could think differently.

Chapter Fifteen

I t was the fall of 1943. Already the workers began to plead for leave. The ones that lived farther away in México asked first. This was understood amongst the men. The one that lived farthest had more days of travel time, more time to lose, therefore his vacation was shorter, and therefore he was allowed to ask first.

Rancho Salinas contained ten thousand acres. Some of it was under cultivation, the rest was for cattle grazing. It consisted of a huge operation, and required camps throughout the entire acreage not just on the main ranch, that was called the Home Ranch.

Chon worked by Don Ramón's side, hoeing weeds in the ranch vegetable garden.

"Mi Choncito, you have come to a very special place indeed. The Salinas family has been in South Texas for nearly two hundred years. As one of the original Spanish colonizer families that came to Laredo in 1755. They underwent Indian attacks that lasted for many years. Somehow they survived. They lost some land, but they were fortunate to hold on to ten thousand acres, that descended to Don Juan Salinas."

The two men worked steady, and the shrill grind of the two hoes, on the sand and weeds, set the tempo for the conversation.

"Most of the Spanish families lost their lands, but not the Salinas. You're gonna see how they work, and how this place hums along like well-greased machinery. When the Spaniards came to Texas they totally accepted the culture they conquered, and intermarried freely. The offspring were known originally as mestizos. As the years passed, they don't call them anything anymore, just Mexican, even if they were pure blood Spanish.

"There were many in South Texas, north of the Río Grande, after the war with México, who had not intermarried with the Indians, who were pure blood Spanish, but were still called Mexicans. Sometimes they were called Tejanos. Most fought bravely for the young Texas Republic. After the war with México, however, a hatred developed, hijo de su madre," the old man cleaned his brow with his forefinger, "for anything Spanish, or Mexican. You hadda watchale. Even Spaniards, whether Tejanos, or not, were persecuted, murdered, plundered, raided, strung up, and pushed to leave the state. Mano, there was mucho hatred."

They stopped intermittently to wipe the sweat off their brow. They kept chinking away at the weeds with the hoes.

"For decades Mexicans were not safe in Texas. To insure safety they traveled in large numbers, with armas, rifles y escopetas, you know shotgats, that shoot the buck shot. Buying provisiones and groceries sometimes was very difficult.

"The Salinas come from such people. Muy fuertes, and got stronger as the decades went by. Tough people, but very kind, unless you cross them, then they are tough and very rough. They are tough as nails, they can fight.

"Families like the Salinas usually stayed on their own ranches. They were able to protect themselves, their animals, and their holdings better that way. There were small grupitos of Mexican population, mostly along the border, and these grew. Within such pockets, the gringo did not dare enter with bad intentions. As the decades passed, the violence subsided, but the hatred, prejudice, bias, and discrimination did not."

As November approached, more and more of the workers left and most would not return until the spring time or until they could no longer stand the hunger, whichever came first. Tonio was already making motions about going back to Durango for the Christmas Holidays.

"Chon, everybody is starting to leave to go home for the cold winter, when are we going to follow. I think we should leave now. We have plenty of money now. We do not need anymore. Let's go on now," Tonio pleaded.

They were sitting in the small kitchen of their house. Chon did not respond. He was quiet, looking down at the floor. After a few minutes, he looked at Tonio.

"Tonito, I have something to tell you, and I hope you will forgive me. I am not going to go back to México. I am going to stay here. I will wait for you, and I hope you come back, but I will not go back. You see, Tonio, I have no reason to return. My father and mother are dead now, and the only family I have is my mean brother, who hates me. So I am not going back at all," Chon explained.

"But, Chon, you can go home with me, and stay with us. My house is your house. We are almost like brothers, you can stay with us," Tonio countered.

Chon was moved momentarily.

"No, Tonio I do not find pleasure in going home, spending all my money, and then returning through the desert, and risking the hostility of the elements and the people along the way."

Chon had found good security at Rancho Salinas. He was so far off the mainstream that he would never be detected. He did not want to create new risk, new exposure.

Tonio was disappointed. He held his head low and said nothing. Chon felt horrible. He had hurt Tonio's feelings. Aside from Akechi san, Nagi san, Sebastian, and others at Tokyo Plantation he had no true close friends, only Tonio. Chon knew that he could depend on Tonio for anything, whether it be to fight side by side, or to confide and communicate. He was a true friend, and Tonio felt the same way.

Chon put his hand on Tonio's shoulder.

"Tonio, we have only known each other about one year, and we have become very good friends. There are still many things that I do not know about you, and there are still many things that I have not told you about me. There are things that I cannot tell you. Little brother, I want to go with you to your home in Durango, but I cannot. It is not that I want to reject you, to the contrary, I would love to go, because I enjoy you and I would enjoy your family, but I cannot go. Believe me, I cannot go, and I cannot tell you why I cannot go. Just believe me, someday I will tell you the reason," Chon said.

Tonio took some comfort.

"It's all right, Chon," he smiled. "I'm sorry, I didn't want to make you feel bad. It's all right, I understand."

But he did not understand why Chon did not want to risk going to México again.

"Hey Chon, when you gonna tell me why you cannot go back to México? Did you murder somebody back there in San Blas or what?" Tonio asked.

Chon looked at him seriously, "I told you someday I will tell you."

"Well, the son of a bitch, he probably deserved it," Tonio mumbled under his breath. "I will be back later, I am going to go find Don Ramón, and make arrangements."

He left in a hurry.

Chon strolled up to the work barns where repairs were made on the tractors and machinery, where he knew that Don Ramón would be.

"Don Ramón I have been wanting to talk to you for some time," Chon started. "I notice that all the men are starting to leave, starting to drift back to the mother country."

Don Ramón thought that another one would be asking for permission to leave.

"I would like to stay here all the time. I am asking permission to be one of those that stays. I do not want to leave. Actually I have nowhere to go. I do not want to be a burden, by staying here, but I really would like to stay," Chon told Don Ramón.

The old man could not believe what he was hearing. Mostly he worried about having enough hands to do the necessary work. Always he worried about having enough men. Throughout the winter he did most of the chores, even the menial ones, himself. How pleasant it would be to have someone good around at all times. And it would not just be anyone, it would be Chon, by far one of the best worker, helper, and friend on the plantation. Still, he did not want the employee to think that it was so important to stick around during the winter time, and that it would be so special to the plantation to have him around. He acted casual.

"Well," he paused as he worked with his hands on a gadget, "I suppose I could talk to Don Juan and ask him if it would be all right. I guess we could say that it would probably be all right, but let me check with Don Juan, and I will let you know."

Don Ramón pretended to stay busy.

Shortly, after, Tonio ran up breathless. "Don Ramón I have been looking for you all over, I have something I need to talk to you about."

Tonio gasped for breath. Chon walked away.

By mid-November, 1943 all the men that were going to leave, were gone. Chon found that the work was a lot less than he anticipated. He settled into a routine quickly. He fed small animals around the plantation, gathered firewood for the main house and for his own. On occasion Don Ramón wanted a field or two cultivated with winter vegetables, cauliflower or carrots or broccoli.

One part of his winter stay that Chon especially enjoyed was getting to know Don Juan, who set the schedule from the beginning.

"Chon every morning at five-thirty, I want you at the main barn."

The first time he did not explain the reason. Chon was at the barn by five. It was dark, and it was cold. Chon lit a fire off to one side of the building. It was the custom on the plantation to light fires for heat supply during the winter. This time only

Chon enjoyed the heat. Chon noticed that Don Juan's pickup truck was parked in the barn. Having nothing else to do, he started it, let the engine warm, and then filled it with gasoline from the supply tank. He returned the truck to the barn. He was bored. He had nothing to do except wait.

Chon could not hear any movement at the main house, but he could see a couple of rooms lit. This indicated that there was activity in the house. Chon remained at the fire, alternating sides to the high flames. He heard the gate to the main house yard open. He waited for his patron to arrive. Don Juan was at the fire within seconds.

"Buenos dias Chon. How are you this fine day? Here help me with these things," Don Juan said, handing over a paper bag full of something soft and heavy, and a huge red thermos. Chon held the two, and Don Juan instructed him to place them in the pickup. Don Juan returned to the house, and in a couple of minutes returned with two rifles, one in each hand. One was a bolt action, with telescopic sight and sling, the other was a short lever action carbine, no sling and no telescopic sight.

"Here Chon, help with this little one, put it in the truck."

"Patron, may I ask where we are going?" Chon queried.

"Of course you can ask. We're going deer hunting. One of my biggest weaknesses. Most of my workers do not know this because they are not here when hunting season starts, but you will get to see all sides of me," Don Juan confided to Chon.

They drove to the far north end of the ranch, where the brush was thick, and the trees were tall. These were original mesquite trees that had been there at least one hundred years. Don Juan had special places that he wanted to hunt. He told Chon to leave him, and return in a few hours. Later he asked Chon to accompany him. When he learned that the ex-commando made no noise as he walked through the monte, he felt no reluctance in inviting him to follow. Chon had seen white tailed deer as he walked through northern México, and South Texas, but he had not seen the huge trophy deers that Rancho Salinas offered. On their first outing Don Juan shot a huge two hundred pound, twelve-point buck. It was a beautiful specimen.

During their times together Don Juan explained his theory of raising huge trophy bucks. He studied the deer and their habits very carefully. He took notes. He followed bucks and herds. After many years, he had reached some conclusions. Mainly his theory dealt with diet, feeding, and the size or population of the herd.

As November passed, Chon and Don Juan became very close, talking and telling each other stories all the time. Of course, Chon kept his guard up and did not divulge his secret, but gradually, he was unable to conceal his intelligence. The farmhand peon role was hard to play. More and more he found himself conversing intelligently and looking people straight in the eye. He would worry about it later, and did not dwell on it.

After an evening hunt, Don Juan began to talk about his two children. He invited Chon into the house for supper, something he had never done before. They sat sipping wine until Doña María Luisa, Mamalu as Don Juan affectionately called her, entered in grandiose fashion. Don Juan stood up and introduced his wife.

"Encarnación this is my beloved, María Luisa," in a fashion he resembled Sebastian in all his flourish. "María Luisa this is my good friend Encarnación. I have told you about him, this is the guy I have been going hunting with these last few weeks."

"Chon, I know you are shocked at my wife's unabashed behavior," he laughed loudly, "but I raised her very different. She says what she feels, and she expresses her love. This is very different in our culture. We are mostly used to the old fat lady staying in the kitchen and never coming out and speaking. Well I am a bit different. I love my wife, and I am not ashamed of her, and I want her to come out and talk to me, and meet my friends and talk with them also, and get ideas from them and from me. In short, I want to enjoy life to the fullest, and

I happen to be one of those individuals who think it can be done better with your spouse at your side. You see, it is a lot more fun to go through life acompañado, and not alone. Don't you think this is a better way?" Don Juan asked Chon, without expecting an answer.

Chon had no choice but to agree with the patron of course, but he was thoroughly shocked. He drew on all reserves to maintain his composure. He was trained for similar situations, although not like this. Still, he could still use the training to help him through this one. He was able to agree and maintain composure.

"Oh, I am finally able to meet you, I am flattered," Doña María Luisa joined in, "a pleasure I am very sure."

She extended her hand out to Chon, who took it in the very Spanish style that Sebastian taught him, gently kissed the hand and bowed. Doña María Luisa was pleased. Not one of Juan's friends had ever greeted her in this fashion.

At first, Don Juan thought that he should be offended and rebuff his visitor, but Chon stood there gentlemanly, straight, dignified. Don Juan had no choice but to respect his guest's good manners and training. After all, he brought him into the house for good reason. First, he considered him a friend, and more important, he thought the young man cultured and well-man-nered enough to introduce to his family.

"The pleasure is mine entirely," Chon replied, and both Don Juan and Doña María Luisa bowed slightly at Chon. The servant girls witnessed all this and they fumed for some time.

Doña María Luisa sat down and the trio began to sip white wine, and they talked about every subject imaginable. Chon knew that he was being observed under a microscope, and that he was flaunting his every quality. He knew that he was drop-ping his guard entirely, but he decided to worry about it later. This was tempting detection; he should be more careful, but he felt daring. After all, why must he always portray the dumb and ignorant farmhand? Tonight he would step out.

"How is it that you are, apparently, so well educated?" Doña María Luisa asked.

Chon was caught off guard, and resorted to quick thinking for an answer. "Well you see madama, I was taught by an old uncle who was almost a Jesuit priest. He took me under his wing, and taught me everything that I know. Although I never passed to the fifth grade he taught me at home, and I guess I picked up a lot."

"We must salute your uncle, he did a good job, and provided a good companion for tonight's dinner," Doña María Luisa responded with a toast, a sip on the wine glass. Before long they were eating, and the couple noticed that Chon possessed impeccable eating manners. The officer was doing well, and impressed the couple.

"Our son Sergio will be home from medical school and our daughter María Elizabeth will be home from college for the Christmas holidays next week," she told Chon, who had not heard much about their children.

Now he found out that the son was studying to be a doctor at medical school at the University of Saint Louis in Missouri, and the daughter was studying to become a teacher at Texas A & I College in Kingsville, Texas, about one hundred miles away.

Naturally, Chon was flattered to be in their home and in their confidence. He had not enjoyed such trust and love since he left Tokyo Plantation. He would savor tonight's glow for quite some time.

As the meal continued they talked about their respective families, histories, upbringing, pasts, and the present. The white wine flowed, they talked, they ate, and the maids stared and glowered. "Dirty mojado!" They whispered to each other.

Chon went home late. He was full of himself. He floated in a glow. He did not care whether the maids liked it or not, or if they talked about him for the next few days. He did not care if he had overstepped his identity. He felt happy and he did not feel threatened.

Chapter Sixteen

The following day, Don Juan and Chon went hunting, as usual, and enjoyed their companionship and friendship even more, having sealed it over a good meal and good conversation the night before. That day, preparations began for the Christmas holidays. It seemed that the entire ranch was in a flurry of activity to get things ready for the great holiday. Chon learned of the American holiday in his Intelligence Service briefing, but did not fully comprehend the exact meaning and the detail of the feast. Don Juan elaborated on the Anglo American custom, which the Tejano population of South Texas accepted with open arms. It was a very special day and everyone got carried away in producing a huge meal, the best meal of the year.

After Don Juan got his kills, they drove down the bumpy ranch road and in an hour arrived at the ranch headquarters.

They hung the deer and the hog that Don Juan had killed on the steel pipe that was the overhead beam on the open shed by the big barn. The steel cable was attached to a pulley and crank, and a few turns on the crank had each of the two animals strung up. They washed out the carcasses, and Chon began to skin the animals. Don Juan said he could not wait any longer.

"I will return later, you keep working, I need to see if my little girl is home," he said as he strode off.

Chon continued to work, and in a few minutes had the deer completely skinned. Then he began on the wild hog. The skinning was more difficult as the skin was thick and tough and full of lard. It took longer. Chon was about half way through with the hog when he heard voices coming from the yard of the big house. He could hear Don Juan's voice and that of a young girl. He was sure it was the Don Juan's daughter María Elizabeth who had been away at college. He did not turn. He pretended to mind his own business.

The father and daughter walked on up to the shed, and still Chon did not turn to acknowledge them. They walked on up to Chon, and father and daughter were talking about the deer and the hog.

"Here is where I shot the deer, right here," Don Juan pointed to the neck area. "See this tiny little bloody hole, that is where the bullet went in. And this here is the hog, and that little hole there in the neck is where the bullet went in on the hog."

Chon stood by skinning. Then he began butchering and deboning the deer. He waited for an introduction but one never came. He finally turned slowly and looked at Don Juan, and saw the young lady for the first time. She was of medium height, had a thin full body, with long auburn hair draping on her shoulders. Her eyes were large, brown and shiny, and almond shaped. She wore a white shirt and a long skirt. Chon looked at her face, it was long and narrow, with the same aquiline nose of her mother's, the curving brown brows complemented the full pink lips perfectly. Chon could not take his eyes off her face.

Don Juan and the young girl kept on talking, and did not acknowledge Chon. He kept deboning the deer, but every small second that he could, he sneaked a look at her face. He was fascinated, he was hypnotized by her beauty. He wished that Don Juan was not there so he could stop deboning the deer carcass and do nothing except look at young María Elizabeth. He kept trying to work, but his mind was spinning. He had never seen such a beautiful face. He finally decided to stop working, lest he might cut off one of his fingers.

He dropped his hand to his side, and turned and looked at Don Juan and María Elizabeth. They were both chattering away about the deer and the hog, and then began talking about the tractors and other things about the ranch. Eventually they walked away and went to other parts of the yard. Chon, in the meantime, just simply stood there with a fool's face looking at María Elizabeth. He was smitten, and did not know what to make of it.

For a long moment Chon stood motionless. He felt a glow.

"What a beautiful young maiden," he thought to himself, "how lucky I am to get to see her. That dirty Don Juan did not even introduce us. He totally ignored me, the son of a gun. I guess I am not good enough to meet his only daughter. I am good enough to go in and eat supper with him and his wife, and I am good enough to clean his deer and hog, but I am not good enough to meet his daughter. That is not right, I must talk to him or at least to Don Ramón about it."

Chon sat down to get over his shock, but after a while he stood up and finished deboning, and stored all the meat in the special freezer that Don Juan kept in the barn. He stepped out into the sun by the barn to see if he could see any part of Don Juan or the young girl. They were gone.

He walked to his cabin to see if anything needed doing. The house was perfectly kept. He had made the bed in the morning before he went on the hunt. The kitchen was spotless. Everything was in its place. There was nothing for him to do, so he laid on his bed, and his thoughts spun around the globe. He thought of Tokyo Plantation, his mother, Akechi san, Sebastian, and the others, and young María Elizabeth, who was also called Mari Liz and Mariquita by her parents. Chon longed to use that affectionate name.

The next day, after a brief hunt, they hurried back to the home ranch by eleven. Chon went off to his house and Don Juan hurried into the house for a festive meal. Chon stayed in his house, lazing around. About two o'clock in the afternoon he heard talking outside. He stepped up to his front door and leaned up against the outer screen door, looked west, and noticed that

María Elizabeth, and three maids were walking down the lane in front of the workers' bungalows. They carried three trays. There were only three homes occupied at this time. Two other workers and Chon. Chon lived in the last of the houses down the lane, so he was the last to receive the surprising attention.

María Elizabeth was carrying out an old family custom. After their dinner, the family always prepared a tray for each of the winter workers. This was a special treat for the workers, it was thought, and it was done in a compassionate way of sharing with others. The trays were loaded down with turkey, creamed peas, candied yams, cornbread dressing, and a special meat dressing, the recipe of which had been in the family for a century. It also included ambrosia, fresh baked sourdough bread, and pecan, pumpkin, and apple pies. Each tray was a feast, and enough for a family. María Elizabeth walked ahead of the three maids, and as they came to the occupied bungalows, she would take a tray from one of the ladies, and walk into the shacks and deliver the goods.

As she walked up to Chon's house, he opened the screen door. The other three ladies waited at the foot of the porch. María Elizabeth entered, stepped through to the kitchen and left the tray on the table, turned around, and walked out of the house. She never spoke one word, and never even looked at Chon. The two maids explained the gesture as an old family custom, and explained to Chon what each item on the tray was and how it should taste, and how it was a part of the holiday meal.

Chon was crushed, the most beautiful woman that he had ever seen was just in his home, left some food, and exited quickly. She did not even speak, nor look at him. He could not believe it. He was hurt.

María Elizabeth walked down the lane with the maids back toward the big house as Chon sighed, seeing her walk away.

He hardly even touched the food, except out of curiosity. He had never seen most of the food on the tray. He knew that it was made from special holiday recipes, but he just tasted. He lost his appetite. He spent the rest of the night listening to the small radio and thinking of María Elizabeth. It was a nice enough way to spend the rest of the day. He had a hard time getting any reception on the radio because there were many football games being broadcast. He learned the basics of the American game during indoctrination training at Intelligence Service School, but he still had a hard time understanding the quick reporting by the broadcasters.

Later that day, Don Juan approached Chon in the camp kitchen and said to him, "Sergio and Mari Liz are both home now. Tonight we will go to midnight Mass, and after that Sergio will go to several parties in Laredo. He'll visit other homes mainly. I want you to drive him. He'll get drunk for sure, and I don't want him to drive. That means that you cannot drink, and you'll probably have to stay in the car, but I want someone with them that can drive and help if necessary. We'll meet you here after Mass. Okay?"

"Of course Don Juan, it will be a pleasure. I'll be here after Mass," Chon replied. It will be a chance to get out and see something besides the ranch, he thought. That afternoon Chon noticed the activity around the big house. He looked for María Elizabeth, as he cleaned areas behind the house, but he did not see her.

Chon walked to his cabin, and as he stepped up into the house, noticed that something was amiss. He could tell immediately that someone had been there. He looked over on one of the beds and saw a brown cardboard box. On the box was a card, which read, "Para un buen amigo. Te deseo una Feliz Navidad, Ramón."

Chon opened the box eagerly and emptied the contents on the bed. A brand new pair of cowboy boots, a pair of dress slacks, a dress shirt, and a beautiful cowboy cut corduroy jacket. The goods smelled special. He looked at each item carefully. He knew about the custom of Christmas gifts from Sebastian. He was moved. He considered Don Ramón one of his best friends.

Chon felt bad that he had not bought a gift for Don Ramón.
Everyone around the ranch knew that Chon was one of three
that did not go home, and one of the few that had no one with
whom to share Christmas. The ladies from the kitchen came
early in the evening to bring Christmas food, he got tamales,
menudo, cookies, bunuelos, and empanadas.

He took a thorough bird bath in front of the hot wood stove.
His cabin was toasty and cozy and comfortable. He dried himself
and put on his new clothes. He took all the food and moved to
the large camp kitchen, where he could use the kitchen refrig-
erator. He built a large fire in the fireplace. He prepared some
of the food for his supper, and listened to the radio for the latest
news on the war. Of particular interest were the battles of the
Pacific Theater of War. He waited for Don Ramón, for the trip
to Encinal to Mass. At eleven thirty, Don Ramón showed up, he
walked into the kitchen, and smiled broadly when he saw Chon.

"Hey you look great in your trapos," he exclaimed. He opened
his arms and hugged Chon in the Mexican fashion, con un abrazo.
He slapped Chon's back several times, and Chon did likewise.

"Thanks viejo, this is just so special. How can I thank you. I
had no idea, and really I have never bought a present for anyone
in my life. I would not know where or how to start. I feel bad,"
Chon said.

Don Ramón interrupted him. "Don't worry hombre, I know
what it is like for you. I just wanted you to have a small gift
from me and my family, something that would help you have a
good Christmas. You don't have to give me anything. The idea
is for everyone to be happy. Now let's go."

When they arrived at church it was almost midnight and
Msgr. Dan Brown was waiting outside, wearing vestments,
ready to enter the church to begin the Mass. The altar boys
accompanied him.

It was almost time for Mass to start so they moved inside.
Don Juan and his wife, Sergio and María Elizabeth were already

there, and sat toward the front of the church on the right side. Don Ramón's family sat at about the same area, but on the left side of the church. During the Mass, Chon could not take his eyes off María Elizabeth, and the homily on the birth of Christianity was wasted on him. He did not hear a word, all he could do was just stare at the young lady. On occasion she glanced over and caught Chon staring at her. She smiled.

After Mass, Chon waited for Sergio in the camp kitchen, listening to the radio. Most stations were playing Christmas carols. He hoped to catch news items on the war in the Pacific, but it seemed that all disk jockeys were out for the night. It was, after all, Christmas morning. Don Juan, Sergio, and María Elizabeth came rushing into the kitchen. They were laughing and talking loudly.

"Chon, my two chiquitos are ready. I have decided to let Mari Liz go. So now you have double trouble. I do not care what time you come back, I just want everyone back by sunrise, and, one specific rule, no side trips to México," Don Juan said with special emphasis on the last rule. "There's a lot of things over there, and most are trouble; drugs, whiskey, whores, and so on. You stay on the American side of the river. Chon do you understand?"

"Yes of course, Don Juan, I understand perfectly," Chon said.

"Well good. I am talking to all of you together, so that you two," he said pointing at Sergio and María Elizabeth, "will not try to talk Chon into going across the river into México."

Chon knew he would never cross to México ever again, no matter what.

"Well let's get going, we have a big night ahead of us," Sergio said loudly.

"Yeah let's go," María Elizabeth joined in.

The family car was a huge Chevrolet Master De Luxe JA 4-Door Touring Sedan. Chon drove and Sergio sat in front with him, while María Elizabeth sat in back. Don Juan waved goodbye as they drove off.

The first stop was at the Ramirez household in Encinal. The brother and sister went in for drinks, food, dancing, and fun. They stayed about an hour, then they returned to the car with Guillermo Ramirez.

Sergio ordered that they move on to Laredo. Chon kept his eyes on the road, and looked at María Elizabeth and Guillermo through the rear view mirror. He listened to their conversations. Before he realized they were driving through Laredo, where the three hopped around from house to house, enjoying different parties.

It was about four o'clock in the morning and Sergio and Guillermo were giggly. Chon could detect that their speech was slurred now, and they were getting louder and more brazen. They decided to go to the Hamilton Hotel. Sergio gave Chon directions on how to get there. The hotel had contracted Sidney Brent, the great Hollywood singer, for the Christmas week. The hotel had a private club that Don Juan belonged to, and the private club always defiantly stayed open beyond permissible hours. The finest lawyers in Laredo belonged to the club, as did all the judges and politicians.

Chon dropped them off and drove to the parking lot where he slid down in the seat to rest. With the hunt, and staying up late, he had not rested as usual and was exhausted. He was parked about twenty yards from the main entrance and did not want to miss them when they came out.

There were many people walking in and out of the hotel. Chon noticed that there were many soldiers and sailors and that made him somewhat uncomfortable, but then it was wartime.

Chon cracked the window slightly so he could hear and get fresh air. He napped and woke often. It was almost six o'clock in the morning. He thought of María Elizabeth. It appeared that Guillermo was brought along as an escort for her, although no one mentioned it. No matter, he was still in love with her. He took a deep breath, sighed, and closed his eyes again. Momentarily, he heard voices.

Sergio, Guillermo, and María Elizabeth were leaving the building, and they shouted and yelled "Merry Christmas, ha ha ha," as they happily waved their arms and began to walk toward the car. Walking toward them from the opposite direction were four soldiers, probably from Fort McIntosh in Laredo, he thought. In similar fashion they too were shouting.

The clash was inevitable. The four soldiers walking down the sidewalk spotted the beautiful María Elizabeth and the young men and were intent on harassing them. By this time Chon was watching every move. He tensely sat up. He rolled down the window to hear and see better.

"Hey greaser Mex, let me see your Señorita there, I wanna Chrishmush kish," the first soldier screamed. The others chimed in.

"Hey, I like that Mexican stuff, it's brown and white, and creamy and greasy," one of the soldiers said. "I hate Mexicans let's get her."

"You take care of one, I'll take the other, and Charlie here will get firsts with the maiden," another soldier chimed in.

"Ooooo, let me see your brownie Señorita. I wanna give her a Chrisshmush, kissh."

The jeers continued, intensified, and got louder.

Sergio and Guillermo prepared for the inevitable. As they came to the forefront, they shoved María Elizabeth back behind them. The weather was cold, but it was hot on the sidewalk, and hot inside the automobile. Chon opened the door. The first soldier faked a right cross at Guillermo, and landed a devastating left hook and Guillermo went down and out of action. María Elizabeth had the sense to back up and start into the hotel. Sergio fared a little better with the two soldiers challenging him, and held them off as they traded punches, but the smaller fighter was no match for the tall soldiers. A fourth soldier, started through the melee, toward María Elizabeth. By this time Chon was ten yards away, and running at full speed. María Elizabeth saw him running up and stopped moving toward the hotel. Chon's legs were pumping and churning harder than he had ever made them work before. Every single possible muscle in his body was tight and working.

Both of his legs flew into the air, accompanied by a deafening scream. The two feet struck the soldier in typical Chon fashion. The first on the chest, and the second on the tip of his jaw. That soldier was out.

Chon came up with a kick and took care of the second soldier, and followed through with another kick and knocked out the third. By this time the first soldier that hit Sergio was prepared. Sergio tended to Guillermo, who was coming around, and María Elizabeth had started toward the safety of the car.

Chon faced the soldier, his eyes were open wide and he had a hateful look on his face, and was breathing deeply and quickly. Chon stood in a Karate crouch and approached quickly. He feigned a charge and the soldier struck with a left. Chon feigned a charge again and the soldier came across with the right cross. Then Chon charged the soldier, while letting out a samurai yell. He battered the soldier with karate chops. With three chops he was on the ground. Instinctively, Chon grabbed his arm and was going to break it on his own knee, but hesitated.

Chon stood, looked around, and realized that the bomb had been diffused. He stood up straight, stared at María Elizabeth, with his brow furrowed, and pointed toward the car.

"I want you in the car immediately," he said in a strong low voice.

Young María Elizabeth darted toward the car. A few people gathered to review the strewn bodies.

"Well they probably got what they deserved. Damn Yankees, they oughtta go home for Christmas," a tall cowboy drawled.

Chon ran over to where Sergio and Guillermo were. By this time, Guillermo was starting to rise.

"Sergio, we must hurry, I have to get you all out of here," Chon spoke firmly. Sergio was drunk and felt like fighting the rest of the night.

"Leave, hell no, we just started. Didn't you see the way we just whipped these bastards. Hell no, we are not leaving. I am a Salinas from Encinal and we don't ever run from no fight."

Chon got Guillermo up on his feet, ignoring Sergio's remarks. Chon threw Guillermo over his shoulder and ran to the car. He opened the rear door and shoved Guillermo in. He glanced at María Elizabeth who was waiting in the corner of the rear seat.

When he returned, Sergio was provoking another fight with the four soldiers who were coming around, but who wanted no part of the driver from Encinal.

"Come on assholes. What was all that shit about my señorita, and greasers, and Mexicans, come on assholes, want some more shit?" Sergio stood over the soldiers demanding a renewed confrontation. Chon walked up behind him and whirled him around.

"I am only going to tell you one time. I want to leave here now. It is not good to stay here, the officials will be here soon, and I do not want to give your father the Christmas present of having you in trouble on Christmas morning. Listen carefully, we are leaving and we are leaving right now. And I said we, and that includes you. Do you understand?" Chon's stare at Sergio was dead serious.

Sergio tried to shake Chon's hand off his elbow, and Chon grabbed his wrist, brought it up to his face. The two were now looking at each other eye-to-eye.

"I said, we are leaving," Chon said slowly and deliberately, his grip tightening on Sergio's wrist. Sergio finally accepted Chon's demand and followed Chon to the car.

They jumped into the car and Chon started up, and backed out with a screech, and drove away. When they were two blocks away, he turned on the car lights. Sergio started to sober up as he realized the gravity of the situation.

"Yeah, I guess you are right. Drive down this street, and take the next right, we have to get back home quickly now, and we do not want to take the main highways," Sergio told Chon.

"That's right, we do not. An excellent idea," Chon replied. "How is your friend Guillermo? And Mariquita, I mean María Elizabeth. Are you both okay?"

Sergio turned to investigate. Guillermo was awake now, but holding his chin. He had taken a knockout punch to the jaw and it did not feel good. María Elizabeth was doing fine. Actually she was very excited, she had just witnessed the biggest fight of her life, and frankly loved it. Besides it was all because of her that the fight started.

Chon sped through the county back roads as Sergio gave directions. Within forty minutes they were driving up to the ranch headquarters at Salinas Ranch. Chon parked the car in the carport and excused himself for the night.

"Sergio and María Elizabeth, I really think you should tell Don Juan everything. I would like to tell him right now, but you are not children so I will leave that decision up to you. But I recommend that you tell him now," Chon said with a tone of an order.

"Yes Encarnación, I think you are right, I will tell him right now. Uh, where are you going to be in case he wants to talk with you?" Sergio asked.

"Well, actually, I was headed for bed, but I will go to the camp kitchen and wait for an hour to see if Don Juan wants to talk with me. Understand this, I have no concern for what I have done. I did what I did because I had to. I am concerned about causing your father problems and the family embarrassment," Chon retorted.

"Well fine, Encarnación, let us go in," Sergio replied as the three went into the big house and Chon went to the camp kitchen. Chon threw more logs in the fireplace and before long the fire was ablaze. He also made coffee and warmed up some food.

Suddenly Don Juan, Sergio, Guillermo, and María Elizabeth burst into the kitchen. They were all laughing and very happy, and they were carrying two bottles of whiskey.

"Chon, I just talked to my attorney and he said we should not have to worry about anything. He is going to call the right people and make sure that this thing does not get out of hand. So, thanks Jack Dempsey for taking care of my two little people here," he put his arms around María Elizabeth and Sergio. "And of course Guillermo over there."

"I am just tickled to death. Now let's sit down so you can tell me how it all happened," Don Juan finished his speech and sat down to share in the refreshments.

Chon begged off, but they would not let him stay in the background. "Really I did nothing except drive us home," Chon explained.

"Drive home. Baloney, baloney," Sergio was not going to let him off the hook. "I have never seen such fighting. Where did you learn to fight that way?"

Karatedo was new in the United States and was not familiar to most people.

"Oh, it's a special kind of fighting, it's called cantina fighting and I learned it from a drunk old man in San Blas," Chon laughed as he made a joke trying to pass of the karate as street fighting.

"Oh, I am so glad I sent you with them," Don Juan said.

Sergio, Guillermo, and María Elizabeth took turns explaining what happened, and each time Don Juan laughed and slapped his legs just thrilled at the night's happenings. Each time he felt like the soldiers got what they deserved, and he slapped Chon on the back. He served up whiskey for everyone. Chon served tamales and menudo, and the five had a roaring party going.

The focus was on Chon. Who was he? Where was he from? Where did he learn to fight? Where did he learn his vocabulary? Where did he learn his English? And on and on. Chon passed it off as having been raised by an old uncle that was almost a

Jesuit priest who taught him everything that he knew. Except
the fighting, that came in the cantina from another uncle who
never saw the inside of a church in his life. The story worked
and they were pleased. María Elizabeth was staring straight at
Chon. He could feel her stare. She was looking straight at his
eyes, and when he glanced up he would take her eyes in. She
would not look away. He had to, because Don Juan, Sergio, and
Guillermo were looking at him and expecting him to converse,
but every chance he got he would look her way and took in a
few seconds of secret and quiet communication.

The fact that he could not concentrate on her look made it more
exciting. Of course, none of this went by Don Juan, who caught
every glimpse, every look. Sergio and Guillermo were still thinking of the fight in Laredo. Before the talk was over, they shifted
their conversation to everything under the sun, from education,
to war, politics, languages, religion, and other topics. By this time
Sergio became very involved in conversation with Chon and was
absolutely enthralled at the intelligence of this new mojado. He
could talk about anything. Anything. It was hard to believe he
could talk about theology, philosophy, science, any subject.

Finally, the night's activities ended. It was high noon on
Christmas Day. Doña María Luisa sent Elvira from the main
house to order them in. Sergio and Guillermo were already
asleep on the kitchen floor, and only Don Juan, María Elizabeth,
and Chon were still talking. All the time, María Elizabeth just
listened and stared at Chon.

"Well, the night is over, the new day has started," Don Juan
laughed, referring to the noon day sun. "Let us go greet the
day or let us go do whatever we need to start this one out right.
Vamonos Mari Liz, into the house you go young lady. You have
already been out later than I like, and seen more than you should.
Into the house you go."

"Good night, Encarnación," María Elizabeth said to Chon
as she was off to the big house.

Chapter Seventeen

Chon awoke late in the afternoon with María Elizabeth's words ringing in his head. "Good night Encarnación. Good night Encarnación. Good night Encarnación. Good night Encarnación." It was all that he could think about. The last words he heard before going to bed, the sweetest, most melodic voice he had ever heard. He kept hearing it over and over. She had finally acknowledged him, and not only that, but she stared at him all night watching his every move, as they sat and talked in the camp kitchen. He basked in the euphoria of love.

He fantasized for an hour, then decided to get up. He was slow in rising because the whiskey had taken a toll. He was not used to drinking alcohol, and now had a severe hangover.

In the house, María Elizabeth and her mother talked about the fight, and chatted about the party at the hotel. The mother returned to the kitchen. María Elizabeth sat on the couch looking at a book, but not reading, thinking only of the "Chinito." She too was in love, she was smitten.

She had many boy friends in the years past. Most were arranged by her mother and her mother's friends or by Don Juan or even by Sergio. Always the companion was a boy from a good family; "a fine family" was the expression used. Always someone who would make a good husband, financially that is, and very little thought was given to personality, character, or intelligence. The only criteria was whether he was from a financially sound family. The result was that most of the time she was matched with a weakling, mentally and physically, who could not converse about anything, did not participate in sports, and could not even dance right. Even Guillermo, who was nice enough actually, and from a fine family, did not converse intelligently about anything, and could just barely dance. The previous night's events had already demonstrated that he could not fight.

It was not surprising that María Elizabeth, faced with the muscular, good looking Chino, who was superbly educated, and obviously intelligent, would fall, and fall hard.

Don Juan caught every motion, every eyebrow, and every look. Although María Elizabeth and Chon probably felt that the world around them could not detect their feelings, there was one person that knew exactly what each was thinking and what was destined to happen, unless obstructions changed course.

The family's dinner was superb, and the four talked and reminisced and had a very special meal. Intermittently, María Elizabeth would think of her Chinito. After the evening meal, the women began to clear the table while Don Juan and Sergio stayed seated several minutes chatting and making small talk. They suggested that they move to the camp kitchen to continue discussions with Chon. Doña María Luisa looked curiously at the suggestion.

"What? You're going out and have a talk with one of the mojados, I don't understand," she said. "It is not often that we have a chance to see each other during the year, and now you want to go out and talk to one of the helpers. Can't you stay and talk to your poor dear mother? And you to your wife? I hardly even talk to you, you are always, and I mean always, out with the workers, and now on a family night, you have to go out and talk to one of the helpers. I don't like it."

"María Luisa, we are just looking for an after dinner pastime, not to leave you and the house for good. Do not make such a big thing out of it," Don Juan replied to her. "Encarnación is all by himself out there, and he makes for very interesting conversation, perfect after dinner conversation. Please try to understand. Let

Elvira clean the kitchen and come out to the camp kitchen, and you will see that we will all have an enjoyable evening."

Don Juan himself felt strange being drawn to the camp kitchen, but he was being drawn, not by force but because there was somebody out there with an indescribable charisma and he wanted to talk with him. That being said, the two men rose to move to the camp kitchen, and María Elizabeth started to follow them.

"And where do you think you're going?" The mother protested.

"Motthherrrr, I do not want to stay and be one of your maids. Please, mother let me join father and Sergio, and you can join us after you get things started here," María Elizabeth pleaded with her mother.

"Well, all right, go on, you should have been born a boy for all the help you give me around here. Go on, I will be out shortly," Doña María Luisa complained, smiling as she saw the rest of her family head outdoors.

The trio burst into the camp kitchen and surprised Chon who was listening to the news on the radio. They all walked in bouncing happily. Sergio carried a huge bottle of whiskey. After a short while, Doña María Luisa came to the door and the madama joined the table discussion. Elvira was left to pick up in the kitchen. "So they could go be with the mojado presumido," Elvira whispered to herself.

The nightly drinking bouts, and philosophical discussions became a ritual and continued for many years into the future, interrupted only by the absence of some of the participants; Sergio at medical school and María Elizabeth at college. Even Doña María Luisa got caught up in the enthusiasm.

It was hard to admit that it was enjoyable to go out and talk to one of the wetbacks, but the truth was that just after supper most of them could not wait to go out and start the conversation. For most of the holiday vacation, almost every night, without even discussing the hour or purpose, they all poured into the camp kitchen. All of this time María Elizabeth did everything she could to be near, or just see Chon. At night, at the discussions, she would get as close to him as permissible under Doña María Luisa's and Don Juan's eyes. During the day, she did not pass up any chance to go hunting with her father. That meant sitting next to the fabulous, the fantastic Chinito. The Chinito of her heart.

Naturally, Chon wanted nothing more than to be able to talk with and hold young María Elizabeth, but that was not to be. The family had high moral standards, and they were not about to let the baby of the family get carried away with anyone, let alone a wetback, no matter how smart, and how different, and how likable, and how refined he might be.

Chapter Eighteen

The next day, as Don Juan and Chon rode in the truck, Don Juan explained to Chon that just after New Year's he was going to host a hunting party for his attorney, Reynaldo García and his law partner County Judge Floyd Trench, who both lived in Laredo. They would bring their office staffs. Other lawyers, bankers, and friends were also invited. It was going to be a long weekend.

He told Chon that he had hosted this party for the last ten years, and he found it to be enjoyable, and extremely helpful politically. To have these men as your friends meant that you did not have to worry about matters that bothered other business-men, such as tax notices, speeding tickets, problems involving families of the workers, and other similar difficulties.

Chon listened attentively and looked forward to meeting the lords of the area. Now, however, he knew that he should not expect special treatment. He was a superior officer of the Japanese Navy, but he had chosen to live a life incognito as a farm peon, and he must keep his place. If detected he would be shot for sure.

"Mariquita and her mother will go off to visit friends for that week, as it is not a good atmosphere for women to be amongst all these men, and all the drinking that will go on," Don Juan told Chon. "Sergio too will go visit some friends in San Antonio during that week. He loves hunting, but has had enough of it during the Christmas holidays. Besides he does not enjoy hunting with so many rifles all over the ranch. The truth, he just wants to get out of all the work involved"

Chon could hardly hide his disappointment but told Don Juan he understood perfectly.

The party would begin January 2 and continue until January 5. That would give all the city boys plenty of time to hunt, and still have a day for New Year's celebration with their families. He had followed this schedule the last few years.

On the morning of December 28, Don Juan assembled the few winter workers in the huge camp kitchen. He wanted to discuss the upcoming party. Don Juan advised Don Ramón, Chon, and the others how he wanted the guests to be treated.

"The jefes that live in Laredo and the surrounding cities, that control the decisions of everything that happens in this area, are coming to Rancho Salinas. I want them to see that we run a good operation here, that we are strong, that we work hard, that we are clean people, and that we enjoy our visitors, our company.

"I want them to hunt hard, to enjoy their hunt. I want them to rest, I want them to eat as much as they want, and I want them to drink as much as they want. When they leave here, I want them to feel like they had a superb time, and I want them to want to come back.

"Ramón make sure that there are plenty of sodas, ice, drinks of all kind, whiskey, beer. Encarnación, I want these men to go to the best hunting spots, and kill the best bucks. I want them to want to come back. You know what to do to make a hunter happy on Rancho Salinas. Do it."

The next day, preparations and cleaning continued for the hunting party. Morale and energy levels were high. The hunters that chose to stay overnight would use the worker cabins that were not occupied. It was Chon's job to clean these cabins for the guests.

The party kicked off at three in the afternoon on January 2. Judge Trench and Reynaldo García were the first to arrive, followed closely by the county sheriff, the county commissioners, the road and bridge superintendent, the superintendent of schools, the tax collector, the tax appraiser, the school board members, and various staff members of these individuals. The district attorney and two assistants and various members of their staff also arrived. There were three district judges from the Río Grande Valley that attended, but they usually only stayed for the first day.

The last day of the party was called Federal day because the Federal District Judge from Houston showed up with his entourage. Also one of the U.S. Senators, the local Congressman, and the U.S. Marshal for the Southern District came to hunt.

The party was held outside in the Salinas' yard. The lawn was green and fresh, and the temperature was perfect. It was somewhat chilly, but brisk and comfortable. Six fires were situated at the perimeter around the party area.

There was much food and drink. The hunt began before dawn and the talk centered on the trophy bucks around the ten thousand acres. The men gathered and talked about horn growth, horn spread, the rut, rattling horns, deer stands, telescopic sights, open sights, rubs, and every imaginable hunting topic. As in every such gathering, there was never a lack of an answer or explanation.

After a few hours passed, Chon managed to get a breather with Don Ramón.

"Now what happens?" Chon asked.

"Well, more than half of these people will not be back, until next year," Don Ramón told Chon. "Of the rest, half will stay here with us tonight, and you and I will have to help take them to bed. Of those, only half will get up in the morning and go hunting. So you see, the group will thin out, although there will be some that will return in the afternoon. Really, only the good friends stay. You can count on the county judge, the abogado García, and the sheriff. Although they may go into their offices in Laredo, they hurry back. These guys you will get to know very well, the others, well, you might."

Later during the night, Chon, Don Ramón, and the other ranch hands helped the drunk dignitaries find their automobiles, or find their cabins. Señor García was feeling good and could still manage to help himself, but needed help with his gear and weapon.

"Como te llamas?" García asked Chon.

"My name is Encarnación Gutiérrez Ayala patron, my friends call me Chon. A sus ordenes."

"Well Chon my man, it is good to meet you. How long have you been here? Where are you from?" The attorney asked.

"I've been here only about a year, and I am from San Blas, in the state of Nayarit," Chon lied.

"That's good. Chon my man let me ask you," the attorney narrowed his questions to the special point of interest, "do you know where the big bucks are, have you been hunting with Don Juan?"

"Yes," Chon chuckled at the obvious motive of the questions. "Yes, I know where the large bucks are and yes I have hunted with Don Juan."

"Then, my good man, Chon, Encarnación, I will see you in the morning," the attorney singsonged, as he handed Chon a five dollar bill. Chon did not know what to make of it but he took it anyway.

"Don't be afraid, take it, take it," the attorney insisted. Chon showed him into the cabin, pulled back the bed covers, showed him the kitchen area, and the latrine and shower area.

"Señor García, the showers are very cold this time of the year, so if you need a bath, tell me and I will get hot water, and you bathe here in the house. It may just be a bird bath as we call it here, but at least you get a bath. Also, if you need to use the latrine, then just use the big bucket under your bed, it will be taken out during the day when you are gone. We call that the thunder bucket," Chon explained and García smiled.

"Chon, thank you for helping so much. Just remember now, no matter what Salinas says in the morning, you are going to help me find the mossy back that has never come out of those woods ever, the one with the thirty inch spread that weighs two hundred pounds. You understand?"

"Yes, yes sir. I understand. I will see you in the morning. I have to help others get to their cabins."

The first two days of the hunting party were hectic for Chon, Don Ramón, Don Juan, and the cooks. They got up at four thirty each morning, prepared breakfast, took juice and hot coffee to the guests' bedside at five thirty, loaded all the gear, helped serve breakfast, and rode out in the cold at six to drop off the hunters. By ten o'clock it was time to return for the hunters. Some sat in deer blinds, others sat in senderos. Usually one or two had killed a buck. The morning finished with Don Ramón and Chon gutting out the bucks, loading bucks, hunters, and gear unto the pickup trucks, and driving back to the main house for lunch. In the afternoon the hunters rested with a siesta and at three o'clock left for the afternoon hunt.

On arrival at the home ranch, the hunters chomped on a hot supper of chicken fried steak and cream gravy, fresh biscuits, mashed potatoes, green beans, or a similar fare. After supper, the hunters listened to the radio and sat around and played gin rummy. After a long day, all the hunters went to bed, except for the County Sheriff Solomon Santos. Sheriff Santos attentively listened to the console radio placed by the fireplace. The fire crackled, as did the radio. The reporters accounted for the week's activity around the world. Most of the activity concerned the war in both the European and Pacific theaters.

Chon listened in the kitchen as he helped the servant Elvira put things away and prepare for the next morning's breakfast. Intermittently Chon listened to the news. His knowledge of English was good. He could understand everything that he read. The spoken word was a little different, depending on the speed of delivery and local colloquial accent. The NBC broadcaster was hard to follow, but Chon understood the gist of the reporting on the battles. It seemed to Chon from the news that the U.S. was rebounding from earlier defeats and that one General MacArthur was the warlord responsible for turning the tide.

He had mixed emotions. In a fashion, he wanted his own country to succeed. After all, he had been a part of the war effort. That and the usual brainwashing that comes with military service. On the other hand, he had psyched himself through deep meditation to leave that part of his life behind, and reform it to a South Texas vaquero, disregarding and ignoring Japan and the war.

The sheriff was an amiable guy. Easy to talk with. He seemed a little out of place. He was younger than the attorneys and judges. He seemed anxious to be elsewhere with more joviality or more activity. Having finished in the kitchen, Chon approached him and started a conversation. The sheriff engaged enthusiastically, and the topics changed, and changed until midnight when exhaustion finally overtook both of them. Despite the weariness, Chon enjoyed the conversation thoroughly. He had not conversed intelligently since talking to the last after dinner session with the Salinas clan.

Just as Chon was about to leave for his cabin, the sheriff begged to be excused for a few minutes. "Chon let me go to the car, I have something that I want to show you. Please wait for me here, I will return in a moment," the sheriff said.

Chon knew that the sheriff was a law enforcement officer. Had the time come for his arrest? Was the sheriff going to get handcuffs? Or, was he going to get information on Chon to ascertain identity? Worse yet, was he going to get the soldiers for the execution? Chon imagined the worse.

Chon noticed that he was the only person in the kitchen. Shortly the sheriff walked in and was carrying a large brown envelope in one hand, and a large black case in the other. He motioned to Chon to join him at a table. Reluctantly, Chon inched up to the table, ready to sprint off running if necessary. The sheriff opened the envelope and the black case, which held a portable typewriter.

"How would you like to be one my helpers?" Sheriff Santos asked Chon.

"I am not sure that I understand. One of your helpers?" Chon asked.

"Yeah. You know I have a lot of power, and in this brown envelope, I have some small pieces of paper that can let you do many things that you cannot do ordinarily. Actually, it is just a small piece of card but there are many people around the entire state of Texas that respect this card as if it were a passport. It will be your passport to many freedoms Don Chon," the sheriff said in a slow and deliberate voice.

"It sounds fantastic and magical to me, if you will honor me with benefits of this precious gift, I will be flattered to receive it, and indebted to you for life," Chon said.

"Very well, then let me fix this. You are about to become a deputy sheriff for Webb County. I am going to deputize you. You must carry this card around at all times. I promise that it will help you in most cases where you think that you have absolutely no help," the sheriff explained, and began typing on the card.

"Now tell me your full name"

"Encarnación Gutiérrez Ayala."

"What is your address?" The sheriff asked.

"Address, well, address, I guess you have to say Rancho Salinas, Encinal, Texas, no?"

"Yeah, I guess so," the sheriff answered and he pecked away at the typewriter.

"Date of birth?"

"November 13, 1920," Chon responded.

"Place of birth?" The sheriff paused. "Well I think we better not put your place of birth on this card. Let me just put that you were born at Rancho Salinas, Texas, because if I put down

San Blas, State of Nayarit this card would be worthless. So here goes, as of today you were born in Rancho Salinas, Webb County, Texas. What do you think of that?"

Chon smiled in amazement at the young warlord. Changing history so easily with a typewriter. The sheriff finished, and pulled the tiny card from the machine, and put it on the table and signed it with the fountain pen he carried in the brown envelope. He put the card on the table, blew on it momentarily drying the ink. Then he picked up the card and ceremoniously handed it to Chon.

"Here. You are now a full-fledged deputy sheriff of Webb County. I am not kidding, and this card is not a joke. Take it and guard it. Keep it in a safe place. When you travel, carry it on your person. You will see that it will help you. I promise."

Chon accepted the card eagerly. He looked at it carefully and read each word on both sides. It looked very authentic. He held it carefully with his index finger and thumb and put it in this shirt pocket. He thanked the sheriff.

"Sheriff, I am not yet sure what your gift means, but it sounds like I am very indebted to you for such a fine gift. I thank you sincerely from the bottom of my heart," Chon said.

"Chon, there is no debt. I gave you this, and I do not expect anything in return. Now let's get on to bed, because I want to get up early and get the big twelve-point mossy back out there that I have trying to get. Good night, hasta mañana," he said, and was off to his cabin.

Chon sat in the kitchen for a few minutes and looked again at the card. He was confused, and amazed. Was it true? Could the card prove to be special? Time would tell.

He was off to bed thinking of Mari Liz.

Morning came too soon. The trucks were ready. The motors were running. The heaters were on. The hunters were having breakfast. It was dark, and it was freezing cold. Chon scurried around cleaning windshields and packing gear. Getting the thermos of hot coffee, and bags of snacks and sandwiches. He saw Don Juan come towards him.

"Chon, I want you to take a special assignment today."

Chon stiffened slightly.

"Reynaldo García and I are very special friends," Don Juan told Chon. "He has been my lawyer for ten years now, and a very able lawyer he has proven to be. He has gotten me out of more messes and problems than I can remember. But never mind about all that. He has been out here for several years now, and he has never killed a big buck. So today I want you to drop everyone else off and leave him for last. Take him to the most special place, where you would go to kill the largest buck.

"So go and do it. Now go into the kitchen and get the hunters and take them out to their blinds. Do not tell the others that we are giving Reynaldo special treatment. Understand? Now go."

Men laughed and filed out of the kitchen, went to their cabins to get their rifles, gloves, binoculars, scarfs, and boarded the pickup trucks.

Chon motioned to Señor García secretly that he should mount his truck. Chon opened the truck's passenger door, and Señor García hurried into the truck cabin. García was thankful for the privilege of riding indoors today. It was bitterly cold, and looked like it might start a winter drizzle.

The last hunter was dropped off and Chon drove off to the most northerly corner of Rancho Salinas, an area where he took no one. It was actually an area that was reserved for the family, but Chon was told to get him a big one, so he went to the most sacred hunting ground.

The pair left the truck, Chon carrying the 30-30 lever action carbine that he was given for the season. García carried a beautiful Winchester bolt action 270 rifle with a fixed four power telescope. Chon examined it and found it a magnificent weapon. It resembled sniper weapons used by the Japanese marines.

Chon and Señor García walked about one hundred yards down a winding trail and came to a deep wooded creek. It was dry and they crossed it without difficulty. They walked quietly through a thicket of wild persimmons. The evergreen canopy blocked out the sunlight. They sneaked through tall grass when they left the thicket. All this time, Chon was motioning to Señor García to be quiet, to step over a log, to not step on dry twigs, to move right, move left. He was the perfect guide.

They walked quietly for ten minutes before coming to a rise in the land, and Chon insisted that they lay on their stomachs and crawl up the rise about thirty yards. García thought that the young man was taking things a bit too serious, but he would wait for a while before voicing an objection. They crawled up the rise. They crested the rise slowly, and just barely peeked over.

As he sneaked a look over the rise, García was glad that he had not complained. He saw a herd of eight deer grazing about one hundred yards away. He dropped his head back immediately and rolled over on his back. Chon was caught by surprise and looked over at his companion. García was laying there suddenly huffing and puffing. His face was flushed, and he smiled in embarrassment. Then Chon recognized what was happening and chuckled. He ducked behind the rise, and giggled. Señor García was having a severe attack of buck fever. The adrenalin flowed heavily. He could not breathe nor keep the rifle steady. They waited for several minutes.

"Do you feel better now?" Chon whispered.

"Yeah, I feel fine now, let's get 'em," García replied in a whisper.

"All right, but remember that we have to be patient and slow. It could be that those animals are all does, and no bucks, so you have to wait for the bucks to arrive. Do you understand? You have to be patient!" Chon whispered.

The two heads slowly protruded over the rise. They scoured the area for minutes. All they could see were five does, and four yearlings. There were no horns to be seen. They continued to search the open area where the animals grazed.

They waited for about half an hour. Another deer joined the herd from the surrounding brush. The pair waited anxiously. The large bodied deer grazed with the rest. Chon did not have binoculars, and he could not tell the quality of the buck. Suddenly from the left of the area they were viewing they noticed a large blur. The animal came to the open area and joined the others. The pair waited anxiously for full view of the visitor.

In a couple of seconds, the big animal looked to all sides, and in doing so displayed a large crown of horns. It seemed as if the crown weighed fifty pounds on a two hundred pound body. It was a beautiful specimen, a trophy in the truest sense of the word. Señor García began to huff and puff again, and Chon was startled as he heard his heartbeat. Though he was two feet away, Chon could hear the blood flow through the diastolic and systolic strokes. He looked at Señor García's neck and noticed that the veins were bulging and the face and neck were very red. Chon became concerned. He dropped below the rise, and pushed Señor García in the ribs. García reacted favorably as he ducked behind the rise. Chon looked attentively, brow furrowed.

"What's wrong?" He asked nervously.

"It's all right Chon, it's just buck fever. Don't worry."

"Buck fever or not, please take it easy. Take ten deep breaths, I don't want you to die out here."

After a few minutes both men peeked over the rise and the huge buck was still there. García looked through the telescopic sight. He took a deep breath. He let half of it out. Chon noticed that he tightened up on the shoulder at the recoil pad. Chon looked down the lane as Señor García squeezed off a round. The rifle cracked loud. Chon knew immediately that it was a good hit.

"Now let's wait about five minutes. Let the animal die. Just lay back and rest. By the way how do you feel?" Chon asked.

"I feel great. I just shot the biggest buck I have ever seen, and I feel just great," García answered.

Back at the home ranch, the hunters went off to take a cold shower. Chon started to hang up the trophy when Don Juan and Señor García walked up.

"Chon, Reynaldo wants to get this deer stuffed, so you need to take him to Laredo to the locker plant. You drive him in."

"But patrón, you must remember that the Migra might get me, the rinches, what do we do about them?"

He thought of the twelve man firing squad. Twelve men at least, maybe more. No blindfold.

"Chon don't worry. Please trust me, you are in good hands, and besides, I am told that you now hold a special card from Solomon Santos, the sheriff. Between Reynaldo here going with you, and the card from Solomon, you could break your way into the pearly gates. Don't worry. Now get along," Don Juan motioned.

Chon and the lawyer boarded the pickup, and drove out of the yard around the main house toward the road a mile away and were on their way to Laredo.

The trip to Laredo was short and quick. They drove to the ice plant where they deposited the lawyer's kill to be stripped of its hide, head, horns, and cape and to be stored until the taxidermist made his rounds later in January.

After the locker plant, the pair drove to the law office that Señor García and Judge Trench shared. The building was a nondescript block building that stood caddy corner from the Webb County Courthouse. Señor García showed Chon his office, a large area.

"Right there on that wall," he pointed to the west wall of the office, "right there is where the monster will hang when I get him back from the taxidermist."

"Chon please sit down, while I make just a couple of phone calls," the lawyer said.

Two calls became twenty. It was January 1944, the United States was in the middle of a World War and people had many legal problems. Chon was fascinated with the man working at his best, calling other lawyers, calling important officials, putting out fires, challenging improper action, setting the stage for future fights, calming distraught mothers, wives, or husbands, soothing businessmen and merchants. He had a good manner.

Finally the short tour was over and they were ready to return to Rancho Salinas. As they drove out of Laredo, about five miles out, Chon spotted a small light green jeep on the shoulder of the road parked perpendicular to the paved highway. There were two U.S. Border Patrolmen stopping traffic. Chon analyzed the situation, and remained calm. Here was the final chapter, he thought, detection at last and undoubtedly execution, whether here in the U.S. or in Japan, if he could ever make it back. He tensed up and prepared for the worse, as he slowed the pickup. The patrolmen approached the truck one on each side.

"Take it easy, do not worry, and just let me do all the talking," García admonished.

The truck stopped and both of the officers stood one at each front door of the truck. "Well hello Mr. García how are you today?" The first Officer asked.

"I am very fine thank you Officer Smith. I have not seen you since court in Laredo three months ago. Has everything been going all right for you?" García asked.

"Just great. We have been catching wetbacks left and right; it seems that the more intense the war gets, the more they want to come over here and work for the war effort. Those already working on farms we leave alone, mostly, but those we find on roads and wondering around, we take in for deportation. With shortages and rationing, and all, things must be pretty bad in México, I guess."

"Yeah. I suppose that's probably true," García responded.

Then the other officer spoke. "Is this man here, legal Mr. García?"

Chon understood and felt like opening the door, breaking and running, but he followed orders and stayed put, waiting for Señor García to take the brunt of the confrontation.

"Oh yeah, this guy is one of the cowboys from over at Rancho Salinas. He's from Encinal actually, born and raised there," García lied, and Chon tensed up some more.

"Where were you born boy?" The agent asked Chon directly. His face was eight inches away from Chon's as he stood next to the pickup truck.

Chon turned slowly and looked at the officer straight in the eye and calmly responded in almost perfect English, "Encinal, Texas."

"Do you have any identification?" The officer asked.

Chon reached into his shirt pocket and pulled out his deputy sheriff's identification card, and again in English responded slowly, "this is all I have right now."

García was surprised to hear Chon speak English, and wanted to see the effect of the exchange. Chon had violated orders but it seemed that the matter was about to be resolved.

"All right, this seems to be all right," the officer replied, "you can go now."

Chon breathed easy. García was relieved that the situation had diffused so easily.

"I'll see you later Smith, you both have a good afternoon," García bid the officers goodbye.

They drove quietly for two minutes, then Señor García could not hold it any longer, and let out a loud high pitched Mexican grito. Then he had a good long laugh.

Chon was still too nervous and upset at almost being detected, and was not quick to join in the laughing until later. Then he sighed, took three deep breaths, then cracked up laughing, and moved his index finger over his brow and whipped it at his side, indicating a very close call.

The next day of the hunt, following Don Juan's orders, Chon alternated between Sheriff Santos and Judge Trench to help each kill a big buck.

Camp closed on the evening of January 5, with a special steak supper. The group had shrunk by now, and only the most avid remained. This night was reserved for reminiscing about the main events of the hunt, and everyone recalled Chon's deputation, and the near miss with the migra.

Spirits were high and everyone enjoyed the evening. Chon spent the afternoon loading gear and equipment. After supper the guests bid farewell, expressed their thanks, and drove away. There was a sudden vacuum, a void, after such an intense atmosphere. Suddenly everyone was gone.

Chapter Nineteen

It was January 6, 1944. Chon noticed the Christmas tree that lighted up each night in the large window of the front living room in the big house. He had read of the custom in his briefing on North America, and Sebastian had described the custom, but he had never seen such a tree until this December at Rancho Salinas. He was intrigued by the tree and the multicolored lights. Doña María Luisa played much Christmas music on the record player, and it could be heard outside. It created a strange, pleasant almost mystical mood. The tree would be left until the Feast of the Three Kings, on January 6.

Now that the hunting season was over, Chon was anxiously looking forward to the return of María Elizabeth. He knew that the holidays were drawing to a close soon.

Sadly, Don Juan informed him that Doña María Luisa and Mari Liz had extended their stay to include a trip to Monterrey to visit old friends and would not return to Rancho Salinas until a couple of days before María Elizabeth was scheduled to return to college. He knew that she would leave on January 15, to begin the last semester of the academic year, and that he would not see her until Easter. He also learned that she was on her last year, that in May she would graduate, and become a full-fledged teacher, and return to Encinal to teach at the elementary school there.

The day after Doña María Luisa and María Elizabeth returned from their trip, Chon awoke at eleven o'clock, showered, and dressed. He went to the camp kitchen and listened to the news while he waited for the others to arrive. He heard about the war around the world. He made mental notes about the war in Japan. Chon also learned that the migra had a camp—a prison of sorts—in Crystal City where they were holding Japanese, Germans, and Italians. Some of the Japanese were sailors, like himself, that had been caught in American ports when the war started. Others had been deported from Mexico and South American countries to the United States. He knew that Crystal City was a little more than an hour's drive from Rancho Salinas. This worried him. He thought that he could be exposed and end up in the camp as well. He wished he could do something for his fellow countrymen, but knew there was nothing he could do. Besides he could not risk being caught and end up at this place himself, or worse since he was not a normal sailor but a spy, a member of the Intelligence Service. He had to put this camp out of his mind; it was his survival that he needed to worry about.

At about noon, Don Juan and Sergio showed up with Doña María Luisa and two other house girls in tow. They brought food for the men to eat while they listened to the game.

The game started at one thirty, and Chon waited for María Elizabeth but she did not show. He dared not ask where she might be lest he be told to mind his own business. He waited and waited. The game went on, and about four thirty the game ended and still no appearance by María Elizabeth. She must be sleeping, he thought to himself. Sergio went to sleep on one of the couches in the kitchen, and Don Juan got up and walked out of the kitchen.

"I am going to take a short nap. I might see you after supper for a talk, I do not know yet," he told Chon.

Chon sat there by himself, and decided to take his own nap at his cabin. He walked slowly. He was tired. He opened the front door and there she was. María Elizabeth was standing in the doorway that separated the front and back rooms. The white

Mexican dress made her sparkle. Chon quickly flung the door open and left it open. He panicked.

"Mariquita, what are you doing here. Do you know I could get killed if you were discovered here?" He spoke quickly.

"I know what I am doing," she responded.

"Well that is what you think, but if Don Juan were to walk in right now, I would be hung from the highest tree, and you know it, and it would not matter that you knew what you were doing," Chon stuttered, he was so nervous.

"I do not care," María Elizabeth responded. She walked forward and met him in the middle of the room. She looked up at his eyes, and grabbed his face with her two hands and laid the biggest, fullest, wettest kiss on Chon's lips that he had ever experienced.

He trembled with fear and passion. María Elizabeth moved her body toward his. She pushed her breasts against his chest, and her thighs against his thighs. He was so scared that he simply held his hands high in the air, he would not dare touch her. He was scared to death, but the sensation of the beautiful kiss slowly took its toll, and his hands slowly grabbed her body and held it close to his. The kiss only lasted for a few seconds, but it seemed like five minutes to Chon. He thought he was going to faint. He knew now that 1944 was going to be one hell of a good year. Finally, the kiss ended, and María Elizabeth moved back, and Chon just stood there.

"I love you Chon Gutiérrez, and don't you dare go anywhere. I will return this Easter. Do you understand? I cannot talk to you because my father and mother and brother do not want me to talk to any man, but I am here and I have told you, and I want you to stay here. Don't you dare leave or go anywhere," she said.

He felt like he was back in the army and had received very strict orders.

"Don't worry Mari Liz, I am not going anywhere. I will be here when you get back for Easter," Chon responded.

She ran out of the house, checking first at the screen door to make sure she was not being watched, then sprinted off to the barns. From there she casually walked into the big house as if nothing had happened.

Chon stood in the same spot for about thirty minutes. He did not want to move. He had never experienced so much passion in his entire life. He felt like he was floating. He was very confused. It seemed that instead of going underground to protect his spy identity, he was surfacing and becoming popular and well known. He was going to have a difficult time staying undetected, he told himself.

Chon rose at daybreak and fired up the stove and the fire place in the camp kitchen. At noon, everyone asked why he did not show up the night before. He admitted that he was too tired. In actuality he just wanted to wallow in the passion he had felt. He knew that Sergio and María Elizabeth would leave in two days. The time was short.

There would be one more late night discussion that evening and that would be it. It went as usual, except that María Elizabeth began questioning Chon in front of her father. She never asked him any kind of question at all in his presence, but now she was pushing an issue, and it made Chon very uncomfortable.

"Chon have you ever been married?" María Elizabeth asked. The question was all right if it were asked by one of the men, but somehow coming from María Elizabeth, it did not seem proper. But he had no choice, he had to answer anything she asked.

He glared at her and answered "No."

"Do you have any children?"

"No, María Elizabeth I do not have any children."

"Do you have any girlfriends?"

"No, María Elizabeth, I do not have any girlfriends," he answered.

"How come a good looking, handsome guy like you does not have any girlfriends?" She asked.

"I do not know what you mean María Elizabeth," Chon replied with a coy smile.

She was grilling him. At first Don Juan thought it was natural curiosity that brought her to ask so many questions, but then he noticed that she was teasing him. He enjoyed it for a while because he was watching María Elizabeth being coy and playing a game, then he tired of it and felt for Chon and brought it to a halt.

"Mari Liz that is enough, you ask too many questions, please be quiet," Don Juan said sternly.

María Elizabeth looked over at Chon and smiled, as if to say that her father saved him for today, but someday soon she would be inquisitive, and he better be ready.

Chapter Twenty

Chon got back to his routine of working with Don Ramón, and thought only of Mari Liz when he was on his own. They began to prepare the machinery for a hard spring of work. They worked on the irrigation equipment also. They purchased and arranged seed. The January freeze was bad, and they combated damage from the freeze. They protected plants, water pipes, and machinery alike.

At night, thoughts of Mari Liz.

Early on, Don Juan and Don Ramón conferred and agreed that Chon should be elevated to assistant foreman. It meant a little better pay. What it meant primarily was that more was expected of him.

On February 20, Chon was working at one of the north fields about five miles from the Home Ranch. He was working on a water pump, and made sure that the tractors turned the soil, all in preparation for tilling for planting. About eleven o'clock in the morning, he heard a loud shrill yell south of where he worked. He looked up and squinted as he tried to find the source of the cry in the fields around him. He heard the yell again. Again he tried to focus in on the commotion. He saw nothing, and after a pause he returned to working on the pump needed to get river water to irrigate the fields.

After ten minutes he heard the shrill yell again. He asked Valeriano, his helper, if he could see where the noise was coming from, and Valeriano shook his head and said that he could not. Chon looked up again and squinted his eyes, and finally in the distance he could see a small figure running toward them. Not knowing what to expect, Chon tensed his muscles. He moved his head side to side, stretching his muscles. He got out of the hole that he was working in. He swung his arms back and forth as a warrior preparing for battle. He reached down for his toes fully stretching his leg muscles.

Again the shrill yell, and still Chon could not see what the matter was. He jumped nervously on the balls of his feet. Whatever it was, he was going to be ready. It would not be as in San Rafael when Luis Carranza almost rode his horse over Chon's body. Could it be the soldiers or someone sent by them? He still could not analyze the situation. Then suddenly he recognized the gait, the lope. It was unmistakable. He could now see his good friend Tonio running toward him.

"Ah good friend, Antonio, hermano, brother of mine, what a welcome sight you are," he thought.

A knot came to his throat and his nose plugged up. Tears came to his eyes. Chon was twenty three years of age, and the poor soul did not have a normal life at all. As a matter of fact he was thrown about like a marble on a hard surface, and it was really sad that his roots and connections were so loose. A young man did not deserve to be so misplaced.

The pair talked and talked and another mojado joined in. They talked about México, family, Christmas, children, tequila, hunting, hiking, crossing the river, and many other things. Finally Chon broke up the chatter.

"Well we can talk tonight around the fire, for now let us get on with our work."

At the night fire all of the men took turns telling tales of the past holiday. Each was applauded or jeered depending on the character of the story. Chon and Tonio joined in, as did Don Juan and Don Ramón.

Chon was jeered on his apparent promotion, and he blushed and apologized to everyone. It was the only thing that he could do and still save face. He knew that he did not have to apologize, but it was the only way to get the others to accept his promotion. The opposite attitude and reaction meant that he would be an adversary. He spoke of the trip to Laredo, the fight, he talked about the lawyer, the judge, the monsignor, and the others. He did not dare speak about Mari Liz, his Mariquita, and their special relationship.

Tonio talked about the hunger and poverty back home in Mexico, how welcome his earned dollars were, and about a meager Christmas.

The spring planting and tending started on schedule. Chon worked hard. He did not want anyone to say that his new promotion made him a lazy or a less efficient worker.

The Easter holiday came upon Rancho Salinas suddenly. Everyone had been working hard, that they hardly noticed that it was upon them. Sergio would not be able to travel such a long distance. Mari Liz did arrive.

With so many people around, and no more late night camp kitchen available, it was impossible for Chon and Mari Liz to be alone. They could see each other in the backyard and barns with the tractors and supplies but there were always many people around. They were barely able to say hello much less speak with each other.

Chon was happy that at least Mari Liz let herself be seen. Earlier he could not even see her. Now at least she would come out and say hello. They were both hoping to be alone longer and to talk. But the opportunity did not arrive. Don Juan noticed the frustration with the two young people.

"It is not my duty to make things easier," he thought to himself. "Nature will take its course."

Chon was like a caged animal, except it was the princess that was in the cage. He could not get in. He contemplated the problem and sought a solution. Finally, he decided that he could trust her to come up with the solution. She did.

On the Saturday before Easter, Chon was working on one of the tractors when suddenly he felt the presence of another person in the garage, he looked up and there was pretty Mari Liz.

"Hello Mari Liz, how are you?" Chon asked.

"I am fine Encarnación, it is truly a delight to see you. Have you been well? I have missed you. I wanted to see you. I want to be with you all the time Encarnación but there are too many people around," she moaned. "I cannot even go to your house because you have a companion that lives with you. What are we going to do?"

"Please slow down, you are talking too fast. Now, may I respond slowly to your many questions and comments? First, I too am happy to see you sunshine. I have been well. I too have missed you," Chon said slowly in a quiet low voice.

"I want to be with you more than you can imagine. You have your classes to keep you busy, all I have are the fields. There is much solitude in my day. Yours should be fully occupied. I know that there are too many people around. And that we cannot see each other. I know of course that you cannot go to my house. But then of course you should not go to my house anyway. What are we going to do Mariquita? It appears to me that we are in love with each other. But are we? Do we even know each other? Who am I Mariquita? Do you really know?"

He was digressing into a long soliloquy. They both stood there looking at each other and yearning to hold each other. They were afraid to be caught. They were afraid to be embarrassed. Tears were coming to their eyes. She did not feel like answering his questions. To begin with, a young girl should not be seen with a man that her father did not approve of for courting. For another, and more importantly, it was thought that it was highly improper for the young maiden of the house to be courted by a common laborer.

Finally, they could stand it no longer. They ran toward each other and hugged tightly for what seemed like an eternity.

There was no kissing. They were content to hold each other. At this moment in their life they did not care who was looking. Fortunately, and luckily and strangely, no one was. He held her hand and pulled her away slightly. He led her to the front of the tractor at the back of the shed. He sat her down. He sat down.

"Mari Liz what are we going to do. In two days you leave for school, then I will not see you until you graduate. For all of that time, I just sit here at the ranch and pine away," Chon told her. "And that is all right, I can stand it. But what I am really interested in, is what happens when you get home and spend the summer here, and decide to stay and teach here at Encinal, or to stay here at the ranch, then what? Do I get to see you? Or, do I have to stay outside the perimeter while you stay within the yard?

"We have to decide if we go on loving each other, or do we stop because it is impossible for us to see each other, because you are the daughter of the patron, and I am just a mojado? These questions have to be answered. I do not feel right hiding behind this tractor right now. If I want to talk with you, I want to be out in the open or not at all. What are we going to do Mariquita?" Chon pleaded.

Mari Liz was in tears. She sobbed. She could not talk.

"Please do not cry anymore. If anyone sees you they are going to think that I hurt you. Please do not cry," Chon pleaded.

Mari Liz quieted down.

"Encarnación, I do not want to lose you. I do not want us to stop seeing each other. I know that you feel bad about us not being able to see each other and talk with each other, but I do not want to stop loving you."

It was quiet for a long time. Only Mari Liz's quiet sobs could be heard. Chon held her two hands in his.

"Encarnación?" She stopped abruptly. "I think I might have been a fool. Do you even love me? I do not think that I have even heard you say anything about loving me."

Mari Liz was speaking loudly and seriously, and defensively.

"Mariquita how could you even ask? Let me tell you that I have never loved anyone the way I love you. The only thing that I can think of is being with you for the rest of my life, and your life too," he added clumsily.

"Well then fine. That settles it, we have to talk to father so he will give us permission to talk to each other and see each other," she said in a stern voice.

"But, no, he will probably be mad, won't he? He will hate me for wanting you and loving you. He will run me off of the ranch. Won't he?" Chon seemed frightened.

"Well if he's going to react that way, we might as well find out now. And who knows he may react well enough. In any event, if we do not ask we will never know, and if we do not ask we will never be able to talk to each other in public," Mari Liz emphasized.

"Well what do we do? What is the next step?" Chon implored.

"The next step is wait, wait, and wait. I need time and I am the one to talk to my father first. I have to talk to him at the right time and explain matters slowly, and make sure he understands. If I do not give him time, I will get a quick 'no, absolutely not, and stop and leave me alone' type of an answer. I must do it with plenty of time. I am leaving in two days and when I get back to school I will have plenty of time to figure out and make a plan. Yes, that will work just fine. Good bye, amor. I am so excited. We are going to make it," Mari Liz reached over and for the second time in their lives kissed Chon full on the mouth, with all the excitement and passion that she could muster. She broke and ran toward the house. Chon watched the thin young girl giggle off to talk with her mother. He was floating on a cloud of some sort. He was happy.

On Holy Saturday, Don Ramón took Chon to the Easter Vigil and, as usual, the Salinas family sat together. Chon stared at Mari Liz the whole time. After the services, Don Ramón and Chon returned to the ranch. On Easter Sunday, the Salinas family had an Easter picnic within the confines of the large back yard of the big house. No outsider was invited, not even Don Ramón. It was strictly family.

Mari Liz was to leave for college that Tuesday morning. On Monday she picked an opportune time to speak to her mother. The madama and her daughter were very close. She raised her daughter to be independent, to be a thinker, to be innovative. Mari Liz knew that if she were to have an ally in getting relief, she must convince her mother first.

"Mother, could we speak for a few minutes. I have something very important to tell you and to discuss with you. I have many questions."

"Why of course, hijita, I can always make time to talk with you. I am always at your side. What is it?" The mother asked.

The pair sat on the huge bed in the master bedroom. Mari Liz checked and she knew that her father was out in the field, and would not be around to interrupt such a delicate conversation.

"Well for starters, I am in love," she said and paused.

"Then to complicate matters my heart's desire is Encarnación, the worker. We are both very frustrated at not being able to see each other and talk to each other. Now, I know that it is very improper for me to be courted by one of the workers. I guess what I am asking is for you to help me with father and to change family and social customs. I want to be courted by the worker. We are in love. And no matter that Chon is a worker, you have to admit that he is very different. He is intelligent, he has excellent manners, it is quite apparent that he is highly educated. I am in love with the man, and I want an opportunity to get to know him better. Is that so horrible?" Mari Liz asked her mother and nervously waited for her reply.

"Well I must say. I would be lying to you if I told you I am surprised at your news," the mother sat down abruptly, and held her hand. "Although thinking back I can see now that you have been spending a lot of time in Chon's presence. Are you sure this is not just an infatuation, something that will go away by the time you graduate? Should we not wait for this matter before having to make such a drastic decision? Particularly shouldn't we wait before telling your father? Why upset him if it is something that will pass?" Dona María asked with sad, pleading eyes.

"Well, I tend to agree with you about being too hasty. If it is an infatuation then you are right, but if it is not an infatuation, and when I get back after graduation in May, I want to know if you and father are going to approve of the courtship or not," Mari Liz pleaded.

"Well I understand what you are asking, and I will do what I can to help you, but I cannot promise what your father will do. For example, let me ask you how long have you known him? Where is he from? What about his parents? What type of an upbringing did he get? Is he a good Catholic? Is he married? Does he have children? These are very important questions that you need to understand, and importantly, you need to be satisfied with the answers. Your father, I am sure will want satisfactory answers also, that is, assuming that he will agree to the courtship, which, Mari Liz, is going to be a very hard proposition. I cannot predict what his reaction is going to be. You are his only daughter. I just do not know."

"Mother, I don't know all the answers, but I do know that a long courtship will help me get these answers, and if the answers are not right, then things can be called off. It is not as if I am a fourteen-year-old girl wanting to run off and get married. I am twenty-two-years old, and I definitely do not want to act like a little girl about all this and run off and get married. For your information mother, I have always been truthful with you, I am still a virgin and I intend to be one on my wedding day. I think that I am being very level headed about this entire thing and I need your help."

Mamalu looked at Mari Liz straight in the eye, paused then grabbed her and hugged her.

"Mari Liz I am very proud of the woman you have grown to be. I am very proud. I am pleased at the way that you want to handle this matter. I will do what I can. You must realize that there are problems that could come up. Your father must approve everything that goes on in this house. In olden times, he would probably send you off to visit for a year or two with one of his brothers or cousins. But your father has always been a very intelligent, pragmatic, and logical person. He is not a person to let social dictates control life. But we just have to wait and see. I cannot predict what he will say nor how he will react. I respect your wishes and I will do what I can to help you. I am happy for you. I know of course what it is to be in love. I am happy for you."

Mari Liz left the room, and Doña María Luisa laid back on the bed thinking. "It will be the shock of the whole county. María Elizabeth Salinas in love with one of the wetbacks. Makes no difference, he is more intelligent, well-mannered, and better educated than the richest, nicest boy she has ever dated."

She chuckled.

"Boy this is going to set the county on its ear."

She giggled.

* * *

Chon immersed himself in his work. It was the easiest way to keep from thinking of Mari Liz. Of course, it was impossible. He dreamed about his love for her, awake and asleep.

The crops were planted and the irrigation had begun. There were about fifty men working the fields, and ten working the cattle. They sat out at night around the huge campfire in the usual custom and told stories. They rose early and worked long, hard hours. Due to the manner in which they were treated by Don

Juan, everyone gave his total commitment. He had experimented on ways to get the most out of his workers and it worked.

On a Saturday morning, Chon was helping the field hands transfer irrigation from one field to another. It was about eleven in the morning and suddenly three green jeeps came onto the field. It was the Immigration and Naturalization Service.

In early years of the Border Patrol, the locals called them Rangers, which ultimately was translated to Rinches. So it was the Rinches that were on the way. Chon looked around and all the hands were running toward the brush land about a mile away. It was a long run, but they did not want to be captured and deported to México. It was a difficult race against a six cylinder motor vehicle.

Chon watched as his crews ran and the jeeps continued to approach him. He felt for his wallet. He carried the deputy card that Sheriff Santos gave him, and never forgot it. He knew that it had special magic, but he also knew that notwithstanding the little card, he was an illegal alien as defined by the American laws, and worse he was a foreign soldier whose country that was at war with the United States. The three vehicles arrived simultaneously. He recognized one of the six officers as Smith, the one that Señor García greeted on the highway last deer season.

"Good morning how are you?" One of the border patrolmen greeted.

"Just fine thank you, what can I do for you?" Chon replied in his best broken English.

"Are you the boss of these people?"

"Well yes, I guess you could say that," Chon replied.

"Well let me tell you why we are here. Ordinarily we would have rounded up all of your helpers and taken them away, and shipped them back to México. You understand?" The officer asked.

"Yes of course, I understand," Chon said.

"Well today we only have a message to deliver. Our Department of War has told us to back off on you fellas and leave you alone. You see we are at war with the Germans and the Italians and with the gooks in the Pacific," the rinche said, to which Chon tightened.

"Well this terrible war is taking a lot of our effort, and it takes a lot of food to feed all them soldiers of ours, and that includes the vegetables and animals that you fellas grow and raise," the officer continued.

"If we keep picking up all you wetbacks, then nobody is going to pick all these crops and our boys are going to go hungry and we ain't gonna be able to beat them Jerrys, Japs, and Wops. So anyway I am here to tell you that we are not gonna be bothering you anymore for the duration of the war, as long as you fellas keep on growing vegetables and raising that beef. After we leave you can tell all your Panchos out there that we don't want them today, but that we'll come and get them after the war is over."

The officer laughed.

The six men mounted their jeeps and were off to another farm. Chon stood in the middle of the field. Slowly all the others drifted back. None had reached cover.

That night the topic was la Migra and the close call they had that morning. Chon explained to them that there would be no pressure as long as the war was on. Some did not believe it, they were suspicious and skeptical.

The talk shifted to the ugly discrimination that some experienced in the cities of South Texas.

"There is much hatred for Mexicans in this part of the country. I worked in a factory in Laredo for two years," Victor explained. "I got to where I walked around the town without any problem with the Migra, until I finally got caught and kicked out to México. But before I got caught we used to go to the theater every Saturday, and they would not let us sit on the ground floor, we had to sit upstairs in the balcony. Only the Gringos were allowed to sit on the main floor. Of course if I were a gringo,

I would not want to sit on the main floor, because we used to spit down throughout the entire movie."

The crowd of m+en roared with laughter.

Again, Chon had been generally briefed on the problem, but had not heard specifics. Victor continued, "And after we got through with the movie, we would try to find a restaurant in the gringo part of town. Forget it. One time we walked in, and sat down, and waited to be served. We waited a long time, and the waitress would not come, and would not come. We would not leave, then finally, she approached and advised that they did not serve Mexicans in that particular restaurant, that if we wanted to eat perhaps we could go around the back and make a deal with the cook. Hearing that they did not serve Mexicans, my friend could not resist and told the waitress that we did not want to eat a Mexican, all we wanted was a sandwich."

Again the crowd roared with laughter.

Most shook their head at the stories not wanting to believe them. Chon also shook his head, but he did not laugh. He had never heard the details of racial prejudice and discrimination and he was just starting to grasp it. Chon wondered how a Japanese would be treated in Laredo, Texas right about this time. He was sure he would be strung up from the highest mesquite tree, if detected.

*＊＊

Doña María Luisa waited for the best moment to talk with her husband. On this morning, she waited until he opened his mail and reviewed the huge check that he received from the produce brokers for the winter's carrot, broccoli, and cabbage crops. He was in a very good mood.

She saw the opportunity and did not mince her words and got to the point immediately. She told her husband of her meeting with their daughter. Don Juan sat quietly at his desk, absorbing every word, every thought.

"I guess we both knew we would have this talk one day. I just never imagined that it would pose a problem," he said shaking his head. "Mariquita, she has been such a joy, but she never makes things easy does she?"

He continued to shake his head. Don Juan paused for a long moment.

"Well, this is going to require much thought, my dear. Right now I just don't even know what to say," Don Juan sighed.

"You have to admit that she is approaching it very intelligently and maturely. She could have run off you know. It's been known to happen," Dona María Luisa pointed out.

"Oh yes, oh yes, she is handling it perfect so far. No one ever accused Mariquita of being stupid. We have a fine woman there Mamalu, I am very proud of her in everything she has done. But this here, well this is a very delicate situation. This is going to require much thought.

"I don't want her hurt. I don't want her life ruined. I am going to need your help on this matter. For the time being let me just think and catch my breath. We will discuss this again. Even if she does it right, and maturely, she could still be picking the wrong guy."

Doña María Luisa walked over to the desk, and kissed Don Juan on the head. He turned up to look at her and they pecked each other on the lips and Doña María Luisa turned to leave the spacious office.

As she approached the door, he called out to her.

"María Luisa, thank you for talking to me about this. And I'm afraid I haven't told you in a long time, but I love you dearly."

"I love you too my dear," Doña María Luisa answered.

Throughout the next few weeks, Don Juan and Doña María Luisa spoke frequently of the situation, posing alternatives to each other, posing possibilities. Each day Don Juan caught himself examining Chon closer and closer. Was this the young man that would be his son-in-law?

Try as he might, he could not find fault with him. He was a fine man. Intelligent, well mannered, and well educated. But where was he from? Who were his parents? Don Juan asked Don Ramón to find out more about the young man, but there was not much to be found. Chon noticed that Don Juan was often scrutinizing him carefully. He imagined that Mari Liz had begun the process, but she did not tell him, so he could not be sure.

Mari Liz arrived from college in late May. The word spread throughout Rancho Salinas that she had graduated, obtained her teaching degree and certificate, and would come to live on the ranch and teach first grade at the public school in Encinal.

Chon did not see her when she arrived. He rose at four in the morning and was out in the fields by five-thirty, moving crews, starting or finishing projects. By that hour the sun peeked through and work could start. The crews preferred to work in the cool of the predawn hours. At four o'clock in the afternoon most of the crews came in for the day. Sometimes there were irrigating crews that worked through the night, but most were in camp by six o'clock in the afternoon.

Chon came in at five that afternoon. He showered in the community shower, then went to the camp kitchen to listen to the radio, and eat supper. He heard the evening news about the war in the Pacific. Most of his fellow workers did not understand why he moved the radio tuner from good polka music to news.

After eating his supper, he heard the cooks talking about Mari Liz. Suddenly he was not tired anymore. He did not want to stay in the kitchen, nor did he want to go to the community campfire. He wanted to see Mariquita, but of course that was not going to be easy. He gulped down the last of his coffee, and walked outside.

It was cool and breezy. He noticed that the men were already gathered for the nightly bull session. The fire was burning. He opted for the shed where one of the big tractors was parked. He pretended to examine the vehicle. He looked toward the big house. It was totally illuminated. He strained for a closer look of people inside the structure, but he could see none. He sat on a small barrel of lubricant.

He wanted to see Mari Liz more than anything in the whole world. She did not come out. He thought of Japan, his mother, Akechi san, Sebastian. How was this romance going to affect his future and his ability to remain undetected? He waited. Time passed. On the west side of the sheds Don Ramón and one of his sons were working on another tractor. He could hear them talk, analyzing the problem and taking steps to correct it. After about thirty minutes, Don Ramón noticed Chon but continued working. After they finished, Don Ramón walked over to Chon and greeted him. He explained that the tractor was repaired.

"We are leaving now Chon, we will see you in the morning."

Don Ramón placed his hand on Chon's left shoulder.

"Chon, I guarantee you that it will work out well. It may not be what you want, but it will work out all right in the end. Good night," he said with a wink.

He bade Don Ramón good night. He sat on the barrel for another hour. By this time the workers began to leave for their bungalows. One thing about getting up early and working hard, there was no worry about the workers staying up late and making noise.

Chon rose and went to bed. Tonio came in a little later, and they chatted for a brief moment. In minutes they were both asleep.

Chapter Twenty One

In the predawn hours, Chon worked feverishly to get off all the tractors and people. He pushed at the kitchen to hurry with breakfast and the sack lunches the men carried out to the fields. He pushed the crew leaders to hurry the men on. Chon knew that he would not be able to see Mari Liz at this hour of the day, so he was not distracted. He left word at the kitchen that if he were needed he would be helping with cattle at the north brush pasture. He informed Don Ramón of his whereabouts. He would return at mid afternoon.

Mari Liz had waited more than two months for this day. She knew that her father would have a decision one way or another. His greeting the night before had been lovable and pleasant, as usual. There was no indication of his feeling on the courting situation. They dined quietly together. She would be returning to the college campus in a week for commencement exercises, and Don Juan and Doña María Luisa would accompany her.

Talk at the table covered many subjects, but there was no mention of the courtship. She realized that her father was not mixing pleasure with business. He would leave the discussion for a more appropriate, serious moment. When? She wanted to ask right then, but she could not bring herself to do it.

She set her alarm for five o'clock. Her father was an early riser, and if she did not get up early she would miss him for the entire day. She wanted to have breakfast with him in hopes that he would address the situation then. The breakfast table was in the kitchen, and was set simply. Don Juan sat at the head of the table and read from a newspaper. Doña María Luisa helped Elvira at the stove. Mari Liz made her entrance and surprised everyone.

"Why are you down so early, Sweet? You should stay in bed and rest. You must be tired after all your final exam studying. Go on back to bed hijita," Mamalu sympathized.

"Well, I could not sleep. And it's beautiful weather outside. It looks like it might rain, and it's cool, so I wanted to be a part of such a beautiful morning. Besides I haven't seen you both in months and I want to see you again, and chat, I missed you," Mari Liz replied.

"Well come and sit princess, I haven't had breakfast with you since I can't remember when," Don Juan said, motioning her to sit.

There was a brief moment of quiet. Don Juan knew exactly why she was up so early. She wanted a quick answer to her questions. He couldn't blame her. Oftentimes he felt the same way with his lawyers and bankers, a quick answer so plans can be carried out or changed as necessary. He got to the point.

"Mari Liz, your mother and I have spoken many times since you left after Easter on the matter of you and Encarnación and the courtship you are requesting. We don't have all the answers.

"You must understand that my primary objective in this matter is to be sure, as much as possible, that you are not hurt. It is hard enough when one marries one of his or her own social class or standing, and one that the family has known for decades. Even these matches don't work out sometimes. In this case it is something entirely opposite. We do not know the young man very well, he is not of our class or standing, and we do not even know his family," Don Juan spoke clearly in a low voice.

"Suppose" he continued, "that he is of a bad moral character, suppose that similarly his family is worthless. How is all of this going to affect you?" Don Juan asked Mari Liz, who simply stared at her father with big shiny brown eyes. She admired and respected him, and the questions made sense. She said nothing. There was quiet for a spell.

"I am not really concerned about the social class and standing issues, about not wanting you to 'marry beneath your class', I believe is the phrase. We are not snobs. The Salinas family has intermarried with the Mexican Indian for the last three centuries, so that is not what I am talking about. What I am talking about is his or your ability or inability to adjust to each other because of the social differences. That is what I mean. And if you cannot adjust, then who gets hurt? My Mariquita, that's who, and that's what I don't want," Don Juan reasoned.

"The other areas, I don't think I have to explain. If he is a criminal on the run, or if he is a bad apple, it's clear what my concern would be," he said.

More quiet. No one spoke.

"If I were my father, I would send you to México City for two or three years, or as long as it took to let you get over this fellow. Or better yet, I would call the Immigration, La Migra, los Rinches, and maybe they would take care of my problem. But knowing Chon, he would be here in twenty four hours," everyone giggled at this observation from Don Juan.

"But, I am not my father. I have a different outlook on life. I sent you to get an education because of that different outlook. Were I like my father, you would have been crocheting doilies for the last five years."

Another pause and no sound.

"My dear, under the most restrictive of conditions, and I repeat, the most restrictive of conditions, I consent to the courtship. Now go get Chon, I want to talk to both of you together."

Mari Liz let out a yelp, and cried for joy. She rushed over and kissed and hugged her father. She kissed her mother as she ran out of the room. Don Juan and Doña María Luisa looked at each other seriously, hoping they had made the right decision.

Mari Liz ran through the house screaming and yelping, she ran through the kitchen, and the cooks, thinking she was hurt, followed her out to the backyard. She continued, ran past the yard perimeter, and to the barns, yelling Chon's name in a loud shrill. She went to the camp kitchen, and there he was sitting drinking a cup of coffee. His pants were tucked into the inside of his cowboy boots, and he wore a small cowboy felt hat, hand formed to a point at the front and at the back. Sweat had permeated the hat band, and a dark gold mud formed along the hat band. She noticed, and she liked it. Quite a rugged cowboy I've got me here, she thought.

"Come quick, Chon, come quick," she was screaming and jumping up and down. "Come, father wants to talk to both of us together. Come quick, come quick, before he changes his mind. Come quick, come quick, come quick."

She was tugging at his left hand as he raised himself from the table. Chon started out the door, she behind him. She turned quickly and announced the news to the occupants of the camp kitchen.

"Father has approved our courtship," she yelled over her shoulder as she followed Chon out the door.

The people in the camp kitchen looked at each other in wonderment. Then it sunk in, and they grinned and chuckled.

Chon and Mari Liz walked side-by-side toward the big house. Mari Liz's hand holding Chon's arm, escort fashion. Chon liked the feel of her hand on his arm, and responded by bending his arm at the elbow and escorting the young lady into her house.

The couple walked through the kitchen, and met with instant hostility in the form of the cook Elvira. It was one thing to allow the help to come into the kitchen and eat. That fact she had gotten used to, especially with the young foreman who had such fine manners, and seemed to be so well educated, but another thing was to allow the cock into the house to court the house princess. The maid was incensed.

"Cabron, igualado, you belong out in the barn, not in here with my darling little princess. Just who do you think you are, social climber!" Elvira said in a firm rough voice. Chon was shocked at the reception.

"Don't pay attention to her, go along, go along," Mari Liz pushed Chon on through the house toward her father's office. The couple entered, and Don Juan and Doña María Luisa sat dead serious.

"Please come in and sit down Encarnación," Don Juan invited to sit in a chair in front of his desk.

"We have a very serious situation here Encarnación, one that my wife and I do not take lightly. Our daughter has told us that you are in love with each other. Naturally, we are not displeased about that. We are worried that she might get hurt, or simply that it would not work out between you, and both of you will be hurt or scarred. We do not know much about you, we do not know anything about your family. You come from different parts of the world, you have different customs," Don Juan explained, not knowing how true his words really were.

"It would be easy for us to send Mariquita off with some relative and banish you from the ranch, or otherwise ask you to leave. But we respect both of your wishes, your desires, and have taken an open attitude to the situation. Starting today, you are permitted to see Mari Liz; it is the beginning of a formal courtship. It can be terminated only by either of you at will," Don Juan explained the rules of the courtship.

Chon and Mari Liz looked at each other's eyes with joy.

"But I do not want this decision misinterpreted. You are not married, and I do not want you to be acting like you are married. I want to see you both in the open at all times. She is not permitted in your house at any time," Don Juan said firmly. "I demand respect at all times. Visiting at night will be in prominently lit places in this house or around it. You are invited, and encouraged to join us for evening meals. Mamalu and I too need to get to know you better."

"Please follow my conditions; do not make me angry. Do not make me change my mind. Above all and finally, Encarnación, you are expected to continue your duties with your usual energies. Your courtship of my daughter does not guarantee your job. You can still get fired if you do not perform. How you court without a job is your business and another matter. Keep working hard. That is all for now. You may both go now," Don Juan concluded.

Chon approached the desk, and bowed deeply in Japanese fashion, and reached to shake Don Juan's hand.

"Don Juan, I assure you that you will not be disappointed in my behavior. I promise to be a total and complete gentleman at all times. Do not fear about my job. I will work doubly hard in appreciation of your trust. I promise," Chon bowed deeply again and turned and walked out of the office. Mari Liz stood behind. She blew kisses at both her parents, and whispered, "I love you," to both as she left the room following her true love.

Chon and Mari Liz walked out and went to the camp kitchen. She was holding his hand, pulling him by the hand actually. He felt embarrassed as she held his hand. They walked into the camp kitchen. She walked to the back of the kitchen and served two cups of coffee. She brought the cups out to the table area, and they sat and had their first conversation as novios.

They made a handsome couple. She was beautiful, he was feo, fuerte y formal. Both were around the same age, and both very much in love. Chon caught much ribbing from the workers in the next few weeks. In fact, everyday a comment was made on the romance. This led to much embarrassment, but he said nothing, hoping that they would leave him alone. Eventually, they did.

It became usual for Chon and Mari Liz to be seen in the evenings on the fully lit back porch, of course, or walking around holding hands during the daytime, when Chon was not working, such as Sundays, and sometimes Saturday afternoons. For a change of pace, Chon took Mari Liz to the camp kitchen, where they enjoyed coffee and something to eat.

He kept his vow to Don Juan. He was working doubly hard now to prove his appreciation of trust. Everyday Chon came in from the fields or from the brush, and rushed out to the community showers, then back to his cabin to change. He then rushed off to join Mari Liz for supper. Sometimes he came so late that only he and Mari Liz ate at the kitchen table, under the watchful eye of the late hour maids. Most of the time, however, he ate with Don Juan, Doña María Luisa and Mari Liz.

Don Juan took the evening meals as an opportunity to interrogate Chon to the fullest. After all he did not know very much about this young hard hombre from San Blas, and he had to try to find out everything he could before he was faced with the more important decisions of the future. The only treat Don Juan got was to become more and more exposed to the tremendous knowledge and intelligence the young man possessed.

Chon ,however, began to tell Mari Liz his true life story.

"Mariquita you know that I came here like the wind, suddenly and full of dirt. I had to walk almost one thousand miles to get here. I have told you about my family in San Blas. I have told you all about my past in México. Now I will tell you the truth."

Chon paused to regain his composure.

"Don't you dare tell me that you are married, Encarnación, or I will kill you with a double barreled shotgun, and then when you are dead, I will kill you again," Mari Liz screamed.

"No, no," Chon chuckled and giggled, "I am not married, and if you kill me once how can you kill me again? No, what I have to tell you is very important. I do not even know where to begin. When I get through you may even be afraid of me, you may even feel like talking to your Dad about me, you may even feel like calling the Rinches, really."

"Chon, nothing that you could say or do will ever change my mind about loving you and being your wife," Mari Liz said.

"That is easy to say with the Encarnación, the Chon that you know, but what about the other, el otro Chon, that you do not know? Are you going to throw me away?" Chon asked her, with a look of exasperation.

"Well get on with it Mr. Monster, what is it that I should know about you," Mari Liz chided.

"Well, before I get started I want two agreements from you. The first is that you will not tell anyone about what I am going to tell you. If it is true that you love me, then at least you will allow me some secrecy in the things that I must tell you. The other agreement is that you will allow me to finish what I am telling you. The first part may seem horrible, but if you let me finish then it may not be so bad. Are we agreed?" Chon asked her.

"We are agreed," Mari Liz answered.

"Well the first thing I must tell you is that my name is not Encarnación Gutiérrez Ayala, it is Tasaka Chon, and I am a lieutenant in the Japanese Navy, the Intelligence Service, to be specific. How's that for starters," Chon declared.

"Nah, nah, I don't believe you," Mari Liz came back. "Go on, go on."

For the next two hours Chon and Mari Liz walked up and down the lanes between the growing crops. He explaining his life history, and she listened with mouth open.

Occasionally Don Juan would peer out over the green vegetation, and spot the couple. "Poor devil," he thought, "it must be hard to just look at the girl and not be able to touch her. Although I am sure he gets in a good kiss and feel on occasion."

By eleven-thirty Chon persuaded Mari Liz to walk in for lunch at the camp kitchen. She had heard the story of a lifetime already but he wasn't finished, and she had agreed that she would not say much until the entire story was over. Still she was distant. She tried not to be, but she was. At the camp kitchen he kept on with the story in a low voice, not wanting anyone to hear him. He whispered at times. Mari Liz simply listened, and committed things to memory. After coffee, they walked again to the fields. Chon kept talking.

"Something that you need to understand is that if I had my wishes, I would have never joined the military, and I would be growing crops on the Tokyo Plantation instead of Rancho Salinas. There is nothing that I have against the U.S. nation or its people.

"Whatever the Emperor or the generals feel against your country, I know nothing of. Mine is a feeling for people. What I want is for you and your family is to be safe, and for my family in Japan to be safe. I do not care which country defeats the other, all I want is for all of us to live happily as long as God permits.

"I rejected my country when I refused to kill myself, and if I am taken back to Japan I will be killed. By the same token if you or your father or anyone reports me to the authorities here in the United States, they will probably execute me for being a spy, which I guess would be justified, as I did find out many facts on México and report them back to the mother country. But I never hurt anyone directly. I have not killed anyone, and I hope that I will never ever have to kill anyone. That's my story, am I condemned to death?" Chon asked her plaintively.

Mari Liz did not say anything for a very long moment. The couple kept walking. Tears formed in her eyes.

"Chon, I have heard your life story, and I must say you have surprised me completely. Your disguise has been perfect. I will say to you that I love you now just as I did yesterday. What I do not know now is if I want to spend the rest of my life with you. Why should your story change anything?

"It should not change anything, love is love, and as the priest says for better or for worse, but you caught me off guard, and I have to think now on whether I want to continue to love you, or try to make myself stop loving you or learn to not love you, or, as they say in the novelas fall out of love with you," she giggled as she finished the sentence.

"Well, I certainly would not fault you for deciding against me, the only thing I beg of you is do not denounce me to the authorities. I mean no harm to anyone, and I do not want to be executed. Also, if I had to, I could move along and be a wetback, a laborer on farms, for the rest of my life, which is really the life I had committed myself to. All this can be done without harming anyone. So if you want me to move on I will. Please do not execute me," Chon pleaded.

The story was still sinking in with Mari Liz. She looked and felt hurt. "Why hadn't you told me earlier," she asked.

"If I had told you earlier, we would have never been able to fall in love. No, let me say that differently. You, yes, you, would have never fallen in love with me. You would have never given me the chance of letting me be myself, and your watching, which is what allowed you to fall in love with me, and besides you would have turned me in. Right? You would have turned me in, right?" Chon asked.

Mari Liz giggled, acknowledging that he was probably right. She would have, she thought.

"Chon, let me ask you now, if my father could get you on a plane to Japan and you would be in Tokyo Plantation tomorrow would you leave?" She laid a trap.

"Of course not, and leave you here, never. I do not want to be without you, and I do not care about Tokyo Plantation enough to leave you," he answered.

"Well, Chon, I must think now. I am very confused, and I am very hurt. I feel like you have played me for the fool," Mari Liz started crying. "I want to go home now, and I want to think. So please let me go, and I will see you tomorrow."

She continued to cry. She hurried off to the big house. Chon remained on the sidewalk by the screen door, and turned and walked to his house.

He opened the screen door to the cabin. Tonio was inside laying on his bed listening to the radio. The announcer on the set was talking about the hard battles in the Pacific that the Americans were winning.

"The Americanos they are beating the hell out of them Japos," Tonio yelled. "What do you think Chon?"

"Oh Tonio, I don't feel good, and I don't like war, so don't even ask me. All I want to do is rest," Chon buried his face into the pillow.

"Ah, I know you have little fight with the Mariquita. I bet thas wha happen, right?" Tonio pried.

"Oh Tonio, just be quiet and let me sleep."

Chon laid back and tried to think the day out in his mind. "Did he handle it wrong?" He thought to himself. "What else could I have done?" He thought. "It would not be fair to not say anything to her," he thought. "Oh hell, I really don't care, if I had to, I would shove off and go to another ranch."

It was one o'clock in the morning and Chon was sound asleep. Tonio laid asleep in the next bunk. The screen door squeaked open. Chon was awake immediately. His muscles tightened. He did not let on that he was awake. He was trained to lay in bed as if asleep, but to prepare to attack and kill if necessary. An Intelligence Service man had never been killed in his sleep. He would not be the first. Was it the Migra or the FBI? Mariquita couldn't stand it. She had to return to me, I bet.

Chon listened in an attempt to analyze the situation in the room. Should he run out the back door? That would be the first place they covered. He could not hear very much. He knew that he was going to have to burst in attack in just a few seconds if he could not analyze the presence.

He felt the weight alight on his bed. He could smell her. It was Mariquita. He turned quickly, and there she sat crying and smiling looking at him.

"How could I not love you," she whispered, "how could I doubt my love for you."

She cried, tears flowing down her cheeks.

"Chon, Encarnación, I love you like you cannot imagine, and I will love you for the rest of my life," she grabbed his hand and kissed it repeatedly. "You old mean Japanese samurai, or Lord, or executioner, or admiral, or Shōgun whatever you are, I love you, and I always will."

She kept crying and sobbing.

Chon did not respond. He waited for her to stop crying. After a while, he felt her body next to his, and he thought he would hug her and bring her to bed with him. He reached over to get her and she moved away.

"No way, no way, Encarnación, you know the rules, the rules that my father laid down, no fooling around until we are married. Now you stay there in bed, I am going to stay here as long as I can, but you stay right there in bed and I am not going to get into bed with you," she whispered gradually and slowly, and very quietly, she did not want to wake Tonio.

"Now that we have the ground rules established, I have a very important question. Let us just say that I did agree to marry you even if you are a Japanese spy, or officer, or samurai, or whatever you say that you are or are not, then how am I able to marry you if I am a Christian, a Catholic? Do you pray to Buddha, or to Shinto or whatever it is you do? Are you going to go up to the altar and lie just like they taught you. Will you say that yes you are a Christian, and you agree to abide by the Commandments? What are you going to do then?" She asked him, and waited for an answer.

Chon pawed at her playfully as if to bring her to bed and lay her down.

"No, no, Señor Encarnación, you must answer the important questions, what are you going to do about Christianity? You need to tell me," she demanded.

"That will have to wait until tomorrow, because that is a very long story also. Unless you want to wake Tonio, and go wake your father also so he can shoot both of us," Chon replied.

"Well, all right, but I want to know about your Buddha or Shinto or whatever it is you pray to. Your other activities I can tolerate. Tomorrow we talk," she whispered loudly and ran out the screen door.

Tonio jumped up at the sound. "Uhhh, who, who, what, wha, wha, wha, gives, Chon what?" Tonio was groggy and not quite awake.

"Go back to sleep Tonio. Nothing gives, the wind opened the screen door and it slammed," he lied to him.

"Oh, Oh, Oh, gnite," Tonio murmured and was out again.

Chon laid in the bed and smiled. He prayed. He dozed off to a deep sleep.

Chapter Twenty Two

It was Sunday, and Doña María Luisa and Don Juan hurried around the big house getting ready for nine o'clock Mass. Don Juan hated to be late. Doña María Luisa could not have cared less, but she hated to see Don Juan get upset about being late, so she hurried.

Don Juan noticed that Mari Liz was sitting at the kitchen table ready and groomed. He paused momentarily and looked at her. She wore a simple pink cotton dress and looked radiant and absolutely beautiful. He was proud.

The three walked into the church and sat at their usual pew about half way in on the right side of the church. They said their preliminary prayers before the Mass began.

After Mass started, Mari Liz casually glanced over to the left side of the church, and there in all his splendor, stood Chon praying the Mass with Don Ramón.

"How can this samurai, son of a samurai, lord, chief spy, whatever he is, dare come in here and pray the Mass. I will tell him about this when I see him back at the ranch," she thought.

After lunch the couple began their usual Sunday afternoon walk through the fields near the big house.

"That was very brave of you to come to my house last night, Mari Liz. Weren't you afraid of being caught?" Chon asked.

"Of course I was afraid of being caught, but I just had to see you. I sneaked out once before when I was in high school. I just had to go to a party, so I sneaked out for two hours. No one ever knew. Anyway are you trying to change the subject, don't

you remember we have something to discuss today?" Mari Liz
fired back.

"How could I forget, and I am not trying to change the subject. Let me begin," Chon reached over and held her hand as
they kept walking.

"When Akechi san brought Sebastian Gutiérrez Ayala to
Tokyo Plantation he let him use a three-room bungalow that
stood inside the yard adjacent to the big house. In fact the big
house was very similar to the big house here, and the yard around
it, except that there in a corner of the yard stood this small house,
a mother-in-law house if you would.

"Every day he would teach me in an open area called the tea
garden just in front of the bungalow. When we were done with
our lessons, he would always take an extra hour to finish the
tutoring of the day. For this instruction we would go inside of
the bungalow.

"The instruction was totally and completely secret. Nobody
at Tokyo Plantation ever knew what he would teach me in
private. There were many suspicions about the private lessons,
and quickly everyone assumed homosexual activity. Since the
instruction was secret and I gave Don Sebastian my word that
I would not divulge its subject matter, no one heard any different from me. I think the one it hurt the most was my mother.
She could not understand any part of the special tutoring, and
the extra session commonly called the 'black hour' by everyone
at the plantation, was especially perplexing to her. She would
become very angry with me when I would not tell her what I
was learning. She threatened several times to go to Akechi san
and expose the 'black hour' but never got up the courage.

"Anyway, Mari Liz, to the question at hand, you will be glad
to hear that during the 'black hour', for three years, almost every
day, I was instructed in the Catholic religion. I know all the
prayers, I know the Commandments, the beatitudes, the sac-
raments, the explanations of the mysteries of the Trinity, the

Immaculate Conception, the consecration of the bread and wine, and all of the others.

"Remember I told you that Sebastian almost took his final vows as a Jesuit priest. He even told me of the Jesuit martyrs like St. Paul Miki and his companions who preached the Gospel to the Japanese people with great success, but when persecution against Catholics became oppressive, he was arrested along with twenty-five others. After enduring torment and derision they were finally taken to Nagasaki and, like Jesus, were crucified.

"Sebastian was not about to let me go without making me a Christian. He baptized me, but said that he could not confirm me, nor could he consecrate bread and wine. He taught me to make a good confession, and in short he taught me everything I need to know to become a good Catholic. I bet you I even know more about the Catholic religion that you do," Chon chided Mari Liz.

"Well, but can you marry in the Catholic Church, or is there something that we need to do?" Mari Liz asked.

"No, I am not quite ready yet. We must talk to Msgr. Dan, when the time gets near, and he must confirm me, and give me other final instructions in converting to the Catholic religion. So you see, Mariquita that part of it has also been taken care of. There are no obstacles except fear and reluctance," he smiled at her.

He piqued her curiosity and now she wanted to know more about his past.

"Tell me about your mother, Akechi san, and Sebastian, tell me more. I must know."

He continued with his story throughout the afternoon. They finished in front of the sheds with him sitting on a low bent tree branch and she on a box. He could not tell a lifetime in one afternoon.

Everyday thereafter he filled in his past a little more. She was fascinated. She reciprocated with her history and they fell deeper and deeper in love.

* * *

Sunday, October 24, 1945, was the wedding day. Mariquita told him two days earlier that it was bad luck for them to see each other on their wedding day. Chon sat in the camp kitchen with Sergio, Guillermo, Tonio, Don Ramón, and a few of the other young men from the camp. They sat around and listened to the radio, football games primarily, and joked and chatted and sipped beer and whiskey.

The wedding would be at seven thirty in the evening at the Immaculate Heart of Mary Catholic Church in Encinal. Afterward, the reception would be in the family garden at the big house. For weeks, Mari Liz and her mother made the plans. Engraved invitations were mailed to their friends throughout all of South Texas. Clearly, the Salinas were not troubled by the wetback issue.

Chon found it better to work hard and submerge himself in his duties so as to not worry about the details.

Sergio came in three days early from medical school. He was proud of having the slugger as his brother-in-law. Chon's refinement made it easy to like the man.

At six o'clock Señor García and his wife arrived to get Chon and take him to the church. They were early, but it was better to be early than to be late. Chon had purchased a small thin gold band, a his and her set, that he gave to Señor García.

Chon looked very dapper. A very handsome, tall, strong, young man. The perfect cowboy in fine clothes. No jeans, no red bugger, but a very well-dressed cowboy off to get his bride.

Chon stood at the foot of the altar waiting for the bride to be led down the aisle by her father. He had not seen her all day. He waited anxiously.

Finally, she appeared in a beautiful white dress, her face veiled. She walked down the aisle with her father. Chon came out to meet her at the foot of the altar, and Mariquita removed her veil and insisted on kissing her father. A goodbye or farewell symbol, Chon thought. The couple walked up slowly to the altar. They stood there, and suddenly the great samurai spy's legs started trembling fiercely.

"What's wrong Encarnación? Do you feel all right?" Mari Liz whispered.

"I feel fine, it's just that I have never been married before, and I am very nervous, and my legs are trembling. You see, I have never been married before," Chon mumbled.

"Well I have never been married before either, and my legs are not trembling. Straighten out love. It will be over soon," Mari Liz comforted him.

They were accompanied on the altar by Señor García as the best man. Mari Liz's best friend Diana Sanchez was the maid of honor, and in keeping with the ancient Spanish customs, padrinos, or godparents, of the kneeling cushions, godparents of the lazo—placed around the married couple after the vows, symbolic of eternal union, the godparents of the arras— the coins symbolizing his financial support, and the ring bearer and flower girl rounded out the wedding party.

After the wedding, a reception was held at the ranch house yard, which was meticulously manicured. The green grass was like a carpet for the guests to walk on. There were many lights hanging overhead on wires from tree to tree. The atmosphere was happy, and lively, and a twelve-men band played popular music in the background. The smell of food permeated the area.

Chon and Mari Liz walked around greeting the guests. After a couple of hours, they paused and sliced the wedding cakes, and sat down to rest and eat. It was the first time on their wedding day that they had a chance to sit, talk, and tell each other how much they loved each other. In following Japanese customs, Chon would not have said anything to the bride and the bride would not have said anything to him. But he read and asked about American traditions and customs, and found that there was no hiding or inhibiting feeling. He was glad he could express his love to his new wife.

Before leaving for the honeymoon, Chon discussed the wetback problem with Don Ramón. How could he go on a honeymoon if he could get arrested for being an illegal or undocumented alien?

"The first thing you have to learn is to act normal. Act as if you are an American, and as if you have an absolute right to be wherever you happen to be. You will find that this attitude will get you by about ninety nine per cent of the time. If you do not speak good English, does not matter. You are still an American and if the gringos don't like it, that's too bad," Don Ramón explained, not knowing that he was giving Chon the answers he needed to hear for disguising a much more serious matter.

About eleven o'clock during the reception, Don Ramón approached Chon and Mari Liz, and whispered to Chon that he had something special for the honeymoon trip.

"Please move over here to the edge of the yard where no one can see us," Don Ramón explained. The three moved over to an edge of the yard next to the oleanders. Don Ramón reached into his coat pocket and pulled out an envelope, he opened it, and pulled out a one page document. He unfolded the paper and showed it to Chon. Chon did not recognize the printed form.

"What is this Don Ramón, please explain, I do not have time to analyze it," Chon said.

"This is your passport to being legal, Encarnación. From now on, whenever your legal presence in this country is questioned, you are to pull out this paper, and remember this. Your name will be Alejandro Narvaez, you were born in Encinal, Texas. Later you should memorize the other data on this birth certificate. You need to memorize it and remember that in a time of trouble you are not Encarnación Gutiérrez, you are Alejandro Narvaez. Agreed?" Don Ramón asked.

Chon and Mari Liz laughed, and thanked Don Ramón for

going to the trouble of getting a duplicate birth certificate. Don Ramón looked for someone that resembled Chon physically and in age, and then went to that friend and told him to go to the County Clerk's office and get a duplicate birth certificate. Chon put the certificate inside his coat pocket.

The party went on and Chon and Mari Liz danced the waltz perfectly. He again charmed the guests. This was no ordinary wetback, everyone, those that got a chance to talk to him, agreed.

The younger kids insisted on knowing which car the bride and groom would use on their departure. Sergio told them that it would be the 1940 two-door black coupe parked under the oak tree in the drive. The young people went and found tin cans, string, and tied these to the car, then with soap wrote words comments, and obscenities on Señor García's car.

By midnight the bride and groom changed to traveling clothes, and exited through the yard giving everyone an opportunity to sprinkle rice on them for good luck. They drove out in Don Juan's four door sedan. The younger crowd realizing that they had been duped into mistreating the wrong car, wanted to know where they were going, so they could follow and harass them during the remainder of the night. Sergio advised them that the married couple would stay at the Hamilton Hotel in Laredo that night before proceeding on a trip to Corpus Christi and South Padre Island. The youngsters took off in several cars for Laredo. They were going to catch up and do things right.

In reality, Chon and Mari Liz enjoyed their first night as husband and wife in bridal suite of La Posada in Laredo. The mob bypassed them and hurried on to the Hamilton Hotel, never finding anyone to harass.

Chon and Mari Liz went on a whirlwind tour of the South Texas Gulf Coast. After the fifth day, they couldn't stand being away from Rancho Salinas and sped back home. Twenty minutes after their arrival, Don Juan insisted that they go on a long drive around the ranch. It was relaxing he said, and they could talk

about the trip, besides he wanted Chon to see some new calves
that were penned up in the north pasture.

The two couples squeezed into the small old four door car
that Don Juan sometimes used for ranch work. They drove
and talked and reminisced. After a few minutes, they came
to the North Pasture, and then to the pens. When they got
to the site, a new yellow brick home stood next to the giant
mesquite tree.

"Where did that house come from?" Chon asked. "I was here
several months ago, and there wasn't anything here."

"Chon and Mari Liz, this is our wedding gift to you," Don
Juan said, looking at his wife with a smile. "It's a small home,
but we've built it for comfort, and we hope you like it."

The house was small but built expertly, and built for comfort.
They named it La Casita de Oro. Don Juan told them a story
for the house's name. He said about one hundred years before,
a Frenchman lived at the location and had established a general
store. He got sick while in France on a visit, and he sent word to
his best friend telling him where he had buried some gold. He told
his friend that he could keep half the gold and asked him to send
the other half to France for his medical expenses. The Frenchman
died in France, and no one knew whether the gold was found.

Soon Chon threw himself into his work at the ranch. He
took over an old project trying to develop a better breed of cattle
for Rancho Salinas. He was intrigued with Don Juan's genetic
studies with the deer herd, and felt that he could do the same,
if not better, with domestic animals in a controlled or semi
controlled environment.

Mari Liz spent much of her time with her mother, developing
a part of herself she had never given much thought to, that of
wife and mother.

To the rest of the employees on the ranch, Chon was their
hero, the one who managed to make impossible dreams come
true. Even the workers, however, realized that Chon was not of

their cut. He was something or somebody else who just happened to work with them momentarily. They loved him, respected him, admired him, and envied him.

Especially loyal, and excited about the whole thing was Tonio. His roommate and buddy had made it, and made it big, and he was very proud. Both Tonio and Chon were extremely busy during the fall, but on Saturday or Sunday on a morning or an afternoon, Chon would go get Tonio, and they would work on a special project at the new house.

Chon and Tonio would talk and joke and reminisce, and built a new fence, or plant new trees, or plant new grass, or just do anything that needed doing. And there was always something to build, repair, or replace.

The newlyweds adjusted to each other quickly. There was a minimum amount of quarreling and arguing. They each respected the other's thoughts and actions, and each was exceptionally tolerant of the other's work hours and obligations.

Don Juan and Doña María Luisa were pleased at what they saw. They saw Mariquita becoming a woman, through and through; she had matured and they were pleased. They worried at first that she would not want, or be able, to fix meals, clean house, iron clothing, or manage the household. Their fears were unfounded. She took to the married life easily.

Although they had consented to the marriage, they still had certain reservations about Encarnación, and they did not know how he would develop with the family, and whether things, or matters about him, would improve or worsen.

Chon's behavior was impeccable. His love for Mariquita was unquestionable. His personality as always was charming. His manner and intelligence was enviable. There were no complaints, and soon they loved him as their own son. Their friends befriended him, and accepted him, and he them.

The war in Europe had ended in June 1944, but the fighting on the other side of the world continued with intensity. Each night Chon and Mari Liz sat in the family room and listened to the news of the fighting. In the South Pacific, General Douglas MacArthur was doing a splendid job for the Americans. When the war with Japan began, the United States was not prepared, and Japan acted at will, taking island after island. With the help of the American Army Air Corps, MacArthur began retaking islands.

The taking was not without price. Thousands and thousands of Japanese and American young men lost their lives in the conflicts of retaking the islands and displacing the Japanese Army.

Chon listened to the radio broadcasts of the blood and guts and brains strewn on the beaches as American troops landed. There were heavy casualties on both sides. He had mixed emotions at first, not because he cared to take sides, but because he was trained to die for Japan, and he was unable—or unwilling—to do so. His wife was an American, his in-laws American, and his child would be an American. Besides, he feared detection very much, and knew that if the Japanese conquered America, and, or México, that soon he would be found and shot. Now more than ever he had frequent thoughts of facing the firing squad.

Late on the night of August 7, 1945, President Truman came on the radio and explained to the nation that on Aug. 6 a bomb—a bomb never before used, never before known to man—had wiped out and devastated the Japanese city of Hiroshima. President Truman explained that the bomb had been a secret project for the last few years, and that the explosion involved the use of atoms and molecules. That the explosion had literally leveled many square miles, and killed thousands of people.

It was hard to comprehend the nature and effect of the new weapon but the President succeeded in informing and communicating that the weapon was ominous indeed. It was frightening.

"Did you hear that, one bomb wipes out an entire city. It

is hard to believe, but I have heard and read about this man Truman, and I do not believe that he would lie about anything much less about something so drastic," Chon exclaimed to Mari Liz.

"Chon, I do not feel good about this war, so many people getting killed, and now this terrible new weapon. Suppose the Japanese have something just as bad, and that now, in retaliation, they use it on us. Let us say a short prayer that this war will end quickly; enough people have already lost their lives," Mari Liz said and began making the sign of the cross.

Chon and Mari Liz prayed. Chon thought as they prayed. Would the secret project Valley, dealing with the invasion of the United States, come to fruition? Did he have a duty to go to the Americans and explain everything he knew? He prayed piously. He did not want his yet unborn baby to fight a war or become a victim of war.

On August 9, the President came on the radio again to announce that another heinous mystery bomb had been dropped on Japan, this time on the city of Nagasaki. The American President was now asking for an unconditional surrender.

The world, including those at Rancho Salinas, stood in disbelief. Was it true? Would it bring the war to an end? Would the Japanese retaliate? If it were true then it appeared that the Americans were probably victorious. If it were not true, then what would happen?

Chon knew that Tokyo was next. Goodbye mama, Akechi san, Sebastian, and Tokyo Plantation. The newspapers reported, and the radio reports likewise described the death and devastation. It was apparently true. In a few days it was announced that the Japanese Empire had accepted the terms of the unconditional surrender, and preparations were underway to formally execute the capitulation.

On September 2, 1945 the powers that had caused each other so much harm, and loss of life, met on the battleship USS

Missouri anchored in Tokyo Bay. The war in the Pacific was over, and everyone celebrated. Even Chon felt a great degree of relief. But now, he thought, the Americans would have plenty of time to find him.

* * *

In December 1945, the family gathered to celebrate Christmas. Sergio arrived from medical school and partied as usual. Chon and Mari Liz joined him for a couple of gatherings. There was no trip to the hotel in Laredo.

Morale and spirits lifted on December 22 when Chon and Mari Liz announced to the rest of the family that next September there would be an addition to the family. Mariquita looked beautiful with rosy cheeks, full bosom, and rounding hips. The baby would be a boy, Chon assured everyone. Everyone laughed. Everyone was happy and very pleased.

It was their first Christmas as husband and wife, and it was very special. Chon and Mari Liz spent their private moments in the family room in front of the fireplace making small things for the baby. Chon made a beautiful crib. Mari Liz knitted tiny socks, shirts, and other garments of soft wool. It was a memorable Christmas; the Christmas of 1945.

The couple worked hard during the coming weeks, Mari Liz began to show, and Chon rubbed her round belly when they sat on the sofa listening to the radio. As the weeks went by Mari Liz got bigger and bigger. On occasion she would go to see her doctor in Laredo and come back with the news that she was doing fine, and that the baby was coming along on schedule.

On September 11, 1946 at three o'clock in the morning, Mari Liz knew that her time had come. She was experiencing labor pains, but did not wake Chon. He was working very hard these days, and she did not want to disturb his rest. By four she could not wait, the time had come, and it was time to go.

"Encarnación, Encarnación," she called, tugging at her husband's arm.

"Huh. Huh. Huh, what's wrong? What's going on?" Chon asked in groggy tones.

"The baby is coming, my water broke. We need to get to the big house and call the doctor, please let's go," Mari Liz told him with an anxious calm.

Chon was up and clothed in seconds. He rushed out to start up the pickup and returned to the house to get Mari Liz.

"Do you feel all right?" He asked.

"Oh, I feel very uncomfortable and the labor pains are quite intensive," Mari Liz replied.

"Well, don't worry I'll hurry," Chon said.

"Don't rush too much, if you hit a lot of bumps it will make matters worse," she said.

They were off and were at the big house in no time. Don Juan opened the door to see what was going on and Chon blurted out the reason for being there at that hour and rushed past him to the phone to call Dr. Holt.

Dr. Edmund Holt had been a friend of the Salinas for decades. He had assisted when Sergio and Mari Liz were born. They too were born at the big house, and the first grandchild would do likewise.

The doctor said he was on his way. By this time Don Juan had awakened Doña María Luisa and Elvira, and all three were at the pickup escorting Mari Liz into the house. They settled her into the guest bedroom on the first floor, and sat around and watched her, each waiting to soothe her every complaint. The doctor arrived in twenty minutes and ordered the men out of the room. Chon thought it very strange that a woman's husband and her father could not see her nakedness prior to delivering their own flesh and blood.

Chon and Don Juan went to the kitchen to make coffee and wait for word.

"The doctor says it will be some time yet. She is having pains but she is not quite dilated enough yet," Elvira came in to tell them.

They drank four coffee pots. By six o'clock other employees who worked in the kitchen arrived. The camp kitchen too was alive with activity, and the word that Mariquita was in labor spread quickly.

Periodically Elvira came to get coffee for the doctor and Doña María Luisa and herself, and gave a status report on the labor to the anxious Chon and Don Juan. They were still waiting on more dilation.

"Is she suffering much?" Chon asked.

"Do not worry, she is doing fine. She is a strong woman, she is a Salinas and she will do fine," Elvira said proudly and emphatically.

Finally, at eight o'clock Elvira hurriedly announced that the baby was coming, the head was protruding. They should get closer to the bedroom.

* * *

In the Mexican custom, the child was baptized within five days. It was not safe to wait longer. His given name was James Tomás Sebastian Gutiérrez. Chon and Mari Liz explained that James was a name they both liked. It was highly unusual to choose a name in English. Santiago or Jaime yes, but not James, and especially not to go with the Spanish Tomás instead the English Thomas. Nevertheless, no one voiced an objection. The other two names were for Chon's alleged uncle Sebastian whose given name was Tomás Sebastian. Chon explained that this deceased uncle was responsible for everything that he was today, and he wanted to show a special affection by naming the child after him.

Actually, Chon and Mari Liz had agreed that each child would have the middle name Tasaka Samurai, but changed their mind when they realized they would have to explain this to everyone.

Instead they settled on Tomás Sebastian, a name whose initials they secretly knew meant Tasaka Samurai.

"Jimmy" occupied everyone's time. He was the subject of conversation for months. Needless to say, he quickly became the apple of his parents' and grandparents' eyes. He was the only thing that occupied their time and attention.

Mari Liz took a leave of absence from the school. She decided to stay out at least until Jimmy began school. Chon and Don Juan were pleased with her decision to stay home.

When Jimmy was a month old, they moved back to La Casita de Oro.

Chapter Twenty Three

The 1946 hunting season was especially joyous for everyone. The war was over. For Chon of course, the season meant renewing his friendships with Señor García, Judge Trench, Sheriff Santos, and other powerful politicians from the area, and going home to his cherished Jimmy, all without the acute fear of detection.

By now all the workers had returned to México. Now with the war over, Chon imagined that upon their return in the spring the Migra or Immigration Service would come back to harass the undocumented workers, the wetbacks.

This was his third hunting season, and he had learned to pace himself, and not exhaust himself as he had the first season. Each year he helped Señor García kill a big buck, but none would duplicate the kill of 1943 that entered the record book as one of the biggest.

Judge Trench became a closer friend, as Chon spent more time with him, helping with his trophy kills. Chon learned a lot about South Texas politics from Señor García and Judge Trench. It was amazing how they loved to talk politics even to Chon, who apparently could not have cared less about the infighting, the back stabbing, the election tricks, the strategy, and the leverage. Not to say that Chon did not listen, to the contrary, he digested every word. Most of the time it seemed as if the politicians were talking to themselves, and not caring who was listening. Chon listened and made mental notes. He tried to learn local politics and started reading the local newspapers.

He constantly asked Mari Liz about people and events. He was slowly becoming a South Texan.

He especially liked it when Señor García, Judge Trench, and Don Juan began reminiscing about past local political events, those currently evolving, and those that could be seen on the horizon. Apparently these men, and others allied with them, controlled whatever occurred in these parts. It was not without opposition, but it seemed they had the intelligence, and power to do things their way, whether it pleased the majority or not.

Although interested in South Texas politics and its workings, he was not a citizen. He had never voted, thinking that he would be pushing his luck a little too far if he tried to vote.

In early 1947, Tonio returned from México, this time with the news that he had married his sweetheart Lupita. He could not postpone it any longer. He was anxious to work harder now, and send money back home.

The rest of the workers moved back and began to work in earnest. It seemed that Chon was stretched very thin, since he was devoting more and more time to the genetics study that he had undertaken.

He discovered that, simultaneously, there was another study going on at Texas A & I College and the sprawling King Ranch near Kingsville. Similarly, they too were trying to develop a better breed of cattle, more hardy, and a faster gainer, and one that could withstand the South Texas heat and environment.

Chon continued his study independently. His experiment centered along the line of developing a red Brahman breed. The Brahman was imported from Africa and India, and did exceptionally well in this country. Chon sought to improve the breed. One of the earlier problems was to reduce the back hump, and that was to be done by crossbreeding with breeds that had no back hump.

Then Chon was faced with creating a longer and taller animal, with a larger carriage, unlike the short Hereford cattle. The problems were many, but he slowly changed methods and procedures and recorded every detail.

By the end of 1947, a second son was born. Juan Tomás Sebastian Gutiérrez, joined Jimmy as the center of attraction at Rancho Salinas and La Casita de Oro. The relationship between Chon and Mari Liz mellowed and solidified well, as did Chon's relationship with Don Juan and Doña María Luisa. Juan's arrival, although being less climactic than his brother James' was not any less exciting and appreciated. "Juanito" resembled his mother more than Jimmy; he was fairer and had a tinge of Spanish blond in his hair.

Although not legalized, Chon took on a confidence that made everyone think that he was a native born Texan. It was all a matter of positive thinking. By now the immigration officers never thought to ask for identification, his appearance and demeanor being totally Texan. His style of dress had not changed much, it was still the tight blue jeans, wide leather belt, khaki shirt, and small crunched up sweaty felt hat, accented by the jeans tucked into the tall cowboy boots. But, neither had his fear of detection.

With the postwar boom, the Immigration and Naturalization Service, the Migra, the border patrol, did not bother cattle ranches and vegetable producers much. Once a year, more or less, they raided farms and ranches as a symbolic gesture.

In 1948, Tonio was arrested and deported to México. Chon became infuriated. He rushed into Laredo to see Señor García. He had become accustomed to visiting Señor García more and more with legal problems.

"Señor García, what are we supposed to do without help? Nobody from the cities want to come out and do farm work, there are very few people that know anything about the work of vaqueros. Is there not anything we can do to keep the border patrol off the ranch? We cannot afford to lose twenty or thirty of our men at one time. This morning they came on and took everyone. It's like Christmas out there," Chon told the attorney, referring to the Christmas vacation when all the workers left for their native México.

"Chon, every once in a while you are going to lose some wetbacks, some laborers. You know that they will come back, and you cannot afford to start a war with the INS, because you know who is going to win. So just get used to the idea that every once in a great while the Border Patrol is going to come on the ranch and pick up a few of your people, period. Besides, don't I remember a young boy about 1943 coming across the river and becoming a hunting guide, and being illegal?" Señor García asked tongue in cheek.

Chon understood perfectly that he was referring to him, and the fact that technically he was still a wetback, an illegal, an undocumented alien, and should not be making war.

"Chon, why don't you let me start immigration proceedings for you. You have been here sometime, you are married to an American, and I understand that you have become a good scientist out there working on cattle breeds or something like that. Let me start your application, and in about eighteen months you will be a legal alien, and then in about three years after that you can apply for American citizenship. I do dozens of these every year and there are no problems, you should let me start," Señor García urged Chon.

"No, uh, no," Chon said nervously, "not just yet, maybe one of these days, but not just now. Well I have to go now, I guess you are right about just having to live with it. Oh, by the way, I hear you are hosting a political rally in Laredo next week. I would like to come and help you?"

"Of course, Chon, I want you to be there, I would love to have you there," Señor García replied.

By now everyone in the area knew that if you wanted anything, or had any kind of business at Rancho Salinas, you would have to go through Chon first. Don Juan gladly delegated duties and

rights and powers over to Chon who readily accepted them and
did a fine job taking over. Since Chon was so entrenched in
the genetics project and the cattle part of the ranch, Don Juan
leisurely concentrated on the produce side of the operation.

Sergio graduated from the University of St. Louis in 1946
and went on with specialized training, and returned to Rancho
Salinas in late 1948 as a full-fledged surgeon. He elected to live
in Laredo, and visited the ranch only on weekends.

Chon became the perfect family man and father. He became
a very devout Catholic, and every Sunday, without fail, one could
see the couple and their children seated about the middle of
the church, on the left side, close to the windows, and the south
easterly breeze. Mari Liz marveled at her luck. She had gotten
a good solid person as her man, and he was kind and pious and
devout. He was an excellent father, husband, and companion.

Jimmy and Juanito were attended by their Nana Isidra, in the
Mexican custom. Isidra, had been Mari Liz's nana and helped
Mari Liz take care of the boys. The pleasure of watching the
family grow made life worth living for everyone.

At first, Isidra could not get used to the idea of the wetback marrying her baby, but with time, just as she accepted the
courtship, she grew accustomed to the marriage. She would
be the first to admit that Don Encarnación was no common
wetback. He was more than a cut above the rest. Isidra's hands
were full, and were to become busier. In the fall of 1949 Sergio
Tomás Sebastian joined his two brothers, in 1951 Mario Luis
Tomás Sebastian named for his grandmother, María Luisa, came
along, and in 1953 Antonio Tomás Sebastian was named for
his godfather Tonio, who had since moved to Rancho Salinas
with his wife Lupita.

In mid-1953, Chon, Tonio, and three other workers from the
plantation added two bedrooms to the east side of La Casita
de Oro. By 1955, in anticipation of another baby, another two
bedrooms were again added to the east side of the once small

cottage. Early December brought along the "Princess," Elizabeth María T.S. named after her mother, but with the first and second name switched to avoid confusion with Mari Liz.

Time passed rapidly. Jimmy was now ten years old. He showed the same talent that his father had shown on Tokyo Plantation twenty-five years earlier. He was agile and muscular, a good athlete, and a straight A student. His younger brothers were no exception, each was a clone of his father, regarding athletics and intelligence. It was as if the young man at Tokyo Plantation had been duplicated five times, in one of his genetics experiments.

He wondered how his mother, Akechi san, and Sebastian would enjoy the six siblings. They reminded him of puppies running around, biting, fighting, jumping, rolling around, sometimes sleeping, and it seemed like always eating.

Jimmy Gutiérrez was used to being the first in his class in everything. He always got straight A's, was president of his class, and the best in every sport, and a leader in every other activity.

Jimmy's brothers and sister followed his footsteps. He was a perfect role model that they strived to imitate. By and large they succeeded. The Gutiérrez children had a reputation within the school district of being the smartest and most able. A reputation in which Chon and Mari Liz took great pride.

Chon watched the children grow. He watched carefully, always making sure that they not go unchallenged. He knew that he should not teach them karate, but he insisted that each participate in sports, and of course work at the ranch. They became excellent horsemen. They became expert hunters and trackers. They learned the deer herd management techniques that their grandfather had started.

The sports available to them at the school system completed their schooling program. Chon loved to watch them play basketball, baseball, football, and run track. Jimmy grew larger, taller, and more muscular than his father, and inherited his speed and coordination. He was thin and wiry, but very muscular. A fine specimen.

In the fall, Friday nights were for football, which was followed by basketball, track, and baseball. The entire family, including Abuelo Juan, Abuela María Luisa, and tío Sergio, were regulars at the children's activities.

Jimmy lettered in four sports as a Freshman. When he brought home four sport jackets, the family knew they had an athlete. Chon was overcome, he was so proud. It was not usual for a boy to earn any jacket as a freshman. For a freshman to earn four of the jackets was unheard of. The red white and gray jackets were an impressive sight, with the bold embroidered "E" for Encinal on the left breast area. Each letter also bore an embroidered hash mark, signifying the number of letters acquired in the sport. Jimmy's therefore only showed one hash mark in each jacket.

With the Gutiérrez brothers, the Encinal Eagles were a force to contend with, winning the district championship each year. As with any team, when you have a strong leader, an excellent athlete, the spark breeds desire, enthusiasm, and momentum. Add to this, the fact that at times you had two Gutiérrez brothers playing on the same team.

Jimmy did not make any all district team as a freshman, but made each all district team, as a sophomore, junior, and senior, as a quarterback in football, third baseman in baseball, forward in basketball, and sprinter in track. Younger brother Juan followed Jimmy by two years, and he lettered as a freshman in every sport and made two of the all district teams. There was a healthy competition between the brothers.

The other youngsters followed Jimmy's example well. Chon was blessed with several samurai, not just one.

On Rancho Salinas, Jimmy was taught horsemanship and marksmanship. He was already getting involved in the genetics program, when he was a ten-year-old. The children were following in their Abuelo Juan's footsteps who knew quite a bit about agronomy and produce. Their mother Mari Liz was their Sebastian, she taught them the finer things in life, and it was understood that they would attend universities when they got older.

Chon was fearful of teaching them Karate Do, lest he might give himself away. The hand-to-hand art of fighting was just barely being heard of in the United States, and if someone saw the fighting method, it might cause unnecessary questions, particularly if someone had already seen the art practiced in Japan. He taught them to box, and the older ones could at least defend themselves, the younger ones would learn later.

Chon, Mari Liz, and the children became the typical ranch and farm family, working hard and enjoying every minute of it. Jimmy often hunted cottontail rabbits, with Juanito in close pursuit.

* * *

Discussion of Japan almost never came up. The postwar period came into full bloom. On occasion there would be an article in a magazine, or something in the news, about Japan, but by and large Japan was not a topic of conversation. This allowed Chon to suppress any feeling for the old country. He had a wife, and his job, and his children to help him forget. But it was not possible to entirely wipe out the old memories. The cultural differences would have made adjustment nearly impossible and lengthy, were it not for the preparation Sebastian and the Intelligence Service provided.

The postwar boom was good for everybody. The factories worked at full force. Everyone had a job, and everyone was spending their money on new consumer goods. More wages to more people meant more spending. Rancho Salinas did not go unaffected, as there were more Americans demanding more meat and vegetables. The operation prospered.

The Salinas and Gutiérrez joined the world of consumers, and enjoyed the new inventions and gadgets along with the rest. The Gutiérrez's bought one of the first black and white television sets in that area of Texas. Everyone in the family was fascinated with the new contraption. To turn on a box and have a part of it light up and then have images of people thousands of miles away, talking, moving, and acting, in the box was something that was hard to imagine and get used to.

Chon became especially fond of the movies, especially the ones made before the beginning of the war, which, he had not seen for some time. And those made during and after the war he had never seen. He had a lot of catching up to do. He especially enjoyed the post war military movies, such as "Flying Leathernecks", starring John Wayne and "To Hell and Back" with Audie Murphy.

About once a month Chon and Mari Liz drove into Laredo without the children for dinner at the Hamilton Hotel. Mari Liz never forgot the night she fell in love with Chon, as he punched and kicked and decommissioned four drunk soldiers to save her and her honor.

On occasion Mari Liz made sandwiches, a jug full of punch, cookies, and other snacks, stuff them in a basket and the entire family went to the drive-in theater in Laredo and watch one or two movies. Chon liked the drive-in theater the best as he could keep his eye on all the children, and the informality, the ability to eat and drink, also appealed to him. They saw other movies, such as James Stewart in "Strategic Air Command" and in "The FBI Story". Chon paid special close attention to the operations of the FBI, since he secretly feared a visit from them. He could visualize a four-door sedan driving up to La Casita de Oro and two officers dressed in suits and ties walk up and knock on the door.

Chon continued his activities with Señor García and Judge Trench in promoting the Democratic Party in the county.

Wherever there was a rally, he was present. Whenever one of their candidates ran for office, he contributed. Still he never took the final step and buy a poll tax and vote. It was noticeable, of course, but no one dared to question him.

Chon compared the political strength of his friends to the ancient shoguns and samurais who kept families together, and cared for their people. He was not opposed to Republicans. In actuality he did not fully understand the two party system. What was important to him was to preserve the status quo, a status quo that favored him entirely, and meant success and security for him and his family. In this part of the country, at this point in time, Señor García and Judge Trench and the Democratic Party represented this guarantee.

Chapter Twenty Four

When President Franklin Roosevelt died in office in 1945, Vice President Harry Truman, from the state of Missouri, took over to finish out the term. In the 1948 election Truman narrowly defeated the Republican Thomas Dewey. The Democratic Party's grip on the nation continued. Through these elections, Don Juan, Señor García, and Judge Trench worked closely with Congressman Lyndon B. Johnson from the Texas Hill Country. The idea was to work hard and get out the vote and deliver it for the Democratic Party.

On a trip to Laredo in 1947, Johnson told them, "If we stay in power we can help our people with grants, colleges, business, international relations, cattle and produce industries. That is, if we stay in power, and the only way we can stay in power is to get the people out to vote. The only way you can get what you need is by showing the powers in Washington that you are a team player and that you delivered at such and such election. It's simple arithmetic. You give the votes, and it comes back in the form of help from Washington, in laws or in money."

South Texas had always delivered well for the Democratic Party. In fact national politicians used the South Texas vote as a barometer. As went South Texas, so went the state. In the 1952 election, after a couple of decades of Democratic Party control, the nation went Republican. For the first time since Reconstruction, Texas voted Republican, with retired General Dwight D. Eisenhower, a Texan by birth, carrying the state.

The pendulum swung, and swung far. The Republicans lost little time in cutting into the Federal programs created under Roosevelt and Truman. Under Roosevelt, and later Truman, Federal involvement and spending had increased to a level never before experienced. This upset the Republicans to no end.

Eisenhower easily won reelection. Although he was very popular with the voters, he did not win over the Washington power structure, what he called the "military industrial complex." They tagged his administration with the "do nothing" label.

The pendulum began swinging the other way, and in 1958 and 1959, Lyndon Johnson, who had been elected to the Senate in 1948, came to South Texas often to meet with Don Juan, Chon, Señor García, Judge Trench, and other leaders. He needed their support. He was going for the big one, he wanted the Democratic presidential nomination.

At one of their meetings they decided to run Judge Trench for the United States Senate seat Johnson was giving up in his run for the presidency. They also decided, unanimously, to commit for Johnson at the precinct and state conventions. The conventions were hard fought and Johnson garnered most of the state delegates. It was all for naught, however, as Johnson could not muster the nomination and a young senator from Massachusetts named John F. Kennedy won the Democratic Party nomination. To strengthen the ticket, Kennedy invited Johnson to be his vice presidential running mate. The move was meant to eliminate polarization within the party.

At the general election Kennedy and Johnson squeaked out a win, and Judge Trench won the Senate seat for the state of Texas. The Trench campaign was hard fought and very expensive. The Trench family went to bat for their favorite son, and their money, plus Judge Trench's impeccable record and unlimited energy, gave him the edge. Don Juan, Chon, and Señor García worked hard and steady during the campaigns, put in long hours, and contributed heavily. It was worth it, as their hunting companion became the United States Senator from Texas.

The young charismatic Kennedy, with Johnson's help, initiated a warm working relationship with the Congress. One of Kennedy's first acts as President was to nominate Federal judges. Kennedy put the word out that he would nominate young, hard working, Democratic Party members. He also let it be known that he wanted minorities represented in the judgeships, this meant that he wanted blacks, Hispanics, and women nominated and appointed.

Aspiring attorneys and judges in South Texas sought out the support of Johnson and Trench. None had the inside lane, none had worked harder and longer for the party, and none was as qualified as the young Mexican American attorney from Laredo named Reynaldo Omar García.

García was sworn in as a Federal Judge in Houston, on March 15, 1961. His parents, brothers, and sisters attended as did his wife Helen, and their three children, and many friends from Laredo and South Texas, including the Salinas and Gutiérrez families. Unbelievably, there had never been an Hispanic, or Mexican American Federal Judge. García was the first ever.

The vibrations of the Battle of the Alamo had taken a long time to quiet.

*　*　*

The Gutiérrez's sat around the breakfast table as Mari Liz scurried around waiting on everyone. The school bus that took them to school in Encinal would come by in ten minutes and she hated the children to be late.

"Jimmy, after the game tonight we will all go out for supper so don't take the bus home. We'll be there to pick you up," Chon said.

"Okay Dad, I'll see you when I get out of the shower," Jimmy answered.

The children finished eating and then picked up their books and began walking out to the front of the house where the bus usually picked them up. Jimmy was the last. His mother called out to him.

"Jimmy, love, good luck in the game tonight, score one touchdown for Momma, all right?" He looked back and they blew each other kisses.

"I'll score two for you Momma," Jimmy yelled as he ran out.

"Now don't get sassy and full of yourself, go on now," Chon lectured him.

Jimmy ran out and in two minutes the bus arrived and the clan climbed in.

The game was the last of the season, and the winner would be the district champion. The coach primed his charges all week and they were so charged, so high, and so full of adrenalin they couldn't wait to get on the field and start warming up. They were fully dressed, but the coach purposely would not let them leave the dressing room. He wanted them impatient and anxious. The boys were quiet but jittery. All one could hear were the clacking of the cleats on the concrete floor, and the managers getting their bags and boxes ready for the bench.

After ten desperate minutes, the coach walked to the front of the group.

"I am just going to say it once. Go out there and win it. Go out there and beat the hell out of 'em. If you don't win district it's your fault, now go get 'em," he yelled.

The team roared as they ran out onto the field, and began their calisthenics. The crowd of spectators had already gathered. The Gutiérrez brothers from Encinal averaged two touchdowns per game each for the season thus far. Jimmy played quarterback and Juanito played halfback. The other team was the Robstown Cottonpickers, and their main threat was senior

Phil McCuskey who had thus far averaged three touchdowns per game.

The crowd expected an offensive display. They were not disappointed. Encinal scored first when Jimmy broke loose on a thirty yard option play around the right end for a touchdown. Juanito crashed over right tackle for the two point conversion.

McCuskey was not to be outdone, and came back and scored three touchdowns as the first half ended.

The team poured into the locker room for the halftime rest and strategy planning. The Encinal coach knew what he had to do. He was hoping to save Jimmy for the remainder of the game, but knew now that he could not.

"Jimmy you are going to play both ways now, offense and defense, and so are you Juanito. We don't have a choice. Juanito, you play defensive halfback and key on McCuskey, play man to man. Jimmy you play safety, and I don't want anything going past. Understood?" The Coach shouted.

The boys nodded.

"The rest of you, all I gotta tell you is that you can still win this game. It's not over, don't give up, you keep playing hard. Actually, you've played a good first half except for three plays and on those three, McCuskey broke away. So with our changes we should be able to get this game behind us, as a victory. I don't want you to wake up tomorrow morning and kick yourselves in the butt for not hustling and winning this game. Put your balls on the line, and get this game won. Leave everything on the field. Don't bring any energy back to the bench. Go get 'em!"

In the third quarter Jimmy broke for two long touchdowns, eighty and seventy two yards, respectively. Juanito and Jimmy contained McCuskey well. The plan was working. McCuskey was feeling Gutiérrez helmets every time he tried to run. The attack was stopped. The game was tied going into the last quarter, and continued tied until the last five minutes when Juanito decided that he was not going to be denied, and rushed five, ten, three, and fifteen yard spurts to score the final eight points of the game.

The crowd went wild. No one dared sit down during the entire game. Don Juan, Doña María Luisa, Chon, Mari Liz, and the rest of the children jumped and yelled all night. The women had lost their voices by the end of the game. Chon was absolutely ecstatic. The boys from Encinal had showed 'em.

"I will be right back, or better yet, why don't you slowly make your way to the locker room, I'll meet you there. I can't wait, I must go see my boys. Sergio come with me," Chon and the younger boy ran to the locker room.

He stepped down into the locker room which was the basement to the gymnasium. He walked through the dark steamy room, naked sweaty bodies everywhere, and everyone yelling and screaming, and replaying the game. Chon made his way until he finally saw Jimmy and Juanito sitting on a distant bench, naked, wet with perspiration taking the tape and bandages off their ankles. He knelt down in front of them smiling.

"Here I'll get that," he started undoing Jimmy's taped ankles and then Juanito's.

"Dad, don't do that, I can get it," Jimmy said, embarrassed at having his father, whom he loved and respected greatly, kneeling in front of him removing the tape. He did not feel worthy. But Chon insisted, and asked little Sergio to help him. Chon and Sergio finished, and the two athletes stood up.

"You two played a super game, and I am very proud of you. I am very proud of you." Chon's chin trembled as he drew a deep breath, a tear welled up in his eye. He cleared his throat. "Go take a shower, we will be outside waiting for you. Let's go eat. Your Mama is outside waiting."

"Thanks Dad and Keko. Thanks. Thanks a lot," Jimmy and Juanito called back.

The large group moved to The Spot, the largest restaurant in town. It was the only place large enough to hold most of the players, cheerleaders, fans, and families. The Gutiérrez's sat at a long table on a side of the large room, looking at the younger set carry on. Jimmy and Juanito sat with the team and cheerleaders. After much consumption of hamburgers, sodas, hot dogs, malts, and ice cream, Jimmy came over to his parents table.

"Mom, Dad, can we stay out late tonight? It was our last game, until bi-district and that's three weeks away, and we won district, and the coach gave us permission to stay out. We won't be breaking training. All the guys are staying out late, huh, please? Can Juanito and I?" Jimmy rattled off his plea.

Mari Liz looked to Chon for the decision.

"Please Dad," Juanito begged.

Chon did not usually permit the boys to stay out beyond midnight or one o'clock, knowing full well that there was a multitude of temptations and trouble waiting for young minds at those early dark hours. Tonight was an exception. He yielded.

"Well, all right, but I want you home by two or three o'clock, none of this staying out until sunrise. I do not want you to go across the river into México, stay on this side," he ordered, knowing full well that as soon as the dance was over, and they took their dates home, they would make a beeline for México, liquor, and the whores. He handed each of them some money, as he shook his head. "Boys grow into men, whether you like it or not," he thought.

As the two boys turned to leave, Jimmy turned back immediately, "Oh, I almost forgot, I have a surprise for you," he exclaimed as he got a chair and sat on it.

"I have been keeping something secret from you," the young man's eyes opened wide as he prepared to divulge the news.

"Six months ago I filled out a lot of papers, and requested something," he said slowly stringing out his words building up the suspense. "And today I finally got a letter at school, answering my application, and guess what?"

He finished and said nothing. All eyes were on him, still silence. Mari Liz could not stand it.

"James you must tell us what you are talking about, I cannot stand it, I cannot wait," she screamed.

Jimmy began in a real slow deliberate delivery. "I have been accepted to the United States Naval Academy in Annapolis, Maryland, and the FBI is coming to investigate our family to see if I can be admitted. Isn't that exciting?" He finished proudly.

The mention of the FBI hit Chon like a hammer in the forehead.

"Investigate our family, FBI, investigate our family, FBI, FBI, FBI, investigate our family, and investigate our family. 'Destroy yourself, do you understand'," Commander Shigeru's words came back to haunt him. "If anything goes wrong, you must destroy everything, even yourself. You must destroy yourself. Do you understand?"

The commander's words rebounded in his head. The group at the table congratulated Jimmy, and Chon broke into a cold sweat. He was stunned. He finally caught himself, and faked a smile and congratulated his son.

Jimmy got up and left for the dance. After idle conversation, the families got up and drove to their respective homes. Chon was silent all the way.

"Is something wrong, Encarnación?" Mari Liz asked, not having caught the import of the announcement about the FBI investigating them, and the inevitable detection.

"Uh, what? Oh, uh, oh, yes, but not here, when we get home I'll explain," Chon answered.

When the children went to bed, Chon explained the gravity of the situation to his wife. He knew that if the FBI checked close enough, he would be discovered. The man he created from San Blas, and the almost priest uncle, would be blown away like the mirage they were. He visualized two men in dark business suits, walking up to La Casita de Oro, and knocking at the door. Mari Liz was sympathetic, but did not have a solution to offer, and did not fully appreciate the panic that Chon was experiencing.

"Well, tomorrow we will have to talk more about this. Now please go to bed Encarnación, it is late and you need your rest."

The couple went to bed. When Chon sensed that Mari Liz was sleeping, he got up and went to the kitchen. He could not sleep, and his mind was racing, searching for a solution. The boys arrived at three, a little on the tipsy side, and bid their father good night. He sat at his desk, and pretended to be working on some bookkeeping. Finally at four thirty he was exhausted, he went to bed and slept.

"Destroy everything including yourself. Do you understand?"

The FBI is coming to investigate us.

By six thirty he was up waiting for the clock to tick off more time so he could call Señor García. At seven thirty he could wait no longer. He called Señor García and woke him.

"Señor García, I am so sorry for bothering you, but I must talk with you, I need about two hours of your time, there is something that I need to tell you, I have a problem. I cannot discuss it on the phone."

Señor García asked him to come to his law office in Laredo. The office was still open for Sen. Trench, to use when he was in town.

When Chon arrived, Señor García was already there, sitting at his old office opening mail.

"Encarnación how good to see you. I haven't seen you since last year's hunt. How have you been? Say I read the paper this morning about the boys, wow, five touchdowns, you must be very proud. Five touchdowns! Wow," Señor García said, patting the proud father in the back.

The men shook hands and Señor García offered Chon a chair and they both sat.

"Señor García, I could not sleep last night," Chon told his longtime friend. Then he launched into his story, beginning with Tokyo Plantation and brought Señor García to the present time.

Señor García could not believe his ears, as he heard the wanderer's adventure. Now he could understand the slight accent that marked Chon's speech, and the slanted eyes that everyone attributed to Mexican Indian heritage. By two thirty Chon had explained about the Naval Academy application and the FBI investigation.

"Señor García, I do not know what to do, and you are one of my closest friends and a lawyer, a judge, surely you can think of a solution," Chon closed his story with obvious anxiety.

"Wow, wow, wow," Señor García said slowly and deliberately, "when you get into problems, you don't fool around, do you? Encarnación, all I can tell you right now is that I will start working on this immediately. With your permission, I must tell Floyd. As a judge I cannot get active in something like this, but Floyd can. But I can assure you that there must be a solution to the problem. I want you to go home, and I want you to relax. It does not do any good to be worrying about the problem if you do not have the solution. I have the solution, or Lyndon Johnson or Floyd will find it, so let us worry about the problem.

"Wow, Encarnación, you have led a very exciting life, wow, some of the stuff you told me is almost unbelievable, but I am sure you would not lie about something so serious, if at all. Wow," Señor García kept shaking his head in disbelief.

Chon drove home. He walked up to the house, and decided not to tell anyone about the problem. For the following weeks he could not concentrate on any of his work. He lost weight, and could not sleep well. Mari Liz noticed his plight, and tried to comfort him at every moment. All he would tell her was that Señor García was trying to find a solution. He called Señor García periodically only to be told that Floyd was working on the problem, and that there was no news.

* * *

Señor García had called Sen. Trench at his Virginia home, as soon as Chon had left his office.

"Floyd how are you? I haven't talked with you for a few months? How's the family?" They exchanged pleasantries. "Floyd, Chon Gutiérrez just left the office, and he has a pretty big problem. Your involvement is indicated, I think."

Reynaldo went on to explain to his former law partner, long-time friend, and United States Senator Chon's predicament.

"Man, you are right, he does have a big problem. Well, let me have my staff look into the matter, and we'll see if we can come up with a solution. I will let you know next week or so, what we have to do," his former partner told Reynaldo.

The following Monday morning, Sen. Trench briefed his staff on the matter, and requested that they inquire from all necessary agencies what the situation meant to a certain Mr. X who is seeking Senator Trench's help.

"Call State, call the Army, call Justice, call Immigration, call the Pentagon, and call wherever you have to, to find out how the government feels about Mr. X. Do they want to arrest him, deport him, or forgive him? Find out!" Floyd meted out the orders.

The Kennedy-Johnson ticket had been a matter of convenience. It was a question of unity, but there was no love lost between Texas and Massachusetts. The worst kept secret in D. C. was that the Kennedys could not stand Lyndon Johnson, and Johnson could not stand the Kennedys. Sen. Trench feared that the antagonism would hurt his attempt to help Chon, since he held Johnson's old Senate seat. Going to Johnson direct, meant an automatic refusal by the Kennedys. Going direct to the Kennedys, meant Lyndon's resentment, and possible sabotage of the plea. He had to work out the matter, and act carefully.

The question was answered for him. A week after the inquiry was begun, the Attorney General called Floyd. "Senator, this is Bobby Kennedy, and I want to discuss this Mr. X that your staff is inquiring about. The Justice Department has been trying to find out who he is but we have come up with nothing. I need to know who he is, you see the President is very interested in this case," Bobby Kennedy demanded.

"Mr. Kennedy, I am sworn to secrecy, I cannot divulge the man's name. I just don't know what to tell you, but I can't give you the name," Sen. Trench replied.

"Senator, you are going to have to decide pretty quickly, or may be charged with harboring a fugitive, and a spy at that. I don't think your constituents would be too pleased to have their Senator harboring a spy. Now would they?" Kennedy rebutted. The north-south rivalry was on, and Floyd was caught in the middle.

"Mr. Kennedy, I am going to have to think about it. I gave my word. I just have to think about it."

"Fine I'll call you tomorrow to see what your decision is, thank you, and goodbye," the Attorney General hung up.

In the Oval Office, President Kennedy, Pierre Salinger, and Robert Kennedy talked. "It's a natural, the guy's a triple threat, quadruple, really if you count him as a Mexican, a Japanese, a spy, and a criminal," Salinger explained.

"I don't want Lyndon to get credit for the splash, and I don't particularly want Trench to get points for helping this guy either. This is going to be a White House push, and no one else gets involved. Tell Johnson and Trench if you have to, that I don't want them in the forefront, understood," the President was emphatic.

"Trench is playing foxy right now, he won't divulge the guy's name. I am having to pressure him with threat of prosecution. But he still didn't bust. He's a pretty solid guy, and I don't know if he'll waffle or not," Bobby Kennedy added.

"Let's keep working on it," the President said.

Sen. Trench sat at his desk when his receptionist advised him that the Attorney General was in the reception area and wanted to see him. Very unexpected and very unusual. Sen. Trench went out to greet him, and walked him back to the office. After exchanging greetings, the Attorney General wasted no time.

"Have you decided to give me the guy's name?" Kennedy asked.

"Mr. Kennedy I have decided not to divulge his name. I have a duty to my constituents to hold their confidences when they ask that matters be confidential. If I were to yield to you, or another agency, and breach confidentiality, there would be many matters that are important to the government of this country that would never be spoken, for fear of bad publicity, injury, or embarrassment, or retaliation. He doesn't want to be arrested, prosecuted, he doesn't want to be deported. So, to answer your question, you don't get the name."

"I'm sorry you feel that way Senator, I'm afraid things might get a bit uncomfortable for you. You could be harboring a fugitive," Kennedy threatened.

Sen. Floyd had been a Texas trial lawyer and politician for twenty-five years, and was not intimidated.

"I myself feel sorry that it has come to this, but you do what you have to do, and I will do what I have to do. I'll take my chances," the Senator said and they bid each other farewell.

Sen. Floyd called Judge Garcia at the Federal Building in Laredo and advised him of the Kennedy squeeze. The next day the judge called the senator.

"Floyd, I've just received a copy of a lawsuit filed in my court about ten minutes ago. It was filed by the Justice Department against a certain John Doe. The suit was delivered personally by a man from the AG's office from Washington. The attorney explained the entire case to me, and explained your involvement in the matter. Of course the attorney did not know that I am also involved. It sets out Encarnación's predicament in much detail, fortunately it does not mention you, and does not mention me."

The judge paused to assess the situation and then continued. "The suit is framed as a petition for deportation, they want him out of the country. They don't know his name but they sure are trying to smoke him out. I'm positive all they want is law and order publicity," the judge said and paused again.

"Floyd, I think this is getting out of hand, I don't know what those sons of bitches are trying to do, but it's getting nasty. I think that you and I are being set up for some embarrassment, especially you right now. But when they find out I initiated this, then the mud's on my face too. Which I really don't mind anyway, but I think we ought to grab the bull by the horns, and get this thing done.

"We still have trial by jury in this country you know, and no jury in the country would convict Chon of jaywalking. I mean the guy is an exemplary person, good husband, good father, good hard worker, community leader?

"I have to agree with you that the bastards are getting nasty, but what the hell, we're all trial lawyers, let's get 'em," Sen. Trench agreed.

"Okay then, from now on I will have to disqualify myself from this case. I am too involved, and it is not ethical for me to stay on. Talk to Chon and see what he thinks. If you act fast enough, we can get this thing put out before it gets too big and out of hand," the judge concluded.

Señor García's brother Justino, also a lawyer, called Chon into the office and explained the details of the lawsuit and the judge's and Trench's recommendation, and the downside of the proposition. He could get deported, and perhaps worse after the conviction.

"If Judge García recommends it, and you and Judge Trench recommend it, then I will go, and hope and pray for the best, whatever the outcome. I have to get this thing behind me," Chon's voice trembled as he agreed to join in the litigation.

Justino prepared pleadings to be filed in the lawsuit, setting out in detail the man's history, and the technical and legal defenses to deportation. In the meantime, Chon had no choice but to tell the Salinas and Gutiérrez families. He gathered the

entire clan, even called Dr. Sergio and his wife, and explained
the story of twenty years ago. The family was shocked. How
could their Chon, their beloved Chon actually be a Japanese
Naval Officer and a spy? They were totally and completely on
his side. Japanese or not, they loved him. He was a fine man,
and they were very proud of him.

Mari Liz and the children stood fast by their man.

One week after Justino filed the explanatory and defensive
pleadings, the government asked for a public pretrial conference.
The government wanted to test the judge's feelings on the case,
and test the defendant's case.

Sen. Trench called Justino and advised him to get Chon prepared for the hearing.

Chapter Twenty Five

T he following article appeared in *The Laredo Post* newspaper on August 15, 1963.

Community in Shock and Disbelief
PROMINENT SOUTH TEXAS RANCHER ARRESTED ON ESPIONAGE CHARGE

LAREDO, Texas--Encarnación "Chon" Gutiérrez Ayala was arrested yesterday following indictment by a Federal grand jury, out of the United States District Court, southern District of Texas, Laredo Division. The indictment charges Gutiérrez with espionage, and entering the United States illegally.

The indictment further alleges that he came to the US in 1942, and has been in the country illegally since. The espionage charge carries a penalty of life imprisonment or death. The immigration charge carries a penalty of five years imprisonment and/or expulsion from the United States.

Press files and reports indicate that Gutiérrez has led an exemplary life as a prominent resident of South Texas. He is president of Salco Land and Cattle Company, a Webb County farm and ranch operation. Gutiérrez has served in various local political organizations, is a member of the board of directors of the Webb County Conservation District, and of Laredo National Bank. Gutiérrez is a board member of the Texas Whitetail Deer Raising Association, and the Texas Cattle Raisers Association.

Gutiérrez is married to María Elizabeth Salinas Gutiérrez, a member of the Salinas family, one of the oldest founding families in South Texas. They have six children, all honor students. The eldest has recently been recommended to attend the United States Naval Academy at Annapolis, Maryland. It is not known if the indictment will affect the appointment to the Naval Academy.

The family is active at Immaculate Heart of Mary Catholic Church in Encinal, Texas. Several friends, neighbors, and residents of Webb County interviewed by the *Post* expressed shock and complete surprise. From information provided by the United States Attorney's office, and other sources, it appears that Gutiérrez's true name is Tasaka Chon, and that he is a lieutenant in the Japanese Navy. He was born and raised near Tokyo, Japan.

His neighbors and friends remember that Gutiérrez came to South Texas in 1942 as a farm laborer, spoke Spanish and English, and claimed to be a resident of México. He never returned to México. In 1945 he married Mary Elizabeth Salinas, and settled on the Salinas family ranch, in north Webb County. The Gutiérrez have lived there ever since.

Gutiérrez has been very active in state Democratic Party activities, and is known as a large contributor to Democratic Party candidates, including Senator Floyd Trench of Laredo. The Senator did not return phone calls to his offices in Washington, D.C. and Laredo.

Tasaka, who is also known as Gutiérrez Ayala, was arraigned yesterday, entered a plea of not guilty, requested a jury trial, and was released on $100,000 cash bond. Trial is scheduled for November. If the allegations prove to be correct, it appears that Gutiérrez Ayala, at least up to this point, has successfully re-invented his identity from Japanese Navy officer and spy to successful South Texas rancher/farmer. The news of the indictment and arrest has taken Laredo by storm. Citizens and neighbors are shocked and in disbelief.

Post surveys taken yesterday at various times during the day indicate that little else is being discussed at schools, banks, and the Webb County courthouse in Laredo.

* * *

Justino García walked with his client, and his family by his side, toward the Federal Building in Laredo. It was a cool day. A norther had blown in the day before, but it was clear and sunny. A perfect day to be hunting, Chon thought. He wondered how long the fight would last. He wanted to wear his jeans and khaki shirt but his lawyer talked him out of it. He wore a dark suit instead, but he refused to take his pants out of his boots. He wore a new scrunched up hat instead of the old sweaty and dirty one. They went up the elevator to the third floor courtroom.

The group walked down the hall and turned at the corner where they encountered about forty newsmen and cameramen. The flashes blinded the group, everyone was asking for a comment or a quote. Justino opened the way for the family to pass, and refused comment. The group went into the courtroom and sat down. Justino explained that in some cases the press appearance was not unusual. Chon was caught completely by surprise, and became very nervous. Mari Liz cried, and had second thoughts about bringing the children. The children were in awe.

They waited five minute. Suddenly there were three loud bangs on the door separating the courtroom and the Judge's chambers. "Oyez, Oyez, Oyez, the Federal Court for the Southern District of Texas, Laredo Division is now in session, the Honorable Reynaldo García, presiding. Please be seated. Order in the court," the bailiff yelled.

Justino was surprised. He knew that Reynaldo was going to disqualify himself, because he was too close to the subject matter, but here he was coming into the courtroom. He feared a setup; were the García brothers to be embarrassed?

Judge García almost ran up the steps to the bench. He looked well, and looked almost happy as he surveyed the parties and their attorneys.

"Does the United States have an announcement?" Judge Garcia asked, looking at the young Assistant United States Attorney from Houston with a smile.

"Your Honor, with the Court's permission, we would like to present this letter from the President of the United States for consideration by the Court."

Justino García jumped to his feet.

"Your honor, I am not sure that all this publicity, all this TV, and fanfare is favorable to my client. He is entitled to an unfettered and fair trial. This letter, uh, uh, we claim surprise. Is it admissible? May I ask what all this concerns?" Justino furrowed his brow.

The procedure was highly unusual, and he was caught off guard, and did not like it.

Judge García countered, "Counselor, please sit down, I think all this will be cleared up in just a few minutes."

Justino was confused and his brother the judge was not helping.

The judge opened the letter and began to read out loud. It was from President John F. Kennedy.

The President went into great detail to explain the Gutiérrez case to the American public.

Chon and Mariquita held hands, and the children watched.

"Finally," Judge García summarized, "the letter finishes as follows, 'by the power vested in me by the Constitution and laws of the United States of America, I hereby grant Encarnación 'Chon' Gutiérrez Ayala, also known as Tasaka Chon, a Presidential pardon. I direct the Justice Department to expedite the application, which, I assume, will be forthcoming, to attain legal status. I will be in Texas soon and I look forward to meeting Mr. Gutiérrez and his family personally. My best wishes to Mr. Tasaka Gutiérrez and his family. Thank you.' Signed John

F. Kennedy, President of the United States of America. End of letter."

The Kennedys had scored another PR splash.

Chon, Mari Liz, the children, Justino, Don Juan and Doña María Luisa all cried openly. Judge García cried, laughed, and smiled. The reporters went wild.

After comment, quote, and interview, Chon and the family and lawyer walked out of the Federal building. One last reporter asked him where he was going.

"I am going deer hunting with my family and friends," Chon replied with a wide smile.

THE END

www.ingramcontent.com/pod-product-compliance
Lightning Source LLC
Chambersburg PA
CBHW031230120726
47905CB00002B/543